Going Down

Also by Vonna Harper

Surrender

Roped Heat

"Wild Ride" in *The Cowboy*

Night Fire

"Breeding Season" in *Only With a Cowboy*

"Night Scream" in *Sexy Beast V*

Going Down

VONNA HARPER

APHRODISIA

KENSINGTON BOOKS
http://www.kensingtonbooks.com

APHRODISIA BOOKS are published by

Kensington Publishing Corp.
850 Third Avenue
New York, NY 10022

ISBN-13: 978-0-7582-2218-3
ISBN-10: 0-7582-2218-1

First Trade Paperback Printing: July 2008

10 9 8 7 6 5 4 3 2 1

Printed in the United States of America

What a ride life has been for us, sis! I can't imagine not having you in my life, especially now that we're parenting our parent. Thank you, thank you for your broad-minded acceptance of what comes out of my fingers and brain.

1

You have one fuckin beautiful bod. What I wouldn't give to rub mine all over yours. Bothered.

Hot, hot, hot! Damn but do you rock. Where the hell do you live? I'd love to take you out—followed by fucking you senseless. Charles.

I dig yur ass an boobs. Thats wut turns me on most. Stu.

Forget her ass and boobs, Stu boy. Look at those eyes. That's a broad what's really into what she does. How about it, Sass? Nutting turns you on like being tied up and whipped by a no nonsense master, right? Lawman.

Tyin her juss the fuckin first act, Lawman. Watch those eyes wen shes climaxing. She dont ever want it to end. Stu.

Hey Sass, I caught your latest at The Dungeon. What a natural submissive. Not damn enough women know their place is at their master's feet, but you do. Watching you squirm and hearing you scream while that dom held a vibrator to your helpless pussy made me cum. If it was me who'd tied you up, I'd never take off the ropes. I'd keep

after you until you passed out. Has that ever happened during in your real life? Hog.

Stifling a shudder, Saree McKeon sipped on iced tea while contemplating letting the men who'd logged into her Sass In Satin chat room know she was at her computer. She'd expanded her Web site to include the weekly live chats because personally connecting with some of those who paid memberships to The Dungeon, where she worked, was the least she could do to thank them for making her one of the successful site's most popular bondage models. Now, after two months of come-ons, occasional filth, and most erroneous, the belief that she truly embraced the submissive lifestyle, she wished she hadn't.

Lawman and Stu, who'd been there almost from the beginning, spent most of their time arguing with each other. Stu's fractured spelling sometimes defied comprehension, and she couldn't help but feel sorry for him. She didn't remember hearing from a Bothered, Charles, or Hog before. Maybe she should acknowledge their comments, especially Hog's, but doing so always left her feeling dirty and uneasy. A few times before she'd caught on, she'd engaged in text conversations with seemingly *normal* men only to discover they were perverts. Thank goodness for the anonymity of the Internet and her alter ego. Because she'd called herself Sass from the moment she'd signed with The Dungeon, she hoped none of the men in her so-called fan club had any inkling who she really was and that she lived in an average-looking house in a middle-class neighborhood a good hour's drive from where The Dungeon's studios were located. These days she kept her comments generic so, hopefully, none of her fans would think she was coming on to them. Yuck!

As for straightening out Hog and others about her lack of interest in the BDSM lifestyle beyond the role playing she did on a regular and well-paid basis for the camera, forget it. Let them believe she spent her life naked, wearing a collar, and spreading her legs for her *master*. Only she needed to know she was currently dressed in a shapeless old cotton shirt, too-big shorts, and mismatched socks instead of the corset and fishnet stockings she'd poured herself into earlier for today's session.

Greetings, she typed. *You know what they say about women always being late. Sorry to be the last to show up, but it's been a crazy day. What is it with modern cars? You'd think they could at least narrow it down when the "check engine" light comes on. Come to think of it, it's probably a conspiracy between the automakers and the mechanics' union designed to fleece car owners. Suffice it to say, I'm running around in a rental until whatever work needs doing on mine is done. I hope everyone's comfortable.*

She'd still been typing when Hog started doing the same.

Let me take care of that for you, Sass. Once you're in my chains and cage, you'll never have to worry about anything again. Except satisfying me, that is. I'm not an easy master. It takes a lot to please me, and you're not always going to like the lessons.

What would she want with you? Sass can have her pick of men, can't you, beautiful? Lawman.

In contrast to Hog's crude comments, Lawman had a sickeningly sweet way of sucking up to her. Keeping to her self-imposed guidelines regarding any kind of personal involvement, she refused to respond. Instead she wrote, *If the counter is right, there are over two hundred of us logged in right now. That's amazing. Obviously we're not all going to be able to talk at once, and since I'm paying for the chat room, I'm going to call the shots. Because this site is linked to The Dungeon, I'm assuming that's how all of you found me. I want to take a minute to let you know what's coming up there. An awesome new set is going to be revealed next week, and we have a couple of guest riggers coming in. I'm going to be working with one of them, and that should be exciting.*

Although several men—at least she assumed they were men—started typing, she kept going, touching on soon-to-be-implemented technical improvements in the video delivery. Because she didn't understand how the video from the handheld cameras used during shoots wound up being posted on the Internet, she relied on what she'd been told when she assured her fans that updating their systems to display even clearer images was a simple and safe matter.

It's amazing what it takes for The Dungeon to be the professional endeavor it is, and of course none of that would happen if not for you, the members, who pay the bills. Everyone associated with The Dungeon has his or her own specialized role but somehow it all comes together. And very well, don't you think?

Yours is the only role I care about. Yours and the other bondage sluts. Only, don't tell me it's a role. No way can you be acting when you climax. Hog.

Damn it, she knew better than to bite. Just the same, her fingers raced over the keys. **This has been discussed here several times, Hog. Of course members want and deserve to know whether they're viewing the real thing or Academy Award–quality acting. I assure you, whatever the camera shows me and the other models experiencing, we aren't pretending. Sexual response is, after all, engrained in most of us.**

Knew it. You sluts really get off on being dominated? A real dom—not those homos pretending to be into BDSM—would have you licking his cock in gratitude. That's what you do in your private life, right? No way you can have so damn much fun on camera and not want to surrender yourself. Got a master? Because if you don't, I'm applying for the job. Hell, maybe I'll just kidnap you and keep you in my basement. Hog.

When setting up her chats, she'd been assured that she could permanently block certain people from participating. One more crude comment from Hog and he'd be added to the list. However, she was still trying to come up with a sharp and civilized reply when someone identifying himself as Reeve beat her to the punch. *Clean up your language. Sass has gone to a lot of effort and is giving her time to connect with her fans. She's a lady, got it. A lady.*

The hell she is. This is one hot bitch ruled by her cunt, aren't you, Sass? Hog.

You don't know me, she couldn't help but reply. *You think the me you see on your screen is as far as it goes, but you're dead wrong.*

*What u sayin? U cant be pretending to—*Stu.

Those orgasms can't be faked, Reeve typed. *But there's more to the lady than the way she earns a living. For all we know she's a lesbian.*

Although she wanted to ensure Reeve that not only didn't she have any lesbian tendencies, she had never participated in a woman-on-woman shoot, she held back. Did loudly protesting ever convince anyone of anything?

No response, Sass? Reeve.

Oh I have one, all right. I'm just not sure you'd believe it. Give me a try.

This was different. Most men either fawned all over her trying to gain whatever they thought they'd gain—not that they'd ever get to first base—or tried to pull the macho male act. Instead Reeve, or whomever he was, wanted to banter, which was a refreshing change. *Fine. Here's the unvarnished truth, at least a bit of it. The me you see at The Dungeon is an employee doing her job. Yes, I love what I do, but when everything else is stripped away, being a bondage model pays the bills, end of discussion.*

Even as she leaned back and studied the words, she couldn't believe she'd laid herself out like that. From the rapid-fire responses coming in, most of the men had missed the point and were arguing over which of them would get the privilege of stripping her and what they'd do once the last article of clothing was gone. Hog's suggestions were particularly vulgar, while Stu either didn't get it or didn't have the necessary vocabulary to express himself. She couldn't help but notice that Reeve hadn't chimed in.

From that, the conversation made a right turn to which other Dungeon models turned them on the most. Then, strangely enough, they started debating what might be wrong with her car. She left her computer long enough to pour herself another glass of tea and check her answering machine. Her sister, Hayley, and the man in Hayley's life were going to be gone this weekend and, since it was going to be hot, would Saree mind watering the plants on the front porch. By the time she'd finished playing telephone tag with Hayley, the hour-long chat was drawing to a close.

Not bothering to catch up on the conversation, she typed, **Sorry to be the one to tell you this, but the powers that be are going to pull the plug on us. I probably don't have to tell you this because you've seen the promo, but I'm going to be featured on this week's update. I worked with my favorite rigger, and if I do say so myself, it turned out very well indeed. At least I was satisfied with a capital S.**

You're talking about the beefcake who wears that lame Lone Ranger mask, aren't you? Much as I hate to admit it, there's good chemistry between you. The two of you play in private? Maybe more than play? He your master? Hog.

No man's my master! Not going to happen, ever! **Why don't you take a poll. Ask the others what they think.**

But will you tell us whether we're right? Hog.

Good question. The answer is, no. Bottom line, it isn't any of your business.

Maybe, maybe not. We see you naked. More than that, we're given up-close-and-personal shots of every inch of your incredible body. You're alive and real, a great smile and huge eyes. Remember, the eyes are the window to the soul. I look into them and it's as if I can hear your heart beat. I know what makes you laugh and cry. Can you blame me for seeing you as more than just some face and body on the screen? Reeve.

For some reason she couldn't quite fathom, it was as if Reeve had reached beyond the Internet and was standing a few feet away waiting for an answer, an honest answer. *You've made another good point. Let me think about your comments and get back to you.*

I'll be waiting.

Although the chat had ended the better part of an hour ago, Saree continued to feel surrounded by it. There wasn't anything that mysterious about aftereffects, was there? After all, as Reeve had said, thanks to modern computers she'd been connecting with countless strangers, mostly sharing tidbits about her life but also theirs. She'd been called a bitch, propositioned, and if she read Stu right, proposed to. Hog had blown it; the next time he tried to sign on, he'd learn that he'd been blacklisted.

As for Reeve—

That's what had her feeling surrounded.

Now that she'd had a shower followed by the sandwich that passed for dinner, she had a better handle on things, at least she believed she'd pinpointed what was different about the short exchange with Reeve. Yes, she was relatively new to this chat business, but so far he'd been the only man to touch on issues that went beyond skin deep. He'd acknowledged that there just might be something between her ears.

Might be hardly said it, she acknowledged as she sat back

down in front of her computer. As an example, the past two weeks had been particularly unsettling. Oh, work was churning at its usual frantically fun pace with some much-appreciated overtime coming up thanks to a scheduled extensive shoot involving her and three other models at a private estate. If Amber Green hadn't dropped off the face of the earth around the first of the month, they'd be in the middle of filming. Unfortunately, the usually dependable and D-cup Amber had stopped answering her phone. When one of The Dungeon's directors contacted her landlord, the landlord had informed him that he'd gotten a call from Amber's father saying there'd been a family emergency and he didn't know how long she'd be gone.

Saree had worked with Amber a few times, and they had gone out for drinks, during which they'd determined that, except for loving sex, they didn't have a lot in common. For one thing, Amber was seriously into BDSM and spent much of her free time participating in the scene. Just the same, Saree agreed with the others who said it wasn't like Amber not to keep in touch with her employer.

So where was she?

Speculation was that she'd found the master she'd joked she was looking for, but although Saree had laughed along with the others, something didn't strike her as right.

Forget Amber.

Not entirely successful in relegating the MIA Amber to the back of her mind, Saree logged into the mailbox set up to receive e-mail from those who'd visited her Web site. There were some fifty messages, maybe a third of them offering her everything from stock tips to penile enlargement products. The rest were legit, although that was a relative term given the content. What was it with some people! When it came to the anonymity of the Internet, nothing was sacred. Were these blatantly pornographic messages written at work or maybe at home with a wife and children in another room?

And yet, much as she itched to immediately delete those with such headings as "Waiting to fuck you," "Screw king," and "Bite your lips," she didn't dare forget that many had memberships at The Dungeon and thus were responsible for her income.

Thanks for getting in touch, she wrote over and over again. And although she wanted to tell them to go to hell, she didn't.

Fortunately, not every message made her feel like throwing up. There were a lot of lonely men out there, horny college students, even respectful voyeurs, if there was such a thing. She didn't forget for a minute that she had no way of knowing what lay beneath a man's surface. He might come across as the most trustworthy gentleman, but she'd never risk her safety and maybe her life by agreeing to meet him.

Better to limit herself to dating those she met in the normal course of her life, not that that often happened.

Well hell, such were the consequences of her unusual career.

Reminding herself that her job had made it possible for her to buy her own home while still in her twenties, she was about to log out when a new message came in. The sender's name stopped her: Reeve.

Just wanted to follow up on what we touched on earlier. I mentioned that being allowed into your sexual world makes people like me feel as if we know you, but that's wrong. Just because we go to movies and see close-ups of an actress's lips doesn't mean we've kissed those lips or know what she does at the end of the day. Your privacy has to be vital to you. In contrast to the very public nature of the way you earn a living, I'm sure you separate your public life from what takes place off-screen. Let me take a flier at this, a mental and creative exercise for lack of a better term. When the cameras are off, you remove your false fingernails and climb into the shower where you soap away the marks left by ropes

and whips. Then you put on a coffee-stained old shirt and ratty tennis shoes. You get into a gas-guzzling SUV and head for a crowded freeway where you fantasize about running over some of the idiots on it. You'd love to take out that cheap broad in the beater who's smoking while her kids are in the backseat. Home is a luxury condo with a state-of-the-art security system and watchmen who tell you about their grandchildren and whom you bake cookies for. Your furnishings are sleek and modern with speakers that can rock the whole building. Your closet is the size of most people's living rooms, and you have a white, long-haired cat that barely tolerates you. As for men, hmm, I'm drawing a blank there, so I'll draw on my imagination. The complex's pool man isn't called ever-ready for nothing, and even the security grandpa is good for an occasional round. The gay couple next door would change sexual orientation if you'd give them a nod, but you're no homewrecker. You nearly got married to the quarterback, in college—you majored in physics with a minor in underwater basketweaving—but you caught him behind the goalpost with the mascot and shoved his engagement ring up his nose. Am I close in any of this?

Laughing, Saree stared at her fingers poised over the keyboard. Should she? Wisdom said no, but hadn't she already taken some huge risks in life, and look where she was, more than solvent with a job she loved, most of the time.

Hi Reeve, not even close, I'm afraid. To set things straight, I was raised by Eskimos and by age ten could reduce a whale carcass to a skeleton in two hours. Unfortunately, that earned me more than a little problem with frostbite, so I jumped on the next cruise ship heading for the tropics. For the next eight years I supported myself selling bait shrimp and moonlighting as a bar-

tender until a gun battle between rival commercial fishermen reduced the bar to rubble. I'd been living with a pirate and thought I had it made, but he tried to sell me to a tugboat captain so I took off for California. The details of how I got into the porn industry are a little hazy, but I do remember waking up on the operating table with spectacular boobs—they are something, aren't they—and deciding to let them earn their keep. Housing is an old warehouse that was cut into apartments. The roof leaks and the plumbing's a joke, but it's cheap. I do have a boyfriend, for lack of a better term, and if you follow professional wrestling, I'm sure you've seen Bubba. He recently changed his hair color from orange to blue, which works better with his eyes. Believe me, you don't want to mess with Bubba. Neither do you want to try to carry on a conversation with him for at least three days after he's lost a match. Now, how about you?

Bubba? You know Bubba? Can you get his autograph for me? Look, I want you to tell him something. I lost a cool twenty grand betting on that loser. I'm planning on being at his next match, and if he blows it again, I'm climbing into the ring and spreading his nose all over his face.

Too late, macho man. Someone already beat you to the punch. That's where he is tonight, trying to get his hands on enough money to get his nose put back together. He didn't say where he was going, and I didn't ask.

That mean you're alone tonight?

Not to you, big boy. Not to you.

Sitting in the dark with the monitor light playing on his features, Reeve Robinson slowly reread what Sass had written. Interesting. Sass, or more accurately Saree McKeon, had a keen sense of humor and was quick-witted, judging by how little time it had taken her to reply to his carefully worded nonsense. He had to admire her because glib rejoinders came easily to her. Granted, his agenda was multilayered, while she was just having fun.

More than having fun, he decided as the minutes stretched out. He intrigued her. Otherwise, she wouldn't have lowered her self-imposed barrier between herself and the faceless, nameless men who fantasized about getting their hands on and their cocks in her. Images of countless hands wrapped around countless cocks made him wish he'd mixed his drink stronger, but that was nothing compared to what went on in certain shadowy rooms—shadowy buildings surrounded by impenetrable security systems.

Turning off the computer, he stood and stalked to the nearest window. Night hadn't finished killing the day, but it wouldn't take much longer and then—

Then the monsters—himself included—came out.

Keep the beast at bay. Damn it, don't let it loose! Do your job.

Yeah, the job. He'd taken a vital step tonight by introducing himself to Saree. Next came learning whether she had the guts and courage for the role he believed he had to force on her. Everything he'd learned about her had pointed to her ability to survive, but just as he wore masks, she undoubtedly had her own.

One thing, the woman embraced forced sex, or at least the pretence of it. The question of whether her submissiveness was genuine or part of her public façade would be answered soon. And did it really matter as long as he got and kept her on her knees?

"I'm hunting you, Saree. Don't look over your shoulder because you won't hear me coming until it's too late. And once we're together . . ."

Damn it! He'd had no intention of grabbing his hurting cock! This was nothing more than another assignment, and he was a pro. Keeping her captive, naked, helpless, and dependent on him wasn't anything he couldn't handle.

Who the fuck are you trying to kid? his cock demanded.

2

The damn dream was waiting for her. No matter that she'd taken a sleeping pill and indulged in a long, relaxing bath—experience told Saree that she wasn't going to get through the night without visiting that place. Too far gone to try to fight her way back to consciousness, she opted for tunneling into blackness. Maybe if she refused to acknowledge what came too close to being a nightmare, it would leave her alone.

There. Soft music from instruments she didn't recognize. The darkness wasn't complete, more like a heavy fog but fortunately not cold. She loved being at the beach while early morning mist coated the world and softened its edges. She could concentrate on planting one bare foot after the other in the damp sand, looking for seashells and the countless prints left behind by shorebirds. Yes, that was going to work, a slow sliding movement in time with the quiet waves. Walking forever, walking strong and alone except for the birds. Add a gentle, salty breeze and a distant, hollow foghorn. She had this beach to herself; maybe the entire world belonged to her.

Good, good and safe. There was no sex here, no delicious

but powerful assaults on her senses, no private moments of wondering whether self-control and direction might be slipping away. Maybe she'd walk into the surf and start swimming, her body weightless and surrounded by warm, caressing waves. No man would touch her, and she would remain alone, safe.

Walking. Walking slow. Something snaked around her ankles and something else connected to that preventing her from taking more than mincing steps. Her arms held against her belly via wrist restraints lashed to the strands of rope around her waist. More rope ran from her cuffs to between her legs, trapping her pussy in sensation. She couldn't stop walking because the shadowed human ahead of her had a firm grip on the leash hooked to her collar.

Collared. Led like a captured animal. Taut heat radiating throughout her sex whenever she tried to move her useless arms. Gagged with a rubber ball wedged into her open mouth.

Caught. Caught and being taken somewhere by someone who'd claimed the right to do this. No more sand to walk on, but at least the spongy vegetation on this trail into hell was easy on her feet.

She'd been here before, maybe not in this particular spot, but in sensation and understanding. The forced journey was about having self-control wrenched away and placed in a stranger's hands, a dark stranger who understood her as intimately as she did herself.

Where are you taking me? What are you going to do with me? Why is this happening and who will I be when you're done with me?

But maybe he'd never finish molding her.

The instinct to fight raced hot and wild through her, but she'd been rendered docile. And with each step, more of the old Saree seeped away to be replaced by need.

Need. Sex. Fucking and being fucked. Legs forced wide to accommodate a cock, arms immobilized to ensure compliance.

Not rape because although she had no choice in the hot act, she wanted it and he knew.

Knew. Understood.

Shadow man stopped. Doing the same, she stood with her head down so she could focus on her lashed-together hands and the soft, pale rope caressing her belly before disappearing between her legs. His. Hate or love this moment, she was his.

"Almost there," he said. "One journey finished so another can begin."

Where are we going, she asked with her eyes. Whether he understood or not didn't matter because he was walking toward her, his grip on her leash warning her not to try to back away.

He touched her, a rough, owning hand raking over her left breast and puckering her nipple. Fighting her quickened breath, she tried to twist away.

"No!" Grabbing her tethered wrists, he forced them away from her body, which tightened the rope's grip on her cunt. Although she sobbed and begged behind her gag, he refused to let up on the pressure until she dropped her head in surrender.

"Lessons to be learned, so many lessons." He touched her right breast this time, the contact gentler but the message just as unshakable. "This is now my body and I'll do what I want with it. For as long as it pleases me, I control it." A thumb and forefinger closed around her hard nipple. "I'm easily pleased, slave. But hard to satisfy."

What was he trying to say? If only she could concentrate! But between the pressure on her nipple and against her labia, she simply blinked away tears and waited.

Waited for her master.

"You know you crave what I offer. No matter how much you try to deny what lies deep inside you, the truth is in your eyes. And here."

Grabbing the rope against her belly, he ran his free hand between her legs. The cunt tie prevented him from reaching her opening, but the promise and potential worked its way through her skin. *Slow and steady, she relaxed, surrendered. Promise and pleasure lay in his fingertips.*

He held his fingers up to her nose. "Smell yourself, slave. No matter how much you might deny it, your pussy speaks the truth."

He knew. Oh yes, he knew!

"Time to start walking again because we have a long way to go. But first, a change because it pleases me to see you in another position."

Vague awareness of the moment's dreamlike quality briefly— at least she thought it was only a few seconds—distracted her. By the time her mind and body connected again, her hands were behind her. A single rope circled her waist and forearms, effectively rendering her arms as useless as they'd been before. More of the same rope was now nestled in her ass cheeks, against her labial lips, and under the rope belt in front, leaving a loose strand to dangle nearly to the ground. The ball gag had been replaced with wood doweling. A separate rope now cinched her elbows so close together that they nearly touched.

The man—her master?—stood a few feet away with his head cocked as he surveyed his work. Only then did she realize that her ankles were free, not that she could run like this. Not that she wanted to.

Wet between her legs and soaking the rope. Heat working deep inside her.

Slave. His slave.

As the word resonated, she concerned herself with what her master looked like. Although bright sunlight filtered down through the heavy vegetation, she couldn't make out his features. His hair was thick and raggedly cut, drifting in the breeze. He was big, outweighing her by seventy or eighty pounds, and many inches taller. His dark shirt clung skinlike to his chest and arms *before caressing his taut belly. Jeans covered his lower body like a lover.*

She longed to be that lover, to welcome him into her hot, wet core.

"You'll see more of me when you've earned the right. You're beautiful in your bondage. Carry that with you as we travel. Your master proclaims you beautiful. And desirable."

Unable to thank him, she nodded. This time she didn't stare downward but kept her head level and her eyes on him.

"I could have kept you unconscious until we were where your training will take place, but I want you to be part of the process. To feel every step of the journey and know how inescapable it is." With that, he picked up the loose rope and pulled her toward him. Loving and hating this latest demonstration of his absolute control, she resisted. Then pressure against her labia forced compliance. Instead of reeling her in, he turned away and struck out, a livestock owner bringing his latest acquisition home.

One step followed by another, a single movement of thigh and calf muscles, mind tunneling inward to where heat waited. No longer alone and free, no longer fighting the beast living deep inside her.

Rejoicing.

"You sound, I don't know, off."

Shaking her head, Saree acknowledged that she should have known better than to try to pull something over on her sister. So much for pretending she'd called Hayley on a whim. "I didn't get my usual eight hours of beauty sleep. You know what a bitch I become when I don't feel beautiful."

"Yeah, right. Look, I don't want to cut this short, but Mazati and I are meeting with the state historical society this afternoon and I need to prep."

Mazati was Hayley's lover, hands down the sexiest man she'd ever known, and unknown to more than 99 percent of the population, a time traveler from ancient Aztec civilization. The story of how he'd claimed first Hayley's body and then her heart was something Saree still didn't entirely understand. What she did know was that from the moment the combustion between the two started, Hayley's fire opal jewelry creations had become works of inspired perfection. Not one for jealousy, Saree wished Mazati could get himself cloned.

"Historical society?" she belatedly thought to ask. "What's this, your jewelry has made you so rich that you've decided to include them in your will? Let me point out that as your one and only living blood relative, it's all suppose to come to me."

"Which is why I've hired a bodyguard," Hayley shot back. "And I'm learning self-defense in case you decide to bump me off. Seriously, you remember that article Mazati and I had published in *World Historian* about the role of precious stones in the lives of the Aztecs? Well, we've been getting calls from all over. People are starting to see us as Aztec researchers. Little do they know the truth."

"Which is that Mazati is how many thousands of years old? How is my almost a brother-in-law holding up? Not aging too fast, is he?"

"I don't have any complaints."

Sighing, Saree closed her eyes as an image of her sister and Mazati staring at each other came to mind. What was it with those two? Not only was the sexual attraction between them so intense it had a life of its own, but even when they were arguing about where to go for dinner, energy radiated from one to the other. Damn! What she wouldn't give to be on the receiving end of that!

Or would she? Maybe because she paid her bills by letting men supposedly use and abuse her body, she wasn't sure she'd ever let a man get that close in her personal life.

"Are you there?" Hayley asked. "You didn't fall asleep, did you?"

"No." She wandered from the living room to her bedroom. "Shit, how'd it get that late? I've got to get ready for work."

"What did you call about?"

On the verge of sidestepping the question, she stretched out on her bed and stared at the ceiling. "I had that dream again. Guess I was hoping you knew of a spell I could use to get it out of my mind."

"*That* dream? Oh, you mean the one where you've been captured by someone you can't see?"

"One and the same."

"Is it really that mysterious? Not only do you make your living fostering the bondage fantasy for both sexes, but I told you a lot about how things started between Mazati and me."

"Maybe." Yes, Hayley had a made a valid point, yet she sensed that dreams of having had control wrenched from her came from somewhere deep inside her—probably because she'd long proclaimed that was the last thing she'd ever allow to happen in the real world. Get serious! What modern and liberated woman wanted to spend her life groveling at the feet of some man who demanded she call him Master?

"Just maybe?"

"I need a vacation," she said before she'd known she was going to. "A break."

"Job burnout? Come on, you love what you do. Who wouldn't adore being well paid to have endless climaxes?"

"Maybe I'm getting old."

"You're twenty-seven. That ain't old."

"It is in this business."

"Bull! Damn it, sis, you're one of the top ten most-viewed Dungeon porn stars. To quote more than one of your fans, except for your boobs, you're genuine, no faking nuttin."

No, she'd never faked an on-camera orgasm, which maybe

was part of the problem. Granted, being helpless while a man who knew what the hell he was doing held a powerful vibrator to her clit guaranteed success, and when she screamed out her delight, she was absolutely and completely convinced she had the greatest gig on earth. Only afterward did she admit that being trapped in a body she had so little control over scared her. Her sister found joy and fulfillment using her hands and creativity to craft exquisite jewelry while she moaned and shook and sweated and sometimes begged the rigger to turn off the damn vibrator before she splintered.

"I should make you president of my fan club," she said, again belatedly. "Hell, I know what it is. I'm jealous of you; you have Mazati."

"You want to amend that. He has me. You'll find Mr. Right. You just have to be patient and keep looking."

How, she nearly asked, but they'd been over this ground. Even Hayley couldn't argue that her career choice limited rather than expanded her potential mates. Most men were intimidated by what they perceived to be her overcharged libido. As for those in the industry, the majority were so self-absorbed they barely gave her the time of day, not that she ever really lusted after a rigger or male porn star.

"If I was on vacation I could look," she offered. "Tropical island, nearly nude native hunks, filthy rich old men burning their fat bellies in the sun."

"With their rich old wives in tow, don't forget. Damn it, sis, you keep talking about taking some night classes. Do it. You never know who else might be taking the same class or teaching it."

"Hmm."

"Don't hmm me. Move beyond work situations in your search for Mr. Right."

"Maybe."

"What do you mean, maybe? I'm just repeating what you've told me."

"I know." She drew out the words. "I was just thinking—the other night this guy joined one of my chats. Then later we e-mailed privately. Great sense of humor, and he kept the conversation out of the gutter, if you know what I mean."

"Humor's good. What do you know about him?"

"That's it." As she reached between her legs, the word *Reeve* echoed in her. "I don't know a damn thing."

"They found a body."

"Where?"

Instead of answering immediately, Agent J stared out at the trio of sailboats in the distance. Although J was in his late fifties, his nude and tanned torso was as lean as when he'd been in his teens. If anyone in the sailboats or the tourist boat closer to shore had taken note of the two men in the luxury craft, they might have assumed the men were wealthy business owners, but although that was Reeve's cover, the truth was that they were members of an organization so secret that the FBI hadn't been able to penetrate all the layers. Fine, let the FBI believe that The Clan's membership was limited to the powerful. Only the members themselves needed to know why they existed.

The craft was Reeve's, at least that's what the financial trail would show. The same was true of R&R, the supposed electronics company he'd founded and recently sold, thanks to those who knew how to create something out of nothing.

It was hot this afternoon, too damn hot to be exposing one's skin to the sun's rays, but when Agent J had sent a coded text message this morning saying he had vital information for Reeve, it was understood that they'd have their conversation far from eavesdropping equipment. Not that either man suspected their covers had been blown, but The Clan succeeded because no member ever took anything for granted.

"Off northbound I-5 about forty miles south of L.A.," Agent J said. "Road workers spotted the body when they were coming to work. She wasn't there when they shut things down last night."

"No doubt she was one of *them*?"

"None."

Despite Agent J's sunglasses, Reeve had no trouble reading the older man's mood. It hadn't been pretty. "She'd been branded?"

"Yeah. S on her left hip, not yet healed."

"What else?"

The *else* included handcuffs and ankle restraints on the naked and gagged woman. She was beautiful, at least she had been before her body hit the highway. The preliminary autopsy report had concluded that she'd been dead when she was thrown from a moving vehicle. Other than the brand identifying her as a slave and the bruising around her neck, she'd been in prime condition—except for faint whip marks on her back, belly, and breasts. Perfectly acceptable, the bastard who'd snuffed out her life would have called them, a necessary element in teaching a slave the nuances of her new world.

What had happened to the dead and so-far unidentified woman had nothing to do with classic BDSM where both dom and sub embraced the master/slave relationship. This was robbing a woman, always a beautiful woman, of her freedom and turning her into whatever her captor/owner wanted her to become.

And if she didn't accept her lot, she wound up dead.

"Who's doing the autopsy?" he asked.

"County coroner's office. I met with the director before coming here. The media's not going to have access to the report."

"But the workers who found her will talk."

"I know." Agent J scratched his reddening middle. "Her killers expect the body to make news. They'd be suspicious if there wasn't anything."

"True." Now it was Reeve's turn to study the sailboats. Having never been in one, he couldn't say whether he'd be able to keep the graceful craft upright, but he'd much rather be giving it a try than what he was doing. "What was it, an in-your-face message to anyone who suspects they exist? Telling everyone they're superior?"

"So far they are. Hell, what do we know about those bastards? That they're rich and powerful, that they consider themselves above the law."

"And that getting into their circle is damn near impossible." The words said, he waited.

"If anyone can do it, you can."

Nodding, although it was the last thing he wanted to do, Reeve continued his study of the sailboats. If he had one, he'd fly a pirate flag because for too long he'd been living with the devil. That was the hell of doing what he did. Yeah, his successes had given him a James Bond reputation, and a book written about his exploits would probably be a best-seller, not that he'd ever risk blowing his cover. But where Bond remained the sophisticated, suave lady-killer, Reeve had spent too much time in and around society's sewers. He knew how to walk hip deep in slime, to mimic the bastards who cared nothing about human life including their own, how to cheat and lie and threaten and kill. When he succeeded at those things and brought evil to justice, his coworkers—who were the only ones who knew what he did—praised him. Sometimes, if he didn't fade into the dark soon enough, victims thanked him; those words kept him going.

But not much longer.

He was tired, burned out, cynical—his heart so deeply buried beneath the harsh exterior that he wasn't sure he still had one. Maybe, like the monster who'd spawned him, he'd been born without one.

Damn it, he wanted to go sailing and fly a kite, do a little mountain lake fishing, have a home, not think about his old man and what he'd done.

"Come back to me, Reeve," Agent J said, his own voice weary. "Don't make me have to say it."

J was right. If they stayed out here much longer, they'd be sunburned. "Don't make me say it either."

"I don't have a choice; neither of us does. Innocent women are being kidnapped and turned into sex slaves by men without regard for human life. So far we haven't been able to crack the walls around whatever the hell they call themselves beyond being fairly sure they're operating in Southern California. You agreed to this cover." He indicated the high-end boat. "We've put too much time, money, and effort into setting it up for you to walk out now."

He shouldn't have said yes back when The Clan could no longer deny the existence of a group of white slavers, should have sensed his soul-deep weariness. But he'd seen the pictures of women in real, raw bondage on the Internet and shared in the frustration of not being able to track the images to their source. He'd seen the helpless fear in the women's eyes, and they'd touched his maybe nonexistent heart and soul.

But if he was going to rescue anyone and bring those he called The Slavers to justice, he'd have to walk back into the sewer.

Not only that, he'd have to drag an innocent woman into it with him, a sexy, beautiful woman who wouldn't be destroyed by what he was forced to do to her.

Saree McKeon.

3

Relax. Relax. Go into that nothing place and wait, simply wait.
Feeling centered now that she'd repeated the mantra she used at the beginning of each session, Saree disconnected from her immobilized body and went deep into her core.

As far as the cameraman, rigger, director, and eventually Dungeon members were concerned, she was being displayed in all her naked glory, a helpless *slave* waiting for what she couldn't escape. No one needed to know or concern themselves with how she managed her emotions.

Even with her eyes closed, she knew what was taking place. Theo, the cameraman who'd been with The Dungeon since its beginning, was standing in front of her while he slowly panned from the top of her head to her naked toes. As he'd done countless times, he'd linger on her face where a gag made of electrical tape wound around her head, trapping her long chestnut hair. Then the camera would slide down to her silicone-enhanced but not off-the-scale breasts, over her ribs, to her hips, and finally to her shaved mons. Because she'd been positioned with her legs widely spread, he'd record an up close view of her sex.

As she saw it, the camera was both impersonal and a lover, the most essential element in what made The Dungeon a success—next to her and the other models, of course. She knew how to play to it, but that would come later once she'd been turned into discomfort, heat, and need. Right now, her body spoke to her and her alone, and only she understood its language.

She was nothing, restrained arms stretched up and out so she resembled an X. Waiting. Exposed and vulnerable. Anticipating.

When she'd started in the business, being rendered helpless in preparation for sexual teasing had unnerved her, but she'd learned to trust those in charge of the production. If a tie cut off circulation or pinched a nerve, all she had to do was tell someone, and if she developed a cramp, a grunt summoned help. Over the past three years, her body had made its peace with what looked like impossible ties and positions. She'd even come to love the lightweight whips that caused her skin to sing and heat because they increased and enhanced her self-awareness.

Floating. Being, simply being.

"So my pretty, been waiting for me, have you?"

Sammy's rehearsed words pulled her into action. Opening her eyes and assuming a horrified expression, she pretended to be trying to free herself. As she clenched and unclenched her fingers and twisted from side to side, the camera marched in to record the details. Mindful of the benefits of sound, she moaned.

"Don't try begging, my pretty." Sammy, who'd recently been hired as a full-time rigger, grabbed her hair and pulled her head down. "You had your warning. I told you, the next time you disobeyed me, I'd punish you. Look around. There's just you and me here."

That wasn't true, not that the members cared. Members preferred shoots that took place outside The Dungeon's sets, which was why they were in the hills above a large park today.

They'd had no trouble finding a secluded setting where she could be tied to trees in any number of innovative ways. Even with the occasional insect, she loved being out of doors, and if a random hiker happened upon them, well, that hiker would certainly have something to tell his or her friends.

Sammy released her hair and started walking around her as is she were some animal he was contemplating buying. Because her role in this B if not C film was to play the not-too-bright bimbo, she kept moaning and struggling.

"When I hired you, I told you you'd be working long hours and I expected you to get adequate sleep, but did you?"

Eyes wide, she shook her head.

"No." Planting himself in front of her, Sammy captured her right nipple. The moment he did, energy and anticipation slammed into her. "You went out barhopping and didn't get home until nearly morning. Now we'll see if it was worth it."

Sammy's grip wasn't firm enough to draw tears, but it wouldn't take much more. Far from wanting to escape, she studied the change in her boob as he drew it toward her. Belatedly, she remembered to beg, at least she made sounds that she hoped people would interpret as begging. However, if they looked into her eyes, they'd know she was turned on.

Just like that, turned on. Feeding off her servitude.

"I'm not a forgiving boss, I told you that from the beginning. By the time I'm done with you, you'll do everything I want. Everything." After tweaking her nub, he released it but only so he could pick up a pair of silver spring-loaded nipple clamps. He ran the erotic contraption over the fullness of her breast while she continued her unintelligible babbling. Smiling like some silent movie villain, Sammy cupped her breast and easily, expertly closed the shiny metal around her nipple. No matter how many times she'd worn clamps, the initial bite made her gasp. Fortunately shock was immediately followed by a familiar river of heat flowing from her breast to between her legs.

Again remembering her role—who had thought up this nonsense anyway—she tried to lunge to the side while throwing back her head. Sammy waited until she stopped struggling and then stroked her left breast with the other clamp. Hoping she looked defeated and resigned and even tamed, she stared while he imprisoned her second nipple. Even as fresh pain hit, she had to admit that the chain dangling between her pale, captured breasts looked great.

Felt great.

Now came what? Although she'd seen the various toys and tools that director Carole Mars had brought for the shoot, she didn't know what would be used when or in what way because keeping the models somewhat in the dark made for real reactions.

"I'm going to start by punishing you," Sammy said. "Then when you're a compliant little bondage slut, I'll give you your reward. And once that's over, I'll let you show me how appreciative you are." With that, he ran his fingers between her legs. Deep in anticipation, she jerked. "Wet here, my pretty. Does that mean you aren't objecting as much as you'd like to have me believe?"

She started to shake her head in denial, then stopped because something among the trees had caught her attention. Because of the shadows she couldn't be sure, but wasn't that a human form?

A voyeur? Hopefully not some high schooler playing hooky or a dirty old man. She could have called the others' attention to the intruder but decided to wait, mostly because at the moment Sammy was tightening the ropes around her ankles and forcing her to increase her stance even more.

A touch, no more than a touch of soft, wide leather strands on her cunt, but that was all it took to haul her attention back to what was happening. Sammy started whipping her exposed labia, his strokes more caresses than blows, the velvetlike leather gliding over her wet tissues. A slow fire spread over her, flames inching down her thighs and over her ass. Wise in her body's ways, she knew she could be kept like this for wonderfully torturous hours. Although she'd masturbated to climax last night, her system had forgotten the incredible sense of release and craved, absolutely craved, the ultimate pleasure. But it wasn't going to happen, not yet, not until she'd been rendered mindless. *Oh boy, gonna be a hell of a ride today.*

Stroke after stroke, gentle and invasive at the same time, occasionally zeroing in on her clit but not often enough to allow her to ride the sensation to explosion. Being teased, damn it, teased! Determined not to be turned into a bleating mound of flesh, at least not yet, she forced her world back into focus.

Yes, a man, no doubting it now. He'd come a little closer, and although the shadows still held him in mystery, she thought she caught an amused look in his eyes. Amused! How would he like it if the tables were turned?

"Getting warmed up, are you? Starting to get the idea, are you?"

Belatedly realizing that Sammy had stopped whipping her, she dragged her gaze off the stranger and onto the experienced rigger. Giving her a superior smile, Sammy ran his nails lightly over her hip bones. *Shit, don't tickle me, don't!* She was still trying to adjust to the change in sensations when he abruptly and confidently spread her labial lips and ran his forefinger into her sodden opening. A moment later a second finger joined the first. The heel of his hand pressed against her mons. Melting. Fucking melting.

"Hmm. Hmm!"

"Like this, do you my sweet?"

Eyes wide and system close to cracking, she shook her head.

"Oh, I think you do!" More pressure, fingers going deeper. And now his other hand pulled the chain linking her breasts so pain and more sparked through them.

"Ahhh! Hmm!"

"I can't understand you. Speak up."

There was no speaking in her and no tamping down the conflicting sensations now running rampant throughout her. Sammy kept after her with pleasure and pain until she thought she'd go mad. When she tried to shake him off, he made a lie of her pathetic efforts before finally, thankfully releasing the chain. The silver thread danced between her breasts, whipping back and forth and creating its own fire. Her nipples begged for mercy and yet ripples of hot need kept her moving. Sammy's fingers were still inside her, possessing her, testing her limits.

Eyes searching for anything to focus on, finding and then locking onto the stranger. *Dance for me,* he commanded with nothing more than a shift of his weight. *Let me understand what you're feeling.*

Something to concentrate on, something to do. Even when Sammy ripped off the clamps and massaged blood back into her throbbing nipples, she shivered and tossed her head for the stranger. Only when the pain receded did she realize she was no longer housing Sammy's fingers. She redoubled her laughable attempts to free herself.

"You love this. You're already becoming a compliant little employee, but I've just begun." Sammy repeatedly slapped her belly. "You need some more warming up and then we'll get on to the fun stuff."

This time warming up began with Sammy selecting a long, thin switch and walking slowly around her while planting stinging slaps wherever and whenever he chose. Each blow was an electrical jolt, adding to the confusion plowing rampant throughout her nervous system. Although not nearly as exciting as sex, the assaults kept her awareness of her body on high alert. Pain followed by pleasure, she kept telling herself. That's what Sammy had promised.

But Sammy's words weren't what fed her shudders. The

stranger—that tall, rangy man with the wide shoulders and solid legs—held her attention, or at least what she had in the way of ability to concentrate. In her mind, his slacks evaporated. With his thighs and calves and butt and erect cock revealed, the stranger became something primitive, maybe as primitive as she was.

As the teasing whipping continued, her body became the stranger's pallet, his tool and toy. He, not Sammy, was controlling and playing with her, discovering her secrets and bringing her heat and cold. She lived not for, but through him, gifted him with her raw emotions.

And in turn he granted her nothing of him.

It wasn't until she heard a buzzing that she realized Sammy had dropped the switch and was guiding a penis-shaped vibrator toward her core. The batteries sounded fresh, and strong. No longer trying to pretend that she was being assaulted against her will, she widened her stance and welcomed the intruder home. Warm and hard, it slid up and in, filled her and brought her memories of flesh and blood invasions. Sammy pressed against the base to keep it in place, and how she loved his firm grip on her buttocks. Waves of rippling movement spun through her pussy.

Pleasure, all pleasure.

The camera plowed close to record her expression; Carole was saying something; an insect kept trying to crawl along the back of her neck. And the vibrator worked its magic, worked her up and out and high and hot. What restraints? What nudity? What existence beyond pure, primitive sex?

Ignoring the camera, she again sought out the stranger. He was even closer now, maybe close enough that he could smell her sweat and hear the vibrator. The bulge between his legs spoke of his arousal while his dark brown eyes remained cool, maybe cold.

Cold? A man with a responsive cock but no heart?

The thought splintered, then evaporated as her climax struck. It built, kept building, shaking her with an intensity she seldom experienced. Long after she should have started returning to earth, she screamed into the gag and fought Sammy and his damnable toy and dug through the stranger's layers looking for his heart. Nothing. Either that or a deeply buried soul.

"Please, please, please!" she begged, body twitching, sweating, dying and being born. "Can't take, can't take."

"Holy shit! You got that on film, right? Look at her go."

"That was incredible," Carole said as she loosened the rope around Saree's right wrist. "What got you going like that? I thought you were going to pass out."

Saree still wasn't quite sure she was conscious, but then what did it matter? Her legs were already free and under her and hopefully capable of supporting her once she could lower her arms. Cooked spaghetti touched on how she felt. Overcooked. "It was incredible," she thought to say. "Sammy, where'd you get those batteries?"

"I'd tell you but then I'd have to kill you. Look, there's some insect repellant in my pack. You can use it while we set up for the next scene."

Good old Sammy, ever the professional. But maybe the rumors about his being gay were right and that's why he could play with women all day and not get a hard-on.

Deliberately not looking to where she'd seen shadow man, Saree slipped her terry cloth robe over her shoulders and grabbed a bottle of water. Several long swallows later, she began to feel like herself again.

"I'll be back in a minute," she said. "Someone I want to talk to."

"Huh?"

Saree pointed for Carole's benefit. "Looks like I have an admirer."

"Fuck. I didn't see him. What the hell is he doing here?"

"That's what I'm about to find out."

"Just don't forget to scream if he tries something."

Behind her laughter, Saree acknowledged a sliver of concern. She couldn't imagine the man grabbing her, but hadn't her chat sessions taught her that caution was the number one consideration? Yes, and yet something about him was pulling her in his direction. Sure, she should have closed her robe in front and cinched up the belt, but one thing about the way she earned her keep, modesty didn't mean the same to her as it did to most women.

Besides, she wanted to see if she could push a few buttons.

It didn't take long to reach him, but once there she couldn't think of anything to say. Maybe it was just her being barefoot while he had on brand-new hiking boots, but he seemed damn big while she, hell, when was the last time she'd felt this small and slight? Up close, it was easy to see that his slacks and shirt were custom made. Even his boots were top class. Okay, at least he wasn't some homeless drunk camped out in the boondocks.

"You want to know how I reacted to watching you come, don't you," he said after a too-long silence. "It was quite interesting."

"Interesting? I don't think I've ever heard it described quite that way."

"Maybe my reaction's unique."

His voice wasn't any deeper than most men's. That being the case, why did it feel as if it was worming its way beneath her skin? About to chalk it up to her just-climaxed state, she amended. It was his eyes, no question about it. So dark brown that there was some ebony in there, they carried an unsettling intensity. Unsettling and exciting. "Do you know what we're doing?" she asked.

"Oh yes. This is a Dungeon production. And you're Sass."

Rocking back on her heels, she wondered if she should have stopped when there was still more distance between them.

"You should feel honored that you're so well known."

"I am." *I guess.* "We, ah, we don't usually have an audience."

When he nodded, a small grin slid over his mouth—his strong, straight mouth. "Did it make a difference? Knowing I was watching made it harder for you to come?"

More like his presence made her come harder. "When I'm working, not much gets between me and giving members their money's worth."

"Working? That's not what most people would call what just happened."

"If you know my name then you know how I make my living."

"Point taken." His gaze had remained on her face. Now they slid over her terry-clad body with her close-to-fully-exposed breasts and cunt and settled on her bare feet. "How long before the next scene?"

"Not long, but then they can't start without me."

Another of his half grins softened his strong-boned features. "You're well named, Sass. You don't back down from anyone or anything, do you?"

"Not if I can help it. There were a couple of bullies when I was in high school who—you don't need to know that and I'm not interested in dredging up the past. Getting to the point, I'm a lot more interested in determining whether coincidence and coincidence alone is responsible for your being here at the same time we are."

"I wondered when you'd get to that. Let me start to introduce myself. Perhaps you remember some recent online correspondence with someone named Reeve."

"You're Reeve?"

"You do remember then."

"Yes," she breathed. This was surreal, and disconcerting.

Before Reeve could elaborate, if that's what he intended, Sammy hollered that he was nearly ready to get going again.

And despite what she'd said about nothing happening without her, time was money. "I have to go. Ah, about getting to Bubba through me so you can recover the bet you lost on that match he blew, I'm afraid we broke up."

"It's all right." Reeve ran his long, strong fingers into his back pockets. "I'm not hurting for money. For the record, that's how I knew where you'd be today—a little greasing of the palms."

"You—"

"I bribed someone at The Dungeon."

"Why?"

He didn't immediately answer, and she had to be wrong, but she had the strangest feeling that he didn't want to say anything at all. "Sass, I developed a highly successful electronics enterprise." Extracting a hand from his back pocket, he handed her a gold-embossed business card. "I'm wealthy, which makes it possible to accomplish things most people are unable to. I indulge my appetites, and right now I want the two of us to share a meal."

"That's it? You want to take me out to dinner?" She'd study the card later.

"Not out. I have a boat, an overpriced and shiny craft docked at Marina del Rey. Do you know where that is?"

Marina del Rey was one of the Los Angeles area's wealthiest communities. "Yes."

"The boat has an extensive galley, and I'm a great cook. That's my offer—lobster and asparagus on the bay while the sun's setting. Friday night. No strings attached."

No strings attached. Could she believe him? "Lobster?"

"And the wine of your choice. I believe you'll find something you like in my collection. What do you say, Sass? Ready for an evening of superb food and incredible views?"

"That's all?"

He didn't answer.

4

"I'm impressed. Very impressed." Trying not to gape, Saree took in the boat's exterior as Reeve gave her a hand onboard. Although she knew next to nothing about anything that managed to float, she knew mahogany when she saw it. She supposed the sleek, dark red wood lavishly used as trim made sense because it was hard enough to withstand what the sea threw at it, but it struck her as over the top when it came to opulence. She would have given the craft her full and measured attention if not for the fingers still wrapped around hers.

Not sure how to extricate her hand from his, she took care not to stand too close to him. His clothing was artfully casual, expensive without making a big deal of the fact that they hadn't come off a department store rack, and although the crisp slacks and nearly new blue shirt enhanced his toned late-thirties body, she was struck by an unsettling thought. He wasn't entirely comfortable in them, as witnessed by his slightly stiff stance. Ego building as it was to conclude that he'd dressed up for her, the explanation didn't entirely fit. A man with this kind of wealth didn't need to impress people.

"Let me take a look at you," he said. Still holding her hand, he stepped back. Then, treating her as if she were his dance partner, he spun her first to the left and then the right. As he did, she patted herself on the back for having selected low sandals with rubberized soles. After more vacillating than she cared to think about and certainly wouldn't admit, she'd chosen white shorts that came nearly to her knees and a loose-fitting yellow blouse that didn't show much cleavage. The wind was doing its best to mold the fabric to her body, but she hoped he wouldn't think she was coming on to him. A wealthy man like him must have women throw themselves after him all the time. No matter what came of this evening, she was determined he not think of her as a gold digger, because she wasn't. She had all the money she needed.

"Well," she said once she was facing him again. "Did I pass muster?"

"Indeed you did." He glanced pointedly at their intertwined fingers. "Hair caught in whatever it's caught in so the wind can't make a mess of things. No heels. You'd be surprised how many women don't think about the damage those stupid things can do to a boat."

When are you going to release me? If this is a game—"Confession. I wasn't thinking about your boat. I just didn't want to fall on my ass."

"Does that happen much at work?" Another glance at their hands sent the slightest shiver down her spine. "Maybe it's an occupational hazard."

"I've gotten pretty good at making sure it doesn't. I hope you don't mind, but I'd just as soon not talk about work tonight. And—" She gave an experimental tug only to discover he wasn't about to give up his claim that easily.

"And what?"

"And I want to make it clear that I'm here for the food, nothing else."

"Are you sure?"

On the verge of telling him she didn't play games, she clamped down on the words because at that very moment he was lifting her hand to his mouth and planting a feathery kiss on the tips of her fingers. Another shiver ran down her spine, this one all electricity. *Careful.*

"Yes," she finally thought to say, but maybe only because he'd finally released her. "I'm not interested in a one-night stand. Also, I don't need anything from you so I'm not going to throw myself at you."

His gaze had had a wary, almost cynical look as if he was waiting for her to do exactly that, but with her comment, she sensed him relaxing. She also caught a hint of surprise. "I appreciate your honesty," he said. "It's not something I get every day."

"I imagine you don't." She was suddenly sorry for this man whose wealth made him suspect everyone's motives. "Maybe you haven't thought of this, but honesty tends to be in short supply in my line of work. For example, the men we both *met* in the chat room, I'd be surprised if anything any of them said about themselves was the truth."

Smiling a smile that did something to the pit of her stomach, he pointed, drawing her attention to a trio of seagulls flying overhead. "I thought you didn't want to talk shop. May I suggest a safe topic—seagulls. Actually it's more of a warning. They don't much care where they let it drop, if you know what I mean."

Returning his smile, she made a show of spreading her hands over her head. "I'm a Southern California girl, I know seagulls. How do you suggest we protect ourselves from unwanted deposits?"

"By going below deck while I fix dinner."

Below deck. Alone with him. "You need any help? I was going to bring some wine as my contribution, but I didn't know what kind you like."

He took a step toward the stairs leading down. "I have more than enough wine for tonight. In fact, I'm going to suggest a light chardonnay I like with fish. I hope you'll agree."

Not sure of the proper protocol for such things, she held back until she was certain he intended to take the stairs first. When he disappeared, for no more than a second she fought the urge to abandon ship. She hadn't had a date in so long that she wasn't sure how people did that anymore, and yet more than uncertainty was at play. Although the marina was filled with impressive boats or ships or watercrafts or whatever they were called, as far as she'd been able to determine, only one other had anyone on it, a couple of elderly men who looked as if they'd recently returned from a day of fishing and drinking. The extensive marina was like being in an abandoned building—abandoned that is except for a man who outweighed her by many pounds and was in prime physical condition.

"Are you coming?" he asked. "I'll take you for the grand tour later, ideally after the gulls have gone to bed."

Hey, sis, guess where I am tonight? Sorry I didn't tell you; I'm now thinking maybe I should have. Anyway, if you get this message, don't hang up. I might want to get back in touch with you.

Calling on the technique that had gotten her through countless bondage scenes, she mentally slipped into her *nothing* place. That done, she planted her sandal on the top stair and started down. It was shadowy below the water level, not totally unlit but far from bright. Fortunately before she could do more than frown, he flipped a switch, illuminating a bead of light that ran around the ceiling of the small but well-equipped kitchen.

"It goes without saying that this is a one-person galley." He demonstrated by extending his arms and nearly touching the opposite walls.

"Galley," she muttered, not bothering to take her eyes off his chest and arms. "I'm going to have to remember that."

"You're a landlubber? Not much chance I can sign you on as a crew member then? Darn, I'm in need of someone to swab the deck."

"I'd make a lousy swabbie." She held up her hands so he could see her artificial nails. "Gotta protect these suckers."

"You have to wear them?"

What did he think of them and of the other enhancements such as breast enlargement that she considered essential to job security? And if he said he considered them a waste of time and money, would she defend her stance or agree with him? Shaking off questions she had no answers to, she made a show of hiding her hands behind her. "Look at it this way. They get me out of doing a lot of manual labor. Hmm. Something smells fantastic."

"Fresh garlic sautéed in drawn butter."

Her mouth watering, she stepped into the galley, careful not to infringe on his space. The garlic was barely simmering, the aroma making her stomach growl. "You really can cook, can't you?"

"One of my many skills."

"I think I love you." Surprised by what had just come out of her mouth, she shook her head. "Anything I can do to help?"

"How are you at uncorking a bottle of wine?"

"One of *my* many skills."

His laughter helped her relax, and when he handed her a high-tech corkscrew, she backed up to give him full access to his work area. A high counter complete with a couple of stools was positioned just beyond the galley, and after pouring two glasses of a light, semisweet wine, she perched on one of the stools so she could watch him work. He'd already made a salad that appeared to be equal parts vegetables and fruit and screamed *healthy*. Much as she hated seeing him drop a couple of live lobsters into boiling water, she forced herself to come face to face with the reality of their meal.

While the lobsters were cooking, he dropped some angel-hair pasta into another pot of boiling water, and when the pasta was tender, he drained it and tossed it with the garlic mixture. Their conversation was light and unremarkable: the weather, whether work on the nearest freeway exit ramp was ever going to be finished, how the city's professional baseball team was doing.

"You know," he said as she replenished their wineglasses, "it's much too beautiful an evening to spend it inside. What say I put up an umbrella to protect us from bird droppings and we eat up top."

Relaxed by the wine, she nodded agreement. In less than five minutes, they were seated opposite each other at a small linen-covered table watching the sun set. Placing the first bite of lobster on her tongue, she closed her eyes and sighed. "It doesn't get any better than this. Of all the things I could be doing tonight, this is at the top of the list. In fact, it's the only thing on my list."

"Because of the view, the food, or the company?"

"Let me get back to you on that." She opened her eyes. The sunset was turning Reeve's features a dusky rose. Beneath the warm glow was a darkness she attributed to the approaching night. She knew nothing about this man except that her body wanted his. Everything, even this expensive craft, might be a lie, but she didn't see how that was possible. Sipping, she acknowledged that she'd slipped into a mental and emotional space she seldom experienced. She was relaxed and comfortable in his presence. Sexual awareness was part of the component of course, giving rise to the question of whether they'd have sex before the evening was over, but she didn't want to just drink his booze and eat his food and jump his bones. She also wanted to get to know him.

"You really aren't married?" she perhaps unwisely started with. "I'd think some woman would have figured out you're a pretty good catch."

Holding a fork full of salad near his lips, he studied her. "I could say the same of you. You're a beautiful and, I suspect, a financially secure woman. Why aren't you married?"

"No reason to, yet. No need to rush, yet." *And no one I've found that I'd want to spend my life with, yet.*

"Your reasons are the same as mine, Saree. In addition, I see marriage as the ultimate compromise. I had to do enough of that in order to make my business work; although I've sold it and retired, I want to remain in control of my personal life."

"It sounds as if you don't have a very high opinion of marriage."

Darkness bled into his eyes; something shut down inside him. "Marriage can be hell, and worse, if the wrong people are involved."

What are you talking about? "It's not like that for everyone; it wasn't for my parents, and my sister has found someone special."

Reeve had been dividing his attention between her and his meal, but now he stopped and stared at her. If anything, his eyes absorbed even more of a midnight hue so that he looked older, and strangely vulnerable.

"What? Don't you believe me?"

"I didn't say anything," he muttered after a telling silence. "There was something in your voice, a wistfulness, sorrow. Are your parents dead?"

It was nearly dark now with night being held back by the marina lights, the day coming to an end, and the promise of sleep's forgetfulness ahead of her. She'd come to terms with her parents' death in the years since they'd been taken from her and her sister. Surely he was mistaken about her tone, or was he? And maybe he was keeping the focus on her and off himself.

Putting down her wineglass, she studied the man who in truth was a stranger. Being around virile men had long triggered a predictable response in her. Not only did her nipples harden, but her senses became more alert, and her pussy heated and softened. Those things had already happened, and every time he spoke, her nerve endings responded, but at the moment she couldn't say what she was or wasn't feeling beyond the tightness in her chest and her questions about him.

"We had an incredible family," she heard herself admit. "There's my older sister Hayley and myself. We were raised by the most loving, committed parents any children could ever want. Our parents were not strict but firm in their beliefs. Neither Hayley nor I ever questioned whether we were loved or what the family standards were. Mom and Dad let us know that our looks—Hayley's a beautiful woman—weren't what was important. Formal education was vital of course, but more than that, we were expected to make the most of our brain cells. 'Be curious'—that's what they always said. 'Be curious and look for the answers.' "

"How did they feel about what you're doing with your life?"

"They—they both died before I really got into the porn business." About to lower her head so she wouldn't have to meet his eyes, she decided she needed to see his reaction. "I have a strong sex drive. It's been that way since I became an adolescent. Back then I didn't know how to handle what I was feeling; I know I was terribly confused and was afraid to say anything to my folks. But they *got* it."

"Hmm. I'd dare say having a nympho for a daughter isn't something most parents want to have to deal with."

"I'm sure you're right," she muttered. *Careful. Don't say anything he might try to twist to his advantage.* "But they came through like troopers. Once we'd opened the gates, there wasn't anything I felt I couldn't talk to them about. They even gave me some coping strategies."

"Cold showers?"

"Cold showers, lots of physical exercise, not drinking when I was on a date, acknowledging and then tuning down the messages my body was giving out as much as possible."

"You're drinking now."

Was this it, the come-on she'd just warned herself against? And the other half of the question was whether she was ready for things between them to move to the next level. The animal-instinct part of her response was a loud and clear *hell yes*, but experience had taught her to keep a tight leash on the beast. "I'm also not sixteen like I was when the hormones were in full rage mode."

"But they're still there. Your work leaves no doubt of that."

Although disappointed because he was insisting on keeping the conversation on sex, she couldn't blame him. After all, in all modesty a man would have to be dead or in a coma not to react to the implied message in her choice of careers. *I'm hot. I'm horny. I'm in a hurry. Let's get it on.* "That's only part of what I am, Reeve. I'm also a daughter."

"A daughter who lost her parents much too young." Parents she loved and respected.

Unexpected tears burned her eyes. Her parents had been dead for five and five and a half years, respectively, and she'd had time to, not get over the loss, but accept what couldn't be changed. Why then was she reacting like this?

Because of the tone of his voice. And the walls around him.

"That's what Hayley and I kept saying." After picking up her glass, she sipped. Then, dividing her attention between the relentless eyes on her and the artificial lighting giving the marina a fairyland look, she told him about losing her father to kidney disease following a long, desperate, and ultimately helpless time. A month later her mother was diagnosed with breast cancer.

"Hayley and I sometimes wonder if Mom lived such a short time—less than a year—because she was so worn down from losing her husband. Much as she loved us, she needed to be with him."

"You'll probably never know that."

"I don't expect to. It's something that sustains me, thinking that they're together again." Her lobster had cooled off while she was talking, but she chewed anyway.

"So you and your sister helped care for your father and then you did the same for your mother?"

There was something about his voice, yet another tone she couldn't quite put her fingers on. She could almost swear he hadn't expected to give a darn about her past and didn't know what to do with the unexpected emotion. If that was the case, it served as proof that he was only interested in one thing—getting inside her pants. Given her mood at the moment, she wouldn't bet on his chances.

"I dropped out of college and moved in with Mom. Earlier Hayley had moved back home to care for Dad so it was my turn. Besides, Hayley was engaged by then, and I wanted her to have her own life."

Between bites of tepid dinner, she spelled out the last months of her mother's life when days revolved around doctor appointments and nights were spent praying for a miracle. But, conditioned by what had happened to their father, neither she nor Hayley truly expected a miracle. Instead, she cleaned and cooked and counted pills and drove to doctors' offices and treatment centers and tried to keep on top of the medical bills. Gentle and accepting to the last, her mother had taught her a valuable lesson in facing the grim reaper.

At the end, Hayley was married, but that didn't mean the two of them didn't talk every day, and on weekends Hayley stayed with Mom so Saree could have a few hours to herself. Close as the two of them had become during their father's illness, their mother's disease had unified them in powerful ways.

"Sounds like your sister had an understanding husband," Reeve said.

"That's what we thought. Unfortunately, we didn't know him, not the real him. The short story is he's behind bars for cheating his investment clients. Hayley divorced him." Distracted by what was probably a past-curfew seagull, she stared at the sky. "That taught us a valuable lesson in not taking people at face value." She sighed. "It's like the men I *meet* in my chat room. I don't buy into anything they say."

"What about me?"

Her mouth was suddenly dry. "What about you?"

"Do you believe I'm who I say I am?"

Water lapped against Reeve's and the other boats. An occasional distant horn spoke of boats out in the harbor, and she could just catch the murmur of male voices, but the night had isolated them. No one, not even the sister she thought of as an extension of herself, knew where she was. "Do you think I'd tell you?"

"Good point. One thing I'd like to run past you. Let's assume that my intentions where you are concerned are less than honorable. Given that, would I have gone to the expense and effort of fixing the meal I did? Why not spring for a drive-through burger before taking you to my hideout?"

"Probably because I wouldn't have said yes to the golden arches." Making out his expression was getting harder so she took what she could get, which she read as a teasing tone. "About this hideout of yours, where is it?"

"In the mountains."

"L.A. is short of what I consider real mountains so I find that hard to believe."

"Point taken. What about an abandoned building or ware-house?"

"Hmm. Distinct possibility, but wouldn't there already be someone holing up in anything that's been abandoned?"

"I'm bigger than them. I'll kick them out."

"You probably could," she conceded. With each breath she took she was relaxing a bit more. Just the same, she wished she hadn't poured two glasses of wine down her throat. "I hope you'll arrange to have this place cleaned before you attempt to take me into it. I do have my standards."

He laughed. And for just an instant, she thought he was going to extend his hand. As for whether she'd take it . . .

"Standards?" he echoed. "That's not the impression I've gotten from seeing you in certain bondage sets. That one isn't really the engine room of some ocean liner, is it? Please tell me that isn't grease on the floor. And that barn stall—hopefully someone cleaned up after the last cow was in there."

"All fake, fortunately. I wish I could say the same for some of the locations they've taken me and other models. Did you see that fishing shed, the one the tide came within inches of? It smelled of dead fish, thousands of dead fish. And the air circulation sucked."

"I remember that, but you didn't look unhappy to me. In fact, you seemed pretty pleased with the hook lodged in your—"

"I know where it was lodged," she interrupted. Just thinking about the sleek hook anchored in her ass compelled her to clench her pussy muscles. It had taken a half dozen sessions to get used to the *toy*, but there was nothing like being fucked while that sucker was in place to at least double her pleasure. "I don't need the reminder."

He stirred through what remained of his salad, speared a bit of melon, and held it out for her to take. Not trying to lie to herself that there was nothing erotic about the gesture, she accepted it. "Do you mind if I ask you a business question?" he asked softly.

"Ask," she said around the mouthful. "I can't promise I'll answer."

"Good enough. All right, when it comes to planning a session, how much input do you have? I mean, ahead of time do you know exactly what's going to happen?"

He cared; he wasn't just making conversation or looking for something to hang a dirty joke on. And once again she had the feeling his curiosity surprised him, which seemed strange to her. But maybe not if he was so jaded that he believed he'd seen and experienced everything there was to see and experience.

"Most times," she answered. "I always know in a broad way what the rigger intends to accomplish. But the steps aren't choreographed if that's what you're asking. If they were, I'd be acting from start to finish."

"And it wouldn't be nearly as much fun."

"Right on. Reeve?" She took a moment to breathe in the sea air. "I meant it. The last thing I want to spend the evening doing is going over the details of my job. Surely you understand; you can't always want to talk shop."

"You're right. I have no interest in talking about what I do for a living."

Didn't you say you're retired? "There's more to me than being a porn star." Hadn't she said something like this before? "It isn't as if it's a career I can stay in until I'm ready for social security."

"A young person's industry."

"Especially for women," she allowed. "The moment I start sagging, I'll be replaced."

"What about plastic surgery?"

Because she saw her breasts as tools of the trade, she didn't hesitate to cup and lift them. "This was the one and only time I went under the knife. From now on, nature can have her way with me."

He cocked his head. "Why? A lot of women don't think twice about regularly going under the knife."

The wise reaction would be to change the subject, but she didn't want the conversation to stay on the surface. For reasons she didn't understand, she wanted to get closer to him, to give him pieces of herself and hopefully get the same in return. "My parents both had multiple surgeries." She didn't bother trying to get above a whisper. "I was there for all of them, the time in recovery, the successes and failures, the hope and pain. I had my boobs done shortly after Mom died. At the time of my surgery, I was grieving, not thinking clearly. Being cut brought back everything my folks had endured." She rubbed the bridge of her nose.

"I'm sorry." Then, as she looked at what she could see of him from between her fingers, he reached out and gripped her wrist. Now that he was holding her, she had the feeling he didn't know what to do with her hand, or even how it had gotten into his possession. Accustomed as she was to having men's paws on her, she wasn't prepared for her reaction. Granted, she'd dumped on him when she'd told him about her parents and that had left her feeling vulnerable. Granted, she'd been turned on since she'd first spotted him tonight, but this wasn't just about itches needing to be scratched. Then what was it?

"So—" He drew out the word. "What are you going to do when the camera catches you sagging?"

That wasn't what he really wanted to say; she was willing to bet on it. Then why had he? "I don't know. That's the hell of it, I don't know."

"Maybe you'll have made enough that you won't need to work."

Like you? The thought of all those purposeless years stretching out in front of her made her shudder. Needing to distance herself from the image of her sleeping away her life, she pulled free. "Porn doesn't pay *that* well, at least not my particular niche of the industry."

"So start your own site. Do porn stars have agents? Maybe that's what you'd like to get into, handling your replacements."

"I've thought about those possibilities, but I really think the time's going to come when I want to get out of the industry. Try something completely different."

"You can turn your back on the sex?"

Yet another of those too-familiar alarms sounded inside her. "On *that* kind of sex, I know I can. There's more to life than a climax."

"But do those other things provide the level of sexual satisfaction you're getting?"

"You tell me," she snapped. Damn him for thinking her existence began and ended with her clit. "Didn't you get as much satisfaction from completing a business deal as bonking some woman you picked up? I don't know. Maybe what's between your ears isn't that important to you, just what's between your legs."

"I've hit a nerve."

"Maybe," she dodged. Then, unbelievably restless, she stood and paced to the back of the boat where a large, sturdy chair had been welded to the floor. Guessing that that's where Reeve or a guest sat when reeling in monster fish, she tried to imagine doing the same herself. But although she loved a challenge, she couldn't fathom ending any creature's life simply because she needed to be entertained.

He'd joined her but damned if she was going to acknowledge him. Damn him for not comprehending that she existed from the neck up.

That's what he'd done, hadn't he?

Why was she so confused?

"Have you talked to anyone about how you feel?" he asked. "What about your sister?"

He wasn't any closer than he'd been while they were eating, but now there wasn't a table between them. Besides, standing put her more in tune with the boat's gentle rocking, more in tune with her body's response to the movement—and him.

"Hayley's a jewelry designer. She creates incredible work, is so talented. I envy her ability, but I'm not creative. What works for her won't for me; I know, I've tried."

"Wouldn't work for me either."

For the first time she really looked at his hands thanks to a marina light. Not that there was a *business* type, but she couldn't begin to fathom those strong hands and that body behind a desk. Was that how he filled his time now that he'd sold his business, working out?

"So no future for you in the arts," he said. "What else have you looked into?"

Wondering if he'd asked his question because he'd sensed what she was thinking, she climbed into the chair and gripped the arms. "What about commercial fishing? Is there a future in that for me?"

"Are you picking something out of a hat, or does working out-of-doors appeal to you?"

"I don't know." He'd positioned himself to her right and was leaning his hip against the armrest, infringing on her space and teasing her nerve endings. "Maybe that's where I should start, deciding whether I need a roof over my head when I'm on the job."

"Maybe you'll get married to someone capable of paying all your bills and then some. Come on, you know it's a possibility. Given your looks, you could have your pick of the sugar daddies."

"Unless the man doesn't want his wife's resume to read the way mine does. Besides, who the hell said I want to live off some man."

Instead of picking up the challenge she'd thrown him, he faced her with his hands gripping both armrests. Not that she was in any danger of course, but he'd trapped her between the chair and his body.

"I'm sorry about your parents. I don't want you to think I don't care."

Blindsided by the unexpected comment, she stared up at him. His form all but blocked out the dark sky, and the way he rocked from side to side in time with the tide put her in mind of a slow, sensual dance. There was just him, and her. And the night. And words that said her pain had reached him.

"I know you do," she managed.

5

Cruising the bay at night was something everyone should do at least once, Saree concluded a half hour later. In addition, said experience was definitely habit forming, especially when the captain of the craft was a deep-spoken, dark, and sexy man. Standing next to him while he maneuvered against the incoming tide both relaxed and sexually charged her. The temperature gave no sign of dropping below a comfortable level, but that had only a little to do with why she was imagining doing this until untapped energy became more than she could handle. Bottom line, the company was responsible for the heat between her legs.

"I'm going to put things into neutral and secure the wheel," Reeve said. "Eventually the tide will bring us back to shore, and since we're the only ones around, we're not in danger of running into anyone."

They were alone, truly alone. Thanks to the newly emerged nearly full moon and countless stars, she had no trouble determining that. "You don't have to keep on entertaining me. Anytime you're ready to take me back to land's fine."

"I'm not in any hurry." Although he no longer needed to, he kept his hands on the wheel. His eyes were on the horizon.

She thought he'd ask about her schedule, but he didn't. She'd made her peace with his extended silences while they were moving through the water, telling herself he needed to concentrate on what he was doing. That excuse no longer carried any weight.

"Why are you doing this?" she asked. Perhaps three feet separated them. At the same time it wasn't nearly enough and a vast distance. "You haven't said that much; I've done most of the talking. You haven't told me much about yourself, nothing that would make me think you wanted me to get to know you." When he made no indication he'd heard her let alone had a reaction, she went on. "Are you always like this? You use silence to force people to open up about themselves?"

"Is that what you think I'm doing?"

"Don't. Don't answer a question with another one."

"I'll try not to. As for my motives, I thought I'd already made it clear that I wanted to fix you dinner."

"And that's all, a meal? If that's the case, why haven't we called it a night?"

For the first time since taking the boat out, he looked over at her. The moon did amazing things to him, painting his dark hair with silver highlights and casting his features in shadow and light so she could barely make out the real man. His body seemed as one with the ocean, flowing with it. He'd changed into something he called seaworthy before they took off, and his faded, loose-fitting T-shirt proclaimed his loyalty to the L.A. Dodgers. The breeze occasionally caused the garment to hug his body. Every time that happened, she was struck anew by how physically toned he appeared. His simple brown shorts covered maybe half of his thighs, giving her a clear view of taut legs and a right knee that had felt a surgeon's knife.

This wasn't a businessman's body, damn it!

Then who was he?

Belatedly remembering that he hadn't answered her question, she took a backward step. She might have taken another if not for the heat in his eyes and her body's humming. "What do you want from me?" she demanded.

More than you'll ever understand.

Telling herself he couldn't possibly have said or thought that, she concentrated on bringing air into her lungs. "Am I going to regret saying yes to your invitation?"

"I can't answer that for you, only you can."

A response with layers of meaning, damn it. "At least give me a hint so I can make that decision."

He was still studying her, and although she'd been looked at by countless men, this felt different. Certainly he was aware of her physical form; that was a given. But he was also looking beneath the surface, maybe as deep as her soul. The question she had to answer was whether she wanted him to.

Yes, her body fairly shouted. *Hell yes!*

Maybe not, her heart whispered.

"I'd like to ask you something," he said just when she'd reconciled herself to his silence. "The way you make your living, the way you handle your sexuality, have you ever wished it was different?"

"Different? How?"

"Now you're the one answering a question with one."

"If I am, it's because I don't know where this is going."

He wanted to touch her. Damn it, she felt the wanting throughout his body. But maybe he knew he risked a knee to his gonads if she so much as thought he was jumping her.

"Is that sex drive you told me about something you can turn on or off depending on the situation? It more than comes in handy at work, but if the situation calls for the opposite, can you plug into nun mode?"

"Why do you want to know?"

"Humor me."

Hell, no, this wasn't about humoring him. She didn't owe him anything, damn it. A thank-you for the meal and cruise was all that was called for, and just because she'd thought he was genuinely interested in her family story didn't mean she was expected to dump everything, right?

Right, yes. And yet—

"To rehash," she said with her senses reaching out for him and her sex heating. "I matured early sexually. By the time I was eleven I needed a bra, but it was more than just my body developing curves. Even before the bra went on, I wanted something I couldn't put words to. It was as if I'd put my finger into a light socket." She paused, debated, plunged ahead. "My mother caught me masturbating when I was ten, but instead of jumping down my throat, she sat next to me and helped me explore why I needed to handle myself that way. Her acceptance allowed me to be free."

She glanced down at her legs, then into his eyes again. "If I have any sexual hang-ups, I'm not aware of them. As long as it's safe and fun and legal, I'll explore it. If my parents had disapproved, I would have taken my needs underground, but they'd still exist. Now, does that answer your question?"

Instead of the yes or no she expected, he leaned toward her and placed his hands on her shoulders. "You had incredible parents. Wise. So wise."

What was that note, envy? Sorrow maybe?

Fighting her reaction to the pressure on her shoulders, she ran her hands along his side. "Yours weren't like that?"

"Doesn't matter."

"What? I—"

"I mean it. I'm not going there."

On the brink of pushing his limits, she reconsidered. He didn't want to bring up the past; only a dead woman wouldn't understand that and she was far from dead. Neither did he want to deal with an ignorant "I'm sorry."

"All right, for now," she whispered.

The tide rocked them, pushing them to the left and then the right, forcing her to widen her stance to keep her balance and increasing her hold on him. In the distance a foghorn wailed its lonely cry. The warm breeze stroked her cheeks, throat, arms, and legs.

And then his legs brushed hers.

Ah shit, gone. Just like that, lost.

Arching her back, she ran her breasts over his rib cage. His hold on her shoulders tightened, and the message couldn't have been any clearer. Whatever he wanted of her, he could get; he was that much stronger.

Didn't matter.

Because she wanted the same thing.

With her breasts still pressed against him, she slid her hands down and around so she could cup his buttocks. At the same time, she moved closer and tilted her pelvis at him. On a hissed breath, he released her shoulders but only so he could spread his much-larger hands over her ass cheeks.

Yes, his cock, grinding against her belly with a message she'd heeded for as long as she could remember. Depending on what was called for at work, at times like this she'd either call up memories of all the cocks she'd encountered or convince herself that the cock of the moment was *the* one, a massive member belonging to *the one* man she'd forsake all others for.

But that had always been fantasy because she couldn't remember when she'd last been in love or even if what she'd felt at seventeen or eighteen truly qualified as love.

Not tonight, she ordered as heat chased along her spine. She wasn't going to pretend or fantasize or recall or even wish. She'd live in the moment. With the man who called himself Reeve.

"I didn't want this," he muttered, his breath warming her forehead. Still gripping her buttocks with iron strength, he pushed at her, withdrew a little, pushed again.

"You—why not?"

No answer, but then she hadn't expected any, and even if he'd handed it to her, would she have been able to make sense of whatever he said?

Probably not, because her arms were now around his neck and she was standing on her toes, and the too-familiar demanding ache gripped her.

Given the right circumstances and even some that were less than perfect, she could climax before the average man did. In an attempt to level the playing field, she'd developed a number of strategies. Granted, most of them took place once clothes were no longer an issue, but something told her she shouldn't wait until then.

Teeth clenched against another kind of clenching in another part of her anatomy, she tilted her head so she could rake her teeth over the side of his neck. His response—predictable—was to release her left cheek so he could grip her hair and haul her head off him.

"What the hell?"

"What's the matter? Can't you take it?" she challenged. "It's called foreplay."

"If you've drawn blood—"

"Then I'll pay for a transfusion." The grip on her hair held her head immobile, but then she was used to being restrained and knew how to use helplessness to feed her libido. "I didn't take you for a weakling."

"Are you always this aggressive?"

"When I want something, yes."

"You want then?"

No more words, action. With her head still forced to a less-than-comfortable angle, she rocked her lower body forward. His cock fought back, a length of hot lumber more than ready to accomplish what she needed it to. No question about it, this man was built for sex. Oh, she might have encountered a larger cock, not that she was into making comparisons, but it was obviously capable of fulfilling its assigned task.

And then?

No, damn it, she wasn't going to let that question intrude tonight! She hated the part of her that insisted on looking beyond the moment, that needed a future.

Sex was good. Sex was tonight's goal.

Nothing else.

Still, as she rolled her pelvis from one side to the other, she didn't entirely succeed in staying in the moment. This man, this gift from the sex gods, was nothing more than another in a long list of prime candidates, and yet he could be.

Maybe.

Releasing her hair, he pressed his fist against the small of her back as if trying to reach her womb. He had to know how close he was, how quickly the pressure had claimed her attention. If he thought he was going to gain control over her this way, he was mistaken. Damn him, mistaken! She wasn't that easy.

Or was she?

Rising onto her toes, she again touched her mouth to his neck, this time sheathing her teeth with her lips. And if her tongue dampened the soft skin there, that was his problem. His sensation to deal with.

When he jerked and tensed, she smiled a secret knowing smile and sucked in a deep breath. Her breasts still pressed against his chest, but the contact was now tentative instead of possessive, a tease and a promise.

The air had a wild smell to it. That coupled with the lonely horn took her far from brightly lit sets and cameramen. There was no director here, no need to pause while some prop was re-arranged, no clamping down on carnal hunger until the lens was in position. This was real, real. Sex for sex's sake.

Suddenly unnerved, she acknowledged that it had been so long since everything had been about her and a man that she'd nearly forgotten sex could be this simple. Honest. Uncomplicated.

And yet was anything more complicated than fucking a stranger?

Acknowledging the danger and adventure inherent in the act, she dove into the dark current.

There was just the two of them and a craft she had no knowledge of. She couldn't even remember where shore was. If something happened to him and she had to take the wheel, could she get them back to safety or would they wind up in the middle of the ocean?

Didn't matter.

Now.

Giving herself a mental shake, she leaned away and brought Reeve back into focus. If anything he looked more formidable than he had earlier. Where before civilization had cloaked him, she sensed that what they were about had penetrated his protective outer layer to mix with his wild nature. This was no oiled-skin dom, no leather clad, whip-wielding master. He was man. Simply man.

And she was woman. Hungry woman.

Growling, she kicked at the inside of his right leg, forcing him to increase his stance. That done, she reached for his cock. Her intention had been to see how much of it fit within the palm of her hand, but before she could do more than spread her fingers over the long thick mound, he clamped his hand around her wrist. "Not going to happen, Saree. These aren't your shots to call."

"Afraid I'm going to hurt you?"

"Not in this lifetime."

Before she could come up with a reply, he forced her hand up and around to her back. Accustomed to such handling, she relaxed and held back the hint of panic that tried to invade her thoughts. Being in a strong man's grip always triggered her libido, and although she sometimes worried that said libido would get in the way of the instinct for survival, the thought barely touched her before she shoved it away.

This was foreplay, fun.

"What's up, big boy, you trying to duplicate what you see on your computer? Bring any handcuffs with you?"

"You love living on the edge, don't you?"

Spinning her around toward him, he lifted her in his arms and carried her to the rear of the boat. Although she ordered herself not to, she rested the side of her head against his chest and drank in his scent. He smelled of the sea and more, of male and arousal, of promise.

When he deposited her in what she now knew was called the fighting chair, she sank back in it and stared up at him. The seat had been designed for someone much larger than her and built to withstand a battle with a fish weighing more than the man or woman who'd hooked it. The chair and Reeve surrounded her, cradling and protecting and diminishing her. She was in Reeve's world, a world of strength and battle.

Running her fingers over the wooden arms, she again studied the man who seemed an integral part of his surroundings. She had no doubt that if she so much as made a move to escape, he'd force her back down, but she didn't want to leave.

Feeling small and feminine instead of the businesswoman she'd worked so hard to become, she extended a hand toward him. "What do you want?"

"You. Willingly."

"You have it. You must know that."

"I don't know anything about you, Saree." The look he gave

her was beyond confusion, almost as if he was lost. "You're not what I expected."

"In what way?" Why wasn't he taking her hand?

"You're more complex."

"And you're not?"

"No. I'm not." He ran his fingers between hers, spreading hers and infusing them with his strength and warmth. "What you went through with your parents was incredible. I never expected . . ."

"You thought I was some oversexed simple-minded bimbo? Instead I turned out to be a real human being?"

"Something like that."

Understanding he didn't want to reveal more than he already had, she contented herself with studying the contrast between his dark, competent fingers and her small, pale ones. Tonight she wasn't playing a role. Nothing was expected of her—except honesty. And although he wasn't giving her the same in return, she'd take what little he granted her.

Not sure what she had in mind, she brought their intertwined hands up to her mouth and planted a series of feathery kisses on his fingertips. The chair was on a riser above the deck floor. As a consequence, she and Reeve were nearly eye to eye. Just the same, she couldn't shake the impact of his larger and stronger body.

Damn it, she was more accustomed to the male form than the majority of women. Certainly she'd had more experience exploring the naked male and should have a familiar if not jaded reaction and response to muscle and bone, but he was far from what she was accustomed to. No experienced dom or rigger, he nevertheless exuded an undeniable alpha air.

Was that it, he was alpha wolf and she his potential mate?

Silently laughing off the absurd notion, she sucked on his fingertips. As she did, she studied him, pleased to note that his self-control was in jeopardy. With a wink as warning, she straightened a leg and slid it between his. He remained in place, prompting her to lift her leg until her shin bone found his crotch. "A warning," he hissed. "Unless you're ready to face the consequences, don't."

"I'm not teasing. Did you think I was?"

"I'm just telling you how it is."

Smiling, she started rubbing her leg against him. "This is my answer."

Although she could have sworn he was about to say something, only silence greeted her declaration. Grabbing her leg at the thigh, he pushed up, forcing her to bend her knee. At the same time, he backed away, causing her to lose contact with him. But instead of releasing her, he continued bending her knee until he'd anchored her foot on the edge of the chair. Holding her in place with a single hand, he flipped off her sandal. That done, he rolled her leg to the outside.

Far from fighting, she slid forward a little in wordless invitation. And although her vision blurred, she kept her eyes open as he ran a hand under her shorts. His rough finger pads on the inside of her thigh made her shiver. "You're tickling—"

"That's not tickling, Saree. If you want me to demonstrate—"

"No." Sucking in sea air, she willed herself to relax. But although she managed to leave her leg in place, she couldn't do anything about the way her nails dug into the chair arms. "I don't want . . ."

Inch by inch, movement by movement, his assault on her thigh continued. Although there was no doubt of his destination, she focused on the journey as he slid toward her core. The sleek skin on her inner leg was so damn sensitive, fragile almost in contrast to other parts of her body. Adding to the unsettling and sensual sensation was the knowledge that she couldn't easily break free. Oh, she could bury her nails in his flesh if fight came to fight, but what if he managed to shake off the pain while—while what?

There he was, his forefinger sliding along her panties, teasing, not asking permission to enter that private zone but demanding. Why hadn't she worn slacks?

But if she had, that would have only delayed the end result. The culmination she wanted.

On a sigh, she slid even closer so now much of her weight rested on her tailbone. Off balance, she accepted that getting away from him would be even harder now. His covered hand retreated, but only momentarily. And when he came at her again, he wasted no time working his fingers under the elastic. Her panties, bare inches of fragile fabric, nevertheless hindered his movement. Her opening remained sacred, virginal, cheated.

If he too felt cheated, he gave no indication as he leaned toward her again. At the same time, a fingertip pressed down on her labia, reaching, stretching, finding moisture. Breathing rapidly, she pushed even farther forward. Her head now rested on the back of the chair, causing her to stare at the stars.

There was just the two of them, them and the night—and hunger.

"Reeve, please."

"Please what?"

Only vaguely aware that she'd spoken, she rolled her head to the side but still couldn't make out his features. She was limp and useless, a toy for him to play with, sex offered.

"Stand up."

"What?"

Not waiting for her to pull herself together, he withdrew his hand but only so he could grip her upper arms and haul her to her feet. She had to spread her legs to keep from losing her balance. "Take off your shorts," he ordered.

Just like that? Forget foreplay?

She was gathering her thoughts so she could tell him he was jumping the gun and she wasn't that easy when he hooked his fingers around her shorts' waistband and flipped the button loose. Afraid he might tear something, she slapped his hands away and handled the unzipping herself. Only then did she acknowledge a certain truth; she wasn't any more interested in foreplay than he was.

Glaring at him for taking her so far so fast, she nevertheless worked both the shorts and panties to her hips. Then, seeing herself from a distance, she stopped. "Why are we doing this?"

"Because we need to."

Ah, of course. That made all the sense in the world. She might have told him she was grateful for his wisdom if he hadn't distracted her by again taking hold of her shorts and tugging down, taking the panties at the same time. He stopped when the garments were around her knees, his head up, eyes digging into her. "What?" she demanded.

"This."

With that, he planted a hand over her belly and pushed, forcing her back onto the chair. She landed with a slap of skin against waterproof material. Instead of telling him he was taking a hell of a lot for granted, she let the chair surround and support her. Watching him, she splayed her legs as much as her clothes allowed. *Now what?* She challenged with her eyes.

This, he answered. Hands out, he planted one foot on the riser. Instead of reaching for her heat, he pulled up on her top so it was now bunched just below her breasts and ran his knuckles over her belly. Trying not to squirm, she again dug her nails into the chair arms. If one or more nails broke, so be it. Despite her efforts to the contrary, her lids slid over her eyes and locked her in the darkness of her mind. She couldn't say she trusted him; how could she when things had happened so fast between them? But need powerful enough to make her think of chain and rope spun around her. For these moments she wanted only one thing—him, his body speaking to hers.

You're making me crazy, she thought to tell him as his finger pads traced the outline of her ribs. This was private, man and woman testing each other's boundaries.

Only, she acknowledged when he dipped a thumb into her navel, he was doing the testing while she sat there like some dumb beast. A dumb, turned-on beast.

Breathing through her open mouth, she wallowed in the feel of his flesh on her skin. He seemed to be everywhere at once and yet not. Yes, he touched her from the base of her bra to just above her mons, but although she sighed and offered it to him, he didn't touch her sex. Cruel, damn him, cruel!

But maybe not. Maybe this was the foreplay they'd proclaimed they wanted nothing to do with.

Unexpected laughter nearly broke free at the thought. In her professional experience, foreplay consisted of being brought to the brink of a climax via a vibrator or expert hands. The riggers and doms almost never bothered touching anything except the maximum in erogenous zones unless it was to whip her there.

Remembered stings to her entire body opened her eyes. She stared at him.

"What?" he asked as he dropped his hands to his sides.

She couldn't keep her eyes off his fingers, couldn't kill the longing to feel them everywhere. "Nothing."

"Regrets? Maybe you don't want this."

"You know the answer to that." She reached for him only to have him pull away. "What's wrong? What the hell is this about?"

Instead of reminding her of the heated moisture between her legs and her puckered nipples pressing against her bra, he shook his head. "Anyone ever call you a witch?"

"A bitch, yes, but if they used the *w* word, I don't remember."

"You are, you know."

Before she could begin to prepare, he'd covered her wrists

with his capable hands, sealing them to the armrests. The familiar sensation of being restrained worked its enduring mood over her. In her world, restraint went hand in hand with sex. As long as he kept her like this, he could do whatever he wanted to her. Experience led her to believe he'd insist on sex, but his desires might be more complex than that.

Complex, yes, she decided as he held her not just with his hands but his dark gaze. She wasn't going to ask him what he was thinking; she wasn't! But if she didn't, maybe she'd never know what lived beneath the surface.

"I didn't want this," he muttered. His voice was so low that the breeze might have stolen it, leaving her with something that hadn't come from his lips.

When he continued to stare at her, any thoughts that she wasn't going to react melted. Surrounded by desire, she straightened and leaned toward him. He rocked away. Then, settling himself back in place and lifting her top over her breasts, he studied her as she strained to rub her body against his. It wasn't going to happen, damn it. His arms were so long, and she couldn't maintain this position.

"You win!" Glaring, she sank back into the chair. "Does that make you happy, knowing I've declared you the winner?"

"This isn't about being happy."

"Then what is it?"

"I don't know. That's the hell of it, I don't know."

He was speaking in riddles—to a woman he'd imprisoned in a fishing chair, a woman with her shorts and panties around her knees and her top above her breasts. "Maybe," she whispered, "I can help. If you'd just tell me what you're thinking—"

"You're complex. I didn't want you complex."

How many times had she sensed that zing of alarm tonight? No matter, it was back again. "You want simple," she teased. "I can do that. Bottom line, I want to fuck you. Sorry but I can't get any more basic than that."

He had the good sense to laugh, and if the sound was forced, she couldn't do anything about it. Being bound to the chair was bringing out the hidden submissive in her. No matter what she told those she trusted, no matter what she firmly believed about herself as the modern and independent woman, a small and—to her mind—weak element craved being controlled.

So feed off what he's uncovered.

No!

Do you have a choice?

Disgusted with and a little unnerved by the internal argument, she refocused on Reeve. "Where is this going?"

6

Funny how quickly things can take a right turn, Saree thought as she watched Reeve shuck out of his shorts. Now, like her, he was naked from the waist down.

The size of his cock didn't surprise her. True, seeing it in all its engorged glory filled in whatever blanks there might have been in her imagination, but she'd known he'd be larger and longer than average. Not only had she touched him there when he was still clothed, but she'd seen enough of the suckers to consider herself an expert.

Strange thing about a man's cock. No matter what individual differences there were, not a one failed to elicit a response from her. Those responses had all boiled down to one thing: she wanted it in her. Whether it took up residence in her pussy or mouth or even her ass didn't matter that much. She'd take her pleasure however it came. But if she had her choice—

"Condom." She spoke the word without hesitation. "You better have one."

"Yeah, I think."

He thought? Did that mean he hadn't anticipated their having sex tonight or had he thought she'd supply the one covering she always insisted a man wore? Maybe—and this possibility made her grit her teeth—he hadn't thought enough of her to concern himself with protection.

It's protection for you, too, you idiot. Just because you think I'm some kind of whore—

No, she wasn't going to go there! Facing how some people thought of her solved and resolved nothing.

Mentally shaking off the argument she knew she'd never re-solve to her satisfaction, she noted that he had picked up his shorts and was going through his wallet. When he pulled out a condom packet, she nodded approval. She even entertained the notion of helping him into it.

His expression unreadable, he opened the package, removed the condom, and rolled it onto himself. Seeing him sheathed like that distanced her from the fantasy element that came with being on a boat on an ocean bay at night with a mysterious and wealthy man. Protection was reality, plain and simple. "Thank you," she muttered.

"You shouldn't have had to ask. I'm sorry you did."

How polite and considerate he was, how normal. Why then couldn't she completely shake the sense that something was going on beneath the surface?

Because you don't do things like this. And because you don't tell strangers about your parents.

She'd been leaning forward watching him, but now she sank back into the chair. Suddenly unsure, she moistened her fingers by putting them in her mouth and sucking. Then, acutely aware of his dark scrutiny, she spread her labial lips and dipped into herself. As strong as it was, the sea smell didn't completely cover her own scent. She was soaked, nearly dripping.

"Is that for your benefit or mine?" he asked, cupping both hands around his cock.

"A little of both. What about you?"

"Just trying to keep myself under wraps until you're ready for the next step."

Once again she was struck by how gentlemanly he was; maybe it came with extreme wealth. Watching him sustain and control his erection via a series of pumping movements kicked her own arousal up a notch. And since there was no reason not to let him know, she splayed her legs even more before pushing deeper into her hole. Her role as a bondage model meant she seldom had access to her body, and although she usually had no problem with that given the ultimate reward, tending to her own needs had become a treat.

Still, she wanted *his* hands on her, not hers.

Maybe he knew what she was thinking when he erased the distance between them and closed his fingers around her wrist. Pulling gently but steadily, he forced her to vacate her hole. Then, his expression intent, he lifted her hand to his mouth and drank from the juices on her fingers.

Suddenly shy, she concentrated on returning his gaze. She couldn't think of a thing to say.

When he pressed his free hand on her mons, her harsh gasp said it all. Unhinged, she struggled to pant through the heady pressure. He wasn't touching her sex; she had no idea when or how or if he'd do that. But it didn't matter because the core of her sexuality rested just beneath his hand, and it was waiting for him. Hungry for him.

There. A finger stroking her wet opening while others spread her sex lips. Something between a cry and a groan escaped despite her efforts to keep at least some small element of her reaction from him.

When the intrusion dove deeper, her head thrashed of its own will. Another crying groan broke free. Desperate to keep from drowning, she reached for his cock, but although her fingertips found it, she couldn't hold onto him. And with his finger in her, she couldn't think, couldn't command her muscles, couldn't see. "Not fair, not fair."

"Tell me to stop then."

Like hell I will. "Later."

Although her attempt at humor earned her a deep chuckle, the sound was forced. Why? Because he'd sensed uncertainty on her part? Damn it, she knew how to turn men on!

But most of the time she turned them on because she was a hell of an actress, if not award-winning caliber, at least sure of her role. This was exploration and hesitation, being in his world with his hands on and in and around her and about to drown in the waves he'd created.

Past knowing how to fight those waves, she dropped her arms to her sides, all but slid out of the chair, and turned herself over to him.

He came at her with fingers and mouth, with his knuckles and breath. All thought of fighting the waves gone, she drifted in a heated sea. If others were out tonight and spotted his boat, they might think they were looking at two clad strangers having a private conversation, but if they came close enough, they'd discover that clothing ended at the waist and the positions were intimate. She hoped the hypothetical others would respect their need for privacy, but even if they turned out to be voyeurs, she wouldn't stop what was happening. She couldn't.

Reeve understood the female body and its needs but lacked the finesse of the pros she worked with. Still, although at times his finger worked too fast or slow and the amount of pressure was off, she wouldn't change anything. His slick finger invaded and withdrew, randomly touching her inner walls as if searching for something. The lack of rhythm forced her to stay with him, in the moment, instead of slipping off into the world created by her body and mind. And yet much as she needed to float, to simply *be,* this way made it possible for her to remain in control. A climax was there, humming in the background and awaiting its chance to break free. She taught it patience by listening to his quick breathing and pondering how his fingers had become calloused.

When he knelt and tongued her labia, she grabbed his hair, half rose, nearly came. But his gift was short—and tentative. He stood, covered her pelvic bones with his palms, and held her in place while nibbling at the side of her freely offered neck. Then that changed.

He was on his knees again, spreading hers and leaning so close that his hair brushed her inner thighs. Moaning, she rolled her pelvis at him. Her arousal seeped from her, prompting her to try to clamp her hands around his head and hold him in place.

"I'm not going anywhere," he muttered with his head between her legs. "Relax. Just relax."

Instead of pointing out that she was hardly a novice when it came to cunnilingus, she ordered her muscles to heed his command. But how could she when a second later, the tip of his tongue slipped between her cunt lips? Her arms had grown so heavy; her legs were like lead. What choice did she have but to sink into the fighting seat and continue to offer herself to him?

This time, instead of the brief and unsettling contact he'd given her before, he stayed with her. His tongue all but milked her, and his lips, his damp satiny lips, pulled her loose flesh into him until she wondered if he might swallow her. Closing his mouth around her, he held her captive, drew back only to release the pressure moments later. She hissed, mewled, gasped, and offered herself to him, handed herself over to him, gave up ownership.

"What do you want? What do you want of me?" The instant the words were out of her mouth, she'd have given anything to have them back because she didn't want him to speak. Not now.

But maybe his answer was in the pressure of his tongue pushing past her outer tissues and finding her waiting heat.

"Yes. Yes. Oh yes."

Floating again, drifting, becoming mist, hovering on the brink, losing herself, mostly losing herself and not giving a damn.

Someday, maybe, she'd teach him the nuances of what he was doing, but this was good. Wonderful. Alive.

An image of her shattering like ice formed in her mind. She'd changed from a woman to a dry dandelion caught in a breeze. Bit by bit she was losing form, parts of her drifting off into the air.

Why was he doing this for and to her? She understood men's needs and egos and had never doubted that they put themselves first. No matter what they might profess, their pleasure came before their partner's. Once a man had climaxed, if he could remain awake, he might return the favor, but the opposite simply didn't occur to any man she'd ever known—unless he was being paid for the performance. Other women might rail about their partner's selfishness, but she didn't blame them for being what nature had intended. After all, wasn't it a man's *job* to spread his seed?

Reeve was as virile as any man. He knew what she was, at least how she earned her living, so surely he'd concluded that she knew what male selfishness was all about. He wouldn't have to pretend to be the sensitive male with her; he could be all stud, all selfish.

Questions about the truth behind Reeve pulled her back to the real world. Not completely of course, but she ceased to exist solely as a drifting cunt and became a woman again. He was still kneeling before her. His tongue continued to draw wetness from her, but she was no longer blind and stupid. Instead, she was determined to get answers. Somehow.

"Your turn," she blurted. "Let me do you. I want—you deserve—"

"Don't you trust me?"

She wasn't sure what made the most impact, the loss of that incredible tongue of his or his question. "I don't know. Should I?"

"No."

No? What the hell did he mean by that? By sending an order to her muscles, she managed to sit up straight once again and closed her legs. And if he was amused because she couldn't keep her hand off herself, to the hell with him. "Is that what you usually do? Off with a woman's clothes and right to the goodies? Get her so hot and bothered she'll let you do whatever you want with her?"

"Is that how you see it?"

He stood, and with his arms folded over his chest, she didn't know whether to laugh at his half-clad state or take his cock into her mouth. "You have me off balance, that's all."

"It works both ways."

Again he planted a foot on the riser. Not sure what he had in mind, she assessed her chances of getting past him: none. Before she could decide what to do with her knowledge, he closed his hands around her waist and lifted her off the chair. At the same time, he stepped onto the riser and turned so his back was to the chair. Easily holding her in place, he sat down.

Being taller than he did nothing to lessen his impact, not that she wanted that. Besides, all it took was a look at his cock to make her decision. He must have known what she had in mind as she straddled his legs because his hold became more a caress and less restraint.

Keeping her eyes on him, she slid closer. Once she was in position, she took hold of his cock and aimed it between her legs. Except for a series of blinks, he didn't react. She supposed she could state the obvious, but she preferred to see whether he approved or stopped her attempt to mount him.

Mount him. What a wonderful thought!

Making sure she was in position wasn't the most graceful thing she'd ever done and probably would have been impossible if she hadn't been in good physical condition. As it was, she had to rely on him to steady her while she stood on her toes. A little careful bending of his nearly unbendable cock and his tip rested against her entrance. A little spreading of herself followed by a cautious lowering of her body—and there! There he was. In her.

Still depending on him for balance, she continued her descent. He filled her, invaded her. She was becoming part of him and, she told herself, he was surrendering himself to her. This union of male and female parts was forever new, forever heady. Her mouth dried, prompting her to swallow. Once she'd replenished the vital moisture, she went back to studying him. Shuttered eyes said it all, shuttered with the window to his emotions locked away. And yet sexual hunger lived in their depths. He was showing her his animal side, nothing more.

Fine. She'd give him animal in return.

Throwing back her head so she'd have ready access to all the oxygen she'd need, she started bending and then straightening her knees. She should have started slow and in control, tested her endurance and the vital alignment, but she was so damn hungry. So eager to feel his gift and feed off it.

Yes, there was the beast beneath the civilized veneer he'd shown her earlier. She felt the wild animal in his body as he repeatedly strained toward her, sensed it clawing its way to freedom via his powerful grip on her hips.

Over and over again she slammed herself at him. Damn the potential for damage to his cock! To hell with giving too much away. This was fucking, fucking on the ocean while the drifting boat contributed its own nonrhythm. There was them and the stars and moon and maybe night birds, sweat and summer's breeze and that distant, lonely foghorn.

The horn's whisper seeped into her to quiet a little of her frenzy. And yet she continued to work. The hot, wet burning in her pussy was as old as time and as necessary as breathing. It became her. She had no existence beyond the sleek scrape of cock against cunt.

Wanted no other existence.

"Shit, shit, shit." Each curse announced the start of a downward plunge. It, like her movements, started strong and hard only to slow as she neared her destination so she could concentrate on the full and beautiful sensation. She wanted her breasts to be free instead of imprisoned inside her bra and yet their confinement added to the experience.

Her thighs were on fire, endlessly burning. She might be able to keep up the pace for the rest of her life, but maybe her muscles were on the brink of collapse, kept going only because her pussy demanded satisfaction.

"Ah! Ah."

His voice. Raw and wild sounds torn from an equally raw and wild throat.

"Fuck me," she begged.

"I am. Goddamn it, I am."

Her hands were against his shoulders without her knowing how they'd gotten there, and although she needed to anchor herself to him, she yanked on his shirt's neckline and dug into his newly exposed skin. She scratched and raked, growling as she did. He answered her attack by kneading her waist with such strength that she guessed he'd leave bruises.

Bruises were good. They spoke of frenzy and fire, of a man and a woman each determined to fuck and be fucked.

That's all this was, she mused, grateful for the breeze on her buttocks and legs. Fucking a man who turned her on.

When he reared back and bared his teeth, she switched her attack from his throat to the hard plane of his belly. Although she continued carving white lines in his flesh, she took care to gentle her attack. Watching his reaction, she worked her fingers closer and closer to his groin. She was within inches of the base of his cock when he snagged her wrist and forced her arm behind her.

Both loving and fearing the restraint, she turned her full energy to burying him as deep and full as she could in her weeping and ready sex. The sweet burning sensation kicked up notch after notch. She'd been swimming, but now a powerful current controlled everything. Tossed about by incredible strength, she closed her eyes. A wave rose up over and around her to steal her strength.

Utterly spent, she collapsed on him. At the same time her cunt began a familiar and equally powerful drive. The finish line! Nothing existed except the waiting explosion, compelling her to sink into its bloodred depths. This was what it was all about, the goal! The reward.

The end.

It lapped at her with a heated tongue, but although she struggled to find the strength to meet it, she'd lost all control over her muscles. It would come; she had no doubt of that. But all she could do was wait and pant and sweat.

Something started shaking her, forcing her to lift her head above the current. The *something* turned out to be Reeve. He was doing all the work now, his much-stronger muscles powering him in and out, up and down, ruling not just her cunt but her entire being.

There! Fast. Hard! Lingering.

Delighted, she dove unafraid into her climax. It came at her in waves, sometimes mountaintop high, other times barely simmering, but for as long as it lasted, there was nothing else.

And she screamed.

Her throat was still raw when she dragged herself off Reeve and all but collapsed at his feet. He'd helped guide her off him, but now he sat slumped in the fighting chair with his fingers clutching the armrest.

"Holy shit," she breathed. "You—I don't remember—did you—"

"Yeah. Hell yeah."

7

Bastard. Damn bastard.

Although they were now below deck with the tiny bathroom a step away, Reeve had no intention of going in there and turning on the light because if he did, he'd have to look at himself in the high mirror. Knowing what he was about to do to the unconscious woman sprawled out on his bed was bad enough and tomorrow soon enough for asking himself why the hell he'd had sex with Saree when that hadn't been part of the plan.

The plan. Damn it, focus!

Instead of mentally checking off the list of what he had to accomplish before daylight, however, he sat next to the limp figure, slumped forward. He was so tired that if he didn't know what was expected of him when and why, he'd have already stretched out next to her. If nothing else, then he wouldn't have to face what he'd done.

Well, he wasn't asleep. She was, not that *sleep* was the accurate term. Thanks to what he'd added to the glass of water he'd given her some twenty minutes ago, she was down for the count. And even when she woke up, she'd barely be able to move until the drug was out of her system.

The drug's muscle-weakening properties were part of why he saw himself as a complete bastard. To be awake and aware but unable to fight had to be a terrifying experience, but it was part of the plan he'd committed to.

A plan he'd approved before he'd known that this supposedly oversexed means to an end had nursed her parents through lingering illnesses, not because the duty had been forced on her but because she'd loved them.

What was that like? How did someone go about loving a parent so deeply that that person's own life came in a distant second? True, he'd once had feelings for his parents, intense emotions that had nearly destroyed him in the aftermath of what—No, damn it, no! Don't go there!

Straightening, he turned toward Saree. He'd given her the doctored drink while they were still on deck, but fortunately she'd had to go to the bathroom before it had kicked in. Otherwise, he wasn't sure he could have safely carried her limp body down the steep, narrow steps. She'd gone to the bathroom, slipped back into her shorts, and washed her face before her eyes started glazing over.

"I'm exhausted," she'd said. Then, swaying, she'd taken a step toward the bed. She'd collapsed on it and rolled onto her side, looking up at him with innocent confusion clouding her eyes. "What . . ."

Down and out. His. About to enter an existence that he hoped would save lives. That's what he had to focus on, not her strong and healthy body locked with his and not her compassion for her dying parents but how he intended to manipulate and use her before eventually returning what was left of her back to her world.

I'm sorry, he nearly said aloud. Instead, he knotted his hands and squeezed until he'd cut off his own circulation.

Then, shaking life back into his fingers, he stood and stepped over to the built-in dresser. Teeth clenched, he opened the top drawer where he'd stored what he needed to do his job.

Bastard. You're a damned bastard.

She was dreaming, had to be.

No matter how hard Saree mentally pushed against it, the fog surrounding her refused to lift. Only a couple of things made sense. One, her memories of the evening she'd spent with a man she'd just met. Two, she couldn't move her arms.

Wait, there were three things, weren't there. Her eyes were closed.

Although she had no doubt that a great deal more about whatever was happening would start to fall into place once she opened her eyes, she held off the moment. The problem, the goddamn scary problem, was that she could no longer delude herself into believing that this was a dream. Not only could she now feel soft but thick leather straps around her wrists, she knew she was on a bed—a bed that smelled like Reeve.

Panic filled her throat, but if she gave into it, she was lost. She had to remain strong and in control, at least as in control as someone who'd been anchored to a bed could be.

Oh God, was this what had happened to Amber Green? Instead of having run away with the man of her dreams, her fellow bondage model had been kidnapped? What happened after kidnapping? Imprisonment, but where? Why? And for how long?

Was Amber still alive? No, she couldn't be dead!

Unable to stop herself, Saree slowly, laboriously opened her eyes. She managed to lift her head, but the effort caused her vision to blur and her muscles to shake. Bile rose in her throat. Drugged. Damn it, she'd been drugged!

Clamping down on panic with every bit of will she possessed, she let her head fall back and breathed through her nausea. When it receded, she turned her attention to her surroundings. She was in Reeve's bedroom all right, or more accurately what passed for one on a boat. The bed was against a wall, a dresser had been built into another wall, and a lamp hung from that wall. Light from the compact fixture was directed on her.

Thank goodness she was still dressed, not that she could stop Reeve from changing that condition when and if he wanted to. Knowing she was the center of attention so to speak made her long to return to the forgetfulness she'd worked so hard to remove herself from.

Why? That was the question that ran endlessly through her—why had he done this?

Testing her ability to track without making herself sick again, she slowly turned her head to the right and then the left. Even as she did she knew she wouldn't see Reeve because her nerve endings told her that she was alone. How long had she been like this?

A humming sound penetrated her racing mind. Listening intently, she determined that she was hearing the boat's motor, and unless she was mistaken, the boat was moving slowly through the water. Where was he taking her?

The tumbling questions without answers threatened to push her over the edge, and yet in a way she found her state laughable. After countless sessions of planned helplessness, shouldn't she be accustomed to having no control?

But those had been *sessions, make-believe.* This, whatever it was, was the real thing.

"Reeve? Reeve, where are you?" Shaken by the fear in her weak voice, she wished she hadn't said a word, but of course it was too late. When he didn't reply, she tried to tell herself he hadn't heard her and she was safe, but she wasn't, was she?

Although she knew what the result was going to be, she nevertheless tested the strength of her bonds, or rather she tried to. Had she ever been so weak? Her arms had been positioned over her head in a classic pose, and even as panic again took a chunk out of her sanity, her body remembered the things that had been done to it countless times in the past when she was like this. He hadn't anchored her legs, not that he couldn't when the mood struck him or the time was right. Maybe she'd tell him that the image of a naked woman tethered spread-eagle to a bed was much more erotic and saleable than the way he'd left her.

The way he'd left her.

All right, she was still clothed, and he hadn't taken away her ability to call out for help. Damn it, why hadn't she focused on those things before now?

Because she'd been remembering a million other things. All those bondage sessions with her tied to a bed had wound up with a common result—she'd climaxed. Sometimes the explosions had been forced from her via toys, while sometimes she'd happily spread her already-spread legs wider so she could take a man's cock into her.

This wasn't real after all, she told herself, at least not the unnerving reality she'd allowed herself to be sucked into when she was regaining consciousness. Instead, she'd been scheduled for a bondage video without being informed of it. Reeve was in on the joke. In a few minutes he'd walk in with a cameraman in tow and what was familiar and exciting and safe would begin. She'd pretend to be furious at whoever had pulled one over on her, but when Reeve started performing magic to and on her body, she'd relent. More than relent, she'd throw herself into the scene.

The boat lurched and slowed, shaking her loose from delusion. And as she waited, she turned her back on the desperate explanation that hadn't been one. Those who ran The Dungeon would never start a session without letting the model know; it was written into every contract.

Listening to the motor growl, she longed to be able to do that. The motor sounded so smooth and strong. It was doing what it had been designed to do while she—she what?

The door opened. Horrified and fascinated, she stared at the newly created space. For too long she saw nothing except the darkness beyond, but then the expected and feared form materialized. Again unable to stop herself, she yanked on her wrist restraints. Nothing.

"Don't bother," Reeve said from the shadows. "They're not going to give, particularly with your muscles as weak as they are."

"What is this?" Oh no, not panic in her voice! "What are you doing?"

"What I must."

Much as she wished she could hang hope on the regret in his tone, to do so would lead to even more insanity. A scream crawled up her throat, but she fought it down. Even if someone heard, which she doubted, her cry would reveal too much about her emotional state, and she wasn't about to give Reeve more of an advantage than he already had. "This isn't a joke, is it? You're serious, aren't you?"

"Yeah."

"Why?" Panic again threatened to take over so she gulped in air before continuing. "You don't have to do this. With your money, you can have any woman you want."

"Not want, Saree. Need. You're the one I need."

Don't do this! About to throw the words at him, she pressed her lips together. She didn't know nearly enough about what was happening, but she was already sure of one thing. He'd tell her what he wanted to when he wanted, and nothing she said or did—not that she could do anything—would change that.

She wasn't going to play into his hands, damn it! If he wanted a sobbing, sniveling captive he was going to be disappointed. Instead, she'd watch and listen and learn, and when the opportunity presented itself, she'd forcefully separate him from his cock and shove what was left of it down his throat.

Irrational strength and courage flowed through her at the thought of exacting revenge. He was into some sick game while she was serious, deadly serious, about tearing him apart.

"What do you mean, need?"

"You'll learn in time—at least you'll learn as much as I believe you should. For now, however, I have to start your education."

She was about to point out that she had three years of college behind her and would have graduated if she'd seen a reason for it, but she decided to keep her mouth shut. The more she tried to get to the point of all this, the more nonsense he'd probably throw at her. She was absolutely positive of one thing— no amount of begging, arguing, cursing, or pleading would loosen his tongue.

Perhaps he'd guessed what she was thinking because he slowly shook his head. "We're going to be back in the marina before long. I need to make sure no one knows what's taking place."

Another wave of dread flowed through her, followed by the absolute certainty that he was going to make good on his declaration because she couldn't do a damn thing about it. He'd been a good lover, a great one if truth be known. As she'd been coming down from her postclimax high, she'd debated suggesting they spend the night together, something she almost never did.

How wrong she'd been about him! How dangerously wrong.

Hayley, wake up! Or if you're in bed but not sleeping, stop what you're doing and listen to me. I need you like I've never needed you before. Somehow I'll let you know where I am so you can round up the cavalry. Please, please, get this message!

Reeve had turned from her and was taking something from the dresser. Sweating, she fixed on what was in his hand. Oh shit, a long strip of cloth! Easily killing the scant distance between them, he sat beside her. Although she turned her head to the side, he gripped her chin and forced it back around. She screamed as the cloth descended, only to hear her cry end abruptly as he forced the fabric into her open mouth. Leaning over her, he kept the pressure going while lifting her head so he could wrap the strip around her a total of three times. When he was done, her mouth was full of dry cotton. He tied the ends off at the side of her head.

She had to be mistaken of course, but she could almost swear he'd held her longer than necessary and there'd been a gentleness to his fingers on her cheeks.

Standing, he returned to the damnable dresser. She had no trouble recognizing the pieces of leather for what they were—ankle restraints. So that's why he hadn't spread-eagled her, because he wanted to bind her legs together. Guessing that his ultimate intention was to prepare her for transport, she prayed for the necessary muscle strength to fight him. She held no delusions that she could outwrestle him, but if she could make enough noise—

"To let you know, you're going to be weak for approximately an hour."

Kneeling at the foot of the bed, he grabbed an ankle. She jerked, or more accurately, she tried to. But although he had to pull her leg back into position, he had no trouble doing so.

Don't do this to me! Please, don't!

The two-inch-wide strap closed around an ankle. She heard something snap into position. A matching strap first caressed and then closed around her other ankle.

No, please, no.

A third snap told her what she'd already suspected would happen. He'd fastened a short length of leather to her anklets, hobbling her. When he released her, she put all her strength into trying to separate her legs. Nothing. Anchored.

"This way you won't hurt yourself." He spoke without emotion. "But there's one more thing I need to do."

A thicker and longer leather strip went around her knees, not tight enough to cut off her circulation but so secure she couldn't bend them. She understood the technology behind what she'd always considered a particularly erotic tie. From the hips down she was more than just helpless; her legs were useless, essentially nonexistent.

"Hmm. Hmmm. Fmm."

Reeve jerked upright, then pushed himself to his feet and checked her gag. She kept trying to make herself heard, crying and cursing at the same time, but if he understood, he gave no sign.

Stepping away from the bed, he cocked his head. "We're about there. I'll be back once I've secured the boat."

When he disappeared, at first she felt overwhelming relief, but that had no sooner settled over her when the other pieces fell into place. She was dependent on him for everything. Until and unless he returned, she would remain anchored to the bed, a silent and helpless captive.

Hayley, I've gotten myself into a world of trouble. I don't think he's a killer. Oh shit, I hope he isn't! I don't know what he has in mind and that's scaring me. Find me, please! Whatever you have to do, find me.

Because she had nothing else to do, she tried to imagine what steps he had to go through in order to return the boat to its assigned slip. The channel was so narrow that as they'd been going out, she'd marveled at his ability to maneuver the bulky beast. While they were out on the bay, the air had had that clean and salty smell she loved, but much of that was being replaced by the less pleasant aroma of gasoline, oil, and stagnant water. Although she strained to listen, she didn't hear any other human voices. What time was it?

A gentle bump followed by a rocking sensation told her he'd reached shore. Perhaps he had to jump off the boat to secure it, not that she could tell. The motor had quieted down just before the bump, probably because he'd again put it in neutral. Then the sound died, leaving nothing except silence. No, she amended, not complete silence, because she could now hear her heart pounding.

Concentrating on getting it down to a more normal pace made her lose track of time. As a result, she wasn't ready for the muted thumps his shoes made on the stairs as he descended. Her heart again raced, and yet she wasn't terrified so much as anticipating. A new chapter in her life was about to begin. And this man could and would dictate every word and action of it.

He was big, big and dark, overpowering. Granted, he didn't quite fill the room, but he commanded it and became her world. Against all reason and sanity, her belly clenched, and she pressed her thighs together in response to the unexpected and unwanted energy there.

His silence was unnerving when she needed him to spell out what he intended to do. Specifically she needed to know where he was going to take her and why. Instead of giving her either of those things, he stepped over to the dresser and retrieved something she had no doubt he intended to use on her. Although she wasn't quite as weak as she'd been when he left, neither was she in any condition to put up a fight. Because all she could give him was her own silence, she turned her head and stared at the wall.

Damn him, he was running his hand over the length of her right arm. Perhaps he guessed that the strain across her shoulders was becoming uncomfortable because he devoted several seconds to massaging her there. He was also quieting her, calming her, lulling her. And against all reason, she loved the sensation. *Thank you,* she longed to tell him even as she acknowledged that he was responsible for her discomfort.

A quick tug pulled her right arm closer to the head of the bed. Although she'd already guessed his intentions, he'd freed her wrist before she was ready. Just as quickly, he did the same to her left. This was her moment! Her only chance at freedom!

Opportunity lost, she admitted as he rolled her onto her belly, bringing her arms down and behind her at the same time. Because leather cuffs already circled her wrists, it took him only a second to snap them together. Biting down on her gag, she tested her handcuffs. No, they weren't going to give.

To her surprise, instead of throwing her over his shoulder Tarzan style, he went back to massaging her shoulders. When he was done there, he spend a couple of minutes doing the same to her arms until full circulation had been restored. From long experience she knew that having her hands behind her would eventually exact its toll on her blood flow, but right now she was comfortable—at least relatively so.

After giving her a pat on her buttocks, he lifted her arms by pulling up on the cuffs. More leather settled around her elbows, and he tightened and secured the leather strip so her elbows were only a few inches apart. Her limbs now couldn't be any more useless than if they didn't exist.

Maybe she should have anticipated what came next, but she didn't. As a result, the blindfold was in place before she knew what he had in mind. It wasn't that tight, but its elasticity molded it to her head so it hugged her eyes.

She was locked in darkness, her body useless, silenced. A nonentity, she no longer existed in the world she'd always taken for granted. Against her will she'd been transported to his world, under his command. But although her heart again pounded in her chest, she wasn't afraid so much as acutely alive. All pretense had been stripped away. So this was what it felt like to belong to someone else, to be less than human, a slave, a piece of property.

He wouldn't have done this to her if he didn't have a purpose.

All she had to do was wait and see what that purpose was.

I'm yours. Bottom line, I'm yours.

When he lifted her and placed her over his shoulder, she didn't so much as try to raise her head. Her skin felt as if it were molding to his. His muscles were so damnable strong, so reliable, powerful enough for both of them. If it had been her trying to climb the steep stairs while carrying a hundred plus pound burden, she would have been huffing and puffing, or more accurately dropping to her knees and crawling up, but not him.

From what she could tell, his breathing didn't change as he brought her up to the night sky. The salty breeze licked over her. By his sure footsteps, she guessed he was convinced that no one could see them, and she mentally stepped off to the side so she could watch.

He was striding the length of the boat, heading toward the front where it had been roped to the dock. He had no doubt his long, strong legs could easily bridge the small gap between watercraft and wooden walkway. He'd held her with one arm around her torso while climbing the stairs but now had both hands on her, undoubtedly to ensure that she didn't try to pull something stupid like struggling. Too bad she couldn't tell him that that wasn't even on her radar. How could she want anything except what she was now, part of him.

No! What the hell was she thinking?

After shifting his hold on her, he let go with one hand, and she imagined him reaching for a railing. When she sensed fresh tension in him, she guessed he was preparing to step onshore. Because she had no wish to wind up in the water, she remained absolutely still. Then he jumped and she jumped with him. He landed on both feet, stumbled, but easily caught himself. If she'd been able, she would have applauded.

When he started walking she tried to conjure up her memories. His craft had been near the end of the deck or walkway or whatever it was called, so in her mind she looked at the various fishing and sail and pleasure boats as they passed them. The walkway under his feet rolled gently, forcing him to widen his stance. He strode tall and confident, a casually dressed wealthy and powerful man with what to the casual night observer probably looked like a rolled-up rug. Only by training a light on his burden could someone tell that said load was a trussed human being, but even if that happened, would someone come to her rescue? After all, this was Reeve's world.

He reached the end of the walkway but instead of turning right toward the parking lot where she'd left her car, he headed left. Because her blindfold let in no light she couldn't tell whether he was walking into darkness or toward a well-lit area. She didn't think it would be the latter, but then anything was possible. Wasn't her captivity proof of that?

Time slipped around her, but whether minutes or seconds had passed she couldn't tell because she was still a nonentity, *his*. When he stopped and fished for something in his pocket, she took note of what he was doing, but it didn't really concern her, did it? After all, it wasn't as if she had a say in things. A series of clicks made her wonder if he'd pulled out his car keys and had triggered the remote control. Her mouth dried.

It was really happening. He was going to take her someplace else. Someplace foreign.

Fear washed over her to drown her earlier lethargy. Before she could put her mind to how she might fight him, he'd lifted her off his shoulders and deposited her on her side on something that smelled like leather. The arm under her scraped over a piece of metal she guessed was part of a seat belt, leaving her to assume he'd placed her in the backseat of whatever kind of vehicle this was.

Trying to keep her head above the fear waves distracted her from what he was doing. By the time she'd pulled it all together, he'd removed the restraints around her elbows and knees. The gesture might have heartened her if he hadn't followed that by securing a seat belt around her middle. Another held her ankles, ensuring that she couldn't sit up. Of course. This way no one they might encounter on whatever road he intended to use would see her.

Nonentity, a *thing* being transported.

Where?

For what purpose?

8

Saree couldn't say for sure whether she'd fallen asleep while Reeve drove. Her memories were just disjointed enough that she guessed whatever he'd put into her drink might still be in her system. One thing she did know, by the time they'd reached his destination, she was more than tired of being trussed up. The arm under her was numb, and her neck ached from the unnatural angle. They'd been on a well-maintained road or highway for a long time, but that had changed to one with more than the normal allotment of potholes, and for what felt like the last mile or so, she was positive they were on dirt or gravel.

The Southern California she knew was urban, but east of Los Angeles were desert hills where the lack of a ready water source was largely responsible for the sparse population. She'd done a little exploring of the area, just enough to make her wonder why anyone would want to live surrounded by cactus, lizards, and snakes. If he was taking her to one of those places—

Again acknowledging that he could and undoubtedly would do whatever he wanted when he wanted, she buried her will under acceptance. Mentally and emotionally fighting what was happening wouldn't change anything. Besides, a part of her—

No! She did *not* want this existence, she didn't!

He hadn't turned on the car radio so when a cell phone chirped, the unexpected sound caused her heart to lurch. It rang a second time.

"Yeah," Reeve said. "No, I've been waiting for you to call." A pause. "Of course I have her. I would have told you if I didn't." More silence during which she guessed the caller was talking. "Not a single problem. And so you don't have to ask, we're nearly there. What's been happening on your end?"

Reeve had an accomplice or partner or something, did he? He wasn't some solitary nut after all. But who was he talking to and how was this person, she assumed it was a man, involved?

"You've been in touch with them already? How'd—oh, you're positive she nailed Saree's voice? Yeah, I know she's good."

Who was good? Did this mean a woman was part of *this* as well? But much as she needed answers, they weren't forthcoming when Reeve switched from asking questions to listening and then describing what had happened since she'd agreed to have dinner with him. The only thing he'd left out was that they'd had sex before he drugged and kidnapped her.

"No, she isn't panicking, at least I haven't seen any sign of it. No, I haven't told her anything. I will when it feels right but no more than absolutely necessary." Pause. "They can't get any righter than she is. She's going to be perfect."

Confused by the tone he used when he called her perfect, she was slow to realize the conversation was over. Not only that, the vehicle was barely moving. They were nearly *there,* wherever there was.

The vehicle stopped, and he threw it into park. Then the engine died. Cloistered within her sightless body, she waited, simply waited.

After opening the door closest to her feet, Reeve unfastened the seat belts. Then he removed what had been holding her ankles together but kept the leather anklets on. He helped her sit up. Before she could do more than think about asking anything of her legs, he pulled her toward him, spinning her to the left at the same time so her feet were outside. Gripping her around the waist, he indicated he wanted her to stand.

She tried, she honestly tried, but between the circulation returning to her legs and the gravel, she wound up leaning against him. For just a moment he let her do so, then he picked her up in his arms. Just enough light now penetrated the blindfold that she knew it was morning, but before she could reconcile that with what she remembered of the drive, he started climbing some stairs. She didn't think there were more than three. Then he put her down but kept an arm around her waist. Sounds told her he was unlocking a door.

Fear of what lay beyond the door washed over her, and like a fool, she tried to break free. Of course it took almost nothing for him to carry her into wherever they were. The light faded, plunging her back into darkness. Whimpering low in her throat, she fought the urge to pummel him with her newly free legs.

"I'm not going to hurt you," he said.

You think I'm going to believe you?

"This is necessary. Otherwise, we wouldn't be here. That's all I can tell you for now, that we don't have a choice."

Who was that last we? Surely not her.

He was walking on something that caused his shoes to make a faint slapping sound, tile maybe. This time when he put her down, he positioned her on either a couch or easy chair, the smell letting her know that it was made of real leather. The air was fresh, probably because a window was open. Wise in the way of desert temperatures, she hoped he'd close it and turn on the air conditioning before much longer.

Instinct told her that he was no longer standing beside her, and if it hadn't, the sounds he was making would have brought her to the same conclusion. Turning her head one way and then the other did nothing to acquaint her with her surroundings. Her feet were more reliable, letting her know that they were indeed resting on tile.

There. Him. Back again. Even before he touched her shoulder, she'd sensed his presence. The gentle contact made her start, but then she forced herself to relax. Damn it, he wasn't going to intimidate her, he wasn't!

He continued to touch her, his fingers on her arms and shoulders, the back of her neck before traveling around to her chin. By concentrating on breathing, she managed not to shiver. She even found herself relaxing a little, not that she'd let him know. Her spine stiff, she waited because she had no choice.

"Get used to my touch, Saree. It's what I must do in order to make your body my possession. I know what I'm doing. Don't ever doubt that I do."

Slow, so slow, he walked his fingers from her chin to her throat and from there to the valley between her breasts. The fact that she was clothed made little difference; his heat burned past the pitiful barriers to her helpless and insanely pliable flesh. Even awareness of her full bladder couldn't stop her from responding. What was it he'd said, that she was going to get used to his touch. She could do that, oh yes, she could.

Instead of unfastening her bra as she thought he would, he worked his way up her arms. After briefly massaging the back of her neck, his hands were on her blindfold. Apathy washed out of her to be replaced by anticipation and, strangely, regret. Fantasy was about to end and reality intrude.

She'd been sweating behind the elasticized blindfold. Between that and getting accustomed to the sudden light, several seconds passed before she could make sense of her surroundings. They were in a living room that looked as if it had been professionally decorated. Several windows reached nearly to the ceiling. She was on a couch all right, new and rich looking. The nearby coffee table was a combination of smoky glass and chrome and, she had no doubt, was expensive. The rest of the furniture spoke of the same commitment to class and quality as did several pieces of original artwork. Other decorative touches consisted of handblown glass pieces and copper and chrome freeform objects, all masculine.

Beyond the living room was a dining area and, at angle to that, a kitchen capable of putting out an elaborate meal. Everything spoke quietly and in a dignified way of *money*. So much for her belief that everything off the grid was lucky to have electricity let alone luxury. If this was where Reeve lived—

Before she could finish the thought, her attention was drawn to her purse, which was on the coffee table. Knowing he'd taken possession of it the same as he had her knotted her stomach.

"You need to go to the bathroom," he announced. "And I need to sleep."

And after that, what?

He once again hauled her to her feet, then stood back and studied her. Bit by bit her bonds were being released. All that was left now were the gag and wrist restraints, and if she hadn't already run through her options, she might have convinced herself that she was close to being able to run. But she was barefoot, had no water, and didn't know where she was. Unless she had a death wish, she had no choice but to stay where she was—for now.

"There." He pointed toward the rear of the house. "Head that way."

Both resenting and grateful for the order, she did as she'd been told. The flooring felt luxurious with each large square slightly different so she knew this was real stone and not some reproduction. Discrete wood blinds had all but been built into the window casings so they nearly disappeared when not in use, which was how they were now. From what she could tell from her glimpses of the surrounding desert, there wasn't another manmade structure around.

She didn't know what the house's exterior looked like but imagined that the colors blended with what nature had designed. And yet it included all the modern conveniences anyone could want as witnessed by the oversized bathroom she'd just walked into. Not only was the shower large enough to accommodate at least four people comfortably, but next to it was a massive tub complete with eight jets. If the sight of the toilet hadn't made its impact on her bladder, she'd have taken all the time she needed to study the room. As it was, she was interested in only one thing.

And yet she was helpless to care for her own needs.

Shooting Reeve a pleading look, she noted that he was in need of a shave, and the bags under his eyes spoke of his sleepless night. "I'm going to release your arms," he said. "I hope it goes without saying that I trust you're not going to try something. You won't win—never doubt that, you won't win."

Nodding, she turned from him so he'd have easy access to her bonds. Thank goodness she was accustomed to being handled; otherwise she might lose her mind before this was over.

When was it going to be over, she asked as he unhooked whatever had been holding her wrists together. *And what's going to be left of me when it is?*

Her arms fell to her sides, prompting her to stare at them. Pins and needles attacked her shoulders, and she bit into her gag. Much as she needed to unfasten her shorts, she couldn't until more feeling had returned to her hands so she flexed her fingers and wondered whether her sister was awake and if she'd tried to get in touch with her yet.

Please have gotten my messages. Even if it means you couldn't sleep last night, feel you have to get in touch with me.

"Are you going to do it or am I?"

Furious, she fumbled with her button. Pulling down on the zipper tab took longer, but finally she pushed her garments down to her knees. Because she'd already known he had no intention of giving her privacy, she settled for averting her eyes while sitting on the toilet. The moment her ass came in contact with the porcelain, she let go. Relief!

Finally done, she wiped herself and reached down for her clothing. "Take them off."

A retort backed up in her dry throat, but she did as he'd ordered because his eyes gave her no choice. She stepped out of her shorts and panties, then at his gesture, she stood and backed against the shower door, giving him access to the toilet. He watched her the whole time he was urinating. That done, he let his shorts slide to the floor. "Your top," he ordered.

Although she'd been anticipating this, she made no move to obey. Instead, she reached for the knot that kept her gag in place. To her surprise he didn't stop her, his silence letting her know that he didn't care whether she called for help because there wasn't anyone around to hear. Much as she wanted to call him every foul name she could think of, when she'd pulled the gag out of her mouth, all she did was work moisture into her mouth and lick her lips.

Then, not thinking, she pulled her top over her head, unfastened her bra and dropped it to the floor next to the rest of her clothes. After studying her with an intensity that no doubt mirrored her own, he pulled off his shirt. For the first time since their worlds had collided, she was looking at him fully naked. Of course she was too, not that it mattered because she couldn't think beyond stone-hard muscles and deeply tanned flesh.

No question about it, this wasn't a businessman's body.

"Give me your hands."

She could have refused, could have fought. But not only would he have won the battle, she needed to see where this was heading. When, damn it, when either she got loose or he released her, she had to be able to tell law enforcement everything.

Holding her arms toward him gave her her first clear look at what he'd fastened around her wrists. The two-inch-wide leather strips bore a resemblance to bracelets but lacked any ornamentation. A metal locking device kept them in place, and she only had to glance at the metal rings imbedded in the leather to know their purpose. There was enough play that she could slide a finger between her skin and the cuffs, which meant she wouldn't have to worry about losing circulation for as long as she wore them.

Taking her right wrist, he turned it so the ring was within easy reach. Only then did she realized he'd been holding something in the palm of his left hand. He fastened the something to the ring with a decisive snap. Then, before she had time to comprehend, he snagged her other wrist and brought the two together. Another no-nonsense snap said everything. He'd looped a metal oval hook through both rings and locked it. Her hands were again cuffed together, in front this time.

"Into the shower."

Being nude and without use of her arms transported her into the familiar world framed by her career. Much like a calf with a rope around its neck, she stood trembling and helpless and alive. She had no thoughts of resisting him but also couldn't think how to obey. He'd made her his; she'd become his responsibility. Let him deal with the aftereffects.

Perhaps he could read her mind because instead of repeating the order, he used his hold on her elbow to force her to the side so he'd have access to the shower. Opening the door, he reached in and turned on the water. Instead of a single shower head, there were three separate sprays. They all pulsed, the water changing from a light mist to a strong jet, drenching the oversized shower in a near river of warmth. And when he guided her into the enclosure she went willingly.

He followed her in as she knew he would, closing the door behind him. Instead of waiting for his orders, she stepped into the spray so it struck her throat and breasts. The pulsating, gyrating water felt as if it were penetrating her outer layers while it searched for her lungs and heart.

If her dumb compliance confused him, he gave no sign. Instead, he slowly turned her in a circle so the water hit every inch of her from the neck down. When he adjusted the nozzle so a strong spray was directed at her pussy, she spread her legs. Having the water slap her there wasn't the only thing responsible for her growing submission; he, her captor, was a vital part of the scene. She'd become his creature, his object. Being tired and lost also played their own roles of course. In addition, although it made no sense, she simply wanted to see where this was heading.

He was maybe eight inches taller than she, hard where she was soft, confident in contrast to her confusion, and when he released her, she made no attempt to move. He reached for a rose-scented bar of soap and lathered a luxurious-looking washcloth. Moving behind her, he indicated that he wanted her to bend forward. Obeying him meant she could no longer see him, but he'd already taught her that he could force her to do whatever he wanted. Water was running into her eyes so she closed them, keeping her stance wide so she wouldn't risk losing her balance.

The soap felt like liquid satin, the scent intoxicating. After lying on her side in the back of a car for hours, having her skin pampered felt wonderful. At the same time she was no fool. Just because he was being gentle now was no reason to believe that would continue. He'd said something about a plan for her, a use he intended to put her to.

Curiosity about that use faded and died when he reached the base of her spine. Up until then his touch had been so light that she'd been hard-pressed to distinguish it from what the shower was responsible for. Now, however, gentleness changed into possessiveness. *You're mine*, his hand around her middle proclaimed as he bent her even farther forward. *For as long as I say*, he added simply by running the cloth between her ass cheeks.

Whether having her head so low that blood rushed to her temple was responsible didn't matter. What did was her reawakening awareness of herself as a functioning human being. This wasn't a movie; she wasn't a well-paid model who'd agreed to have her most intimate parts exposed. She was in the hands of a powerful and perhaps dangerous man, and she was a fool to have tried to delude herself into thinking anything else.

The washcloth was between her legs, suds coating her labia and running down her inner thighs. Over and over again he stroked the length of her pussy, each journey forcing a sigh from her. The formerly soft terry cloth now scraped her unbelievably sensitive flesh, bringing her onto her toes in an insane attempt to put distance between herself and what was both pleasure and pain. No matter how much she tried to keep it trapped inside her, a long and low moan rolled out of her.

"You're going to be so easy," he muttered. The words were no more than just out of his mouth when he grabbed her hair and jerked her upright.

Sharp pain on her scalp separated her from stimulation, that and the fact that he'd removed the washcloth from between her legs. She tried to look back at him only to have her head held firmly in place. The fear she'd been able to briefly deny seeped into her. Fingers clenched and her thoughts locked on how much damage she might be able to inflict with her hands together like this, she concentrated on breathing without bringing too much water into her nostrils and mouth.

"You remind me of a horse I broke once," he said with his mouth near her ear. "As long as I kept a rope on him, he'd let me do everything I wanted. He led me to believe he'd accepted that I was in charge. But the moment he was free to run, he was hell to capture again. I'm keeping my ropes on you, Saree. Let them teach your body their own lessons."

His ropes on her, lessons for her body to learn. Instead of recoiling from the implications, she all but crawled into the words.

She heard the washcloth hit the floor. Then he released her hair and pushed her forward until she was directly under the spray, her instantly drenched long hair in her face. No matter that it was hard to breathe, she wasn't about to make the mistake of trying to move where he didn't want her. Instead, she stood with her fingers still clenched and her hands pressing against her mons, listening, waiting, anticipating.

Another possessive tug on her hair pulled her back and against him. Tense, she tried to blink water out of her eyes. A new aroma, this one a heady vanilla, calmed her a little. She relaxed even more when she realized the smell came from the shampoo he was putting on her hair. Standing straight and still, she followed his every move. He'd started by soaping the top of her head and was now working the suds down the strands. To her relief, he'd pushed her hair off her face and was taking care not to get shampoo near her eyes. When she was a small girl her parents had pampered her by shampooing her hair, and although this experience was quite different, there was a single common ground.

She felt cherished.

Cherished? What a fool she was to believe that of a man who intended to mold her in ways she couldn't begin to comprehend! She *had* to pull herself together and see this moment for what it surely was, his manipulation of her emotions.

Her grip on her senses slightly firmer than they'd been a minute ago, she vowed to separate her mind from what was happening to her body. Her determination got her through the rest of the shampooing and rinse. She managed to return his stare while he carefully washed her face, and if her composure slipped when he turned his attention to her throat and breasts, she told herself that he was studying his handiwork instead of her. Another point in her favor; his erection was growing. True, he might decide to bury it in her, but at least he wasn't immune to what he was doing.

When it came time to wash her legs, he backed her against the tile and propped her foot on his thigh. Then, a slightly bemused expression softening his stern features a little, he covered every inch of her from crotch down with soapy foam. The slow and thorough process forced her to draw comparisons between herself and ice left in the sun. She was losing form and definition and taking on the contours of whatever container she'd been placed in—or more accurately, parts of her seemed to be sloughing off so he could pick them up and mold them to his needs.

Finally, thank goodness, he must have decided she was clean enough for his exacting standards because he directed her to stand in a corner while he washed himself. He showed no sign of being embarrassed by his erection; neither did he give her any indication that he intended to use her to reverse its condition.

Good. The last thing she wanted or needed was to have sex with him.

9

Saree sat on a high stool across the kitchen island from where Reeve was cooking breakfast. After they'd gotten out of the shower, he'd directed her to towel dry her hair and wrap the oversized towel around herself, no easy task. Then he'd refastened her hands behind her. Being essentially naked while he wore a fresh shirt and shorts was disconcerting but not nearly as much as having again been robbed of the use of her hands.

She didn't like any part of what was happening—except for the wonderful aroma of sautéing onions and mushrooms. Had he stocked the kitchen before coming after her or was one of his *partners* responsible?

Thoughts of who else was in on *this* caused her to replay the short phone conversation he'd had earlier. Now that she'd run it through her mind, she believed the woman he'd mentioned had managed to replicate her voice, thus convincing her employers that they'd spoken to her.

"This isn't going to work," she blurted. "You can't just kidnap me and expect to get away with it."

"You haven't been kidnapped. You accepted the invitation

of a wealthy and persuasive man you've fallen in love with to be with him for the foreseeable future."

The words thudded around her. Although she opened her mouth, nothing came out.

"I'm going to tell you several things because I believe you'll be better equipped to focus on what happens between the two of us if you've accepted certain realities."

"What realities?" Her throat was dry.

"A woman pretending to be you called management at The Dungeon. Because of the timing, I'm guessing she left messages on their answering machines either last night or early this morning. I have no doubt she was quite believable. Her acting abilities are considerable, and she's been watching your videos long enough to have your speech patterns and word choices down. The short story, the mysterious man who showed up on a set the other day has swept you off your feet. You don't know how things are going to work out between the two of you, but you're excited about doing whatever needs to be done in order to explore the possibilities. People aren't to try to get in touch with you because you don't know where you'll be when. It's all about spontaneity."

Suddenly dizzy, she dug her toes into the footrests. Reeve had helped her onto the high seat, and although she'd both enjoyed and resented his assistance, she now understood why he'd done what he had. She couldn't get down without risking a fall.

"No one's going to be looking for me?" she whispered. *At least no one at work.*

"Correct. Don't worry about your mortgage and utilities; they'll be paid. Fortunately you don't have pets. You might lose some inside plants but thanks to your yard service, your neighbors won't become alarmed."

Had *they* thought of everything?

"Some of your friends within the industry will feel slighted because you didn't personally get in touch with them, but the less contact we have with them, the less chance of a slipup."

If only the dizziness would lift! It was nearly unbelievable that *they'd* made it possible for her to drop off the face of the earth. There'd be no missing person's report, no worried neighbors or colleagues, no one afraid for her.

Except for her sister.

"How—how long will this last?"

He'd been concentrating on the vegetarian omelet, but now he looked up at her. "I don't know."

"Days?" She swallowed. "Weeks?" Another swallow. "Don't tell me you can't ever let me go. Please, don't."

His darkening eyes left no doubt that he'd caught the panic in her voice. "It depends."

"On—what?"

"How well the two of us do our jobs. And on whether eventually you'll believe that we did the only thing we could."

This didn't make sense; surely he understood that. "And if I don't?"

His mouth a white slash, he turned his back on her. "Don't go there."

"How can I not? Damn it, this is my life we're talking about!"

Whirling back around, he glared at her. "We're not talking about anything. I'm damn sorry I let you speak."

"Why did you?"

His silence said nothing and everything, and because she knew better than to try to press him, she only watched while he dished up their breakfast. After placing her share in front of her, he unfastened her wrists. He sat on the adjacent stool, his presence enough to kill any and all thoughts she'd had about throwing herself at the front door. Not only did she have no doubt that it was locked, the unknowns remained. She didn't know where she was or where, if anywhere, she could go for help.

And there was something else, an intangible life force between them, primitive and powerful.

Although she didn't think she'd be able to so much as taste the omelet, the moment it touched her tongue, she sighed in approval. Calmed and quieted by the mix of flavors, she chewed and swallowed. "What about my relatives? What is the woman pretending to be me going to tell them?"

"You have only one, a sister. The answer is as little as possible."

It won't work, she nearly told him, but her freedom and possibly her life depended on her sister. "Oh."

His scrutiny nearly forced her to drop her gaze. "For the record," he said, "our operative has already left a message for Hayley. You're beyond in love. You believe the man you had dinner with is the one you've been looking for all your life, and you don't want anything to get in the way of getting to know him."

Fighting down the impulse to laugh, she nodded.

"What is it?" he demanded with a forkful of omelet inches from his mouth. "You don't think it's going to work?"

"I didn't say anything."

"You don't have to."

"Good," she snapped, just barely stopping herself from jumping to her feet. "because I'm not going to. You and whoever else is in on this insanity think you have it all figured out. Far from me to try to tell you different."

They'd finished eating in silence, thank goodness, because if he'd pressed her she might have said something that could put Hayley in jeopardy. As it was, she had no doubt that Hayley wouldn't begin to buy that cock and bull story because finding *the* man had never been one of her goals and Hayley knew it. What she didn't know was what Hayley would do with her concerns, or how she'd go about trying to find her.

One thing for sure, no matter how desperately she wanted to believe in a wordless communication between the two of them, she couldn't tell her sister where to send the cavalry because she didn't know where she was. Oh, technically there was no doubt of her physical body's exact position—next to a sleeping Reeve on a queen-size bed. Damn it, that sexual zing shouldn't still exist. She didn't want to be near him, she didn't! Only tell that to her nerve endings.

Unlike him, she wasn't free to sprawl out because he'd wrapped a rope around her waist and tied her hands to it in front. In addition, he'd loosely but effectively secured her feet to the bottom of the bed. Even if she managed to sit up without waking him, there was no way she could use her hands to unlock the restraints around her ankles.

She'd actually fallen asleep shortly after he'd finished positioning her, but forgetfulness hadn't lasted long. Instead of trying to claw her way through the many questions about the mysterious others' plans for her, she kept imagining the conversations at work. The management knew her. She'd worked hard to develop her reputation as reliable. At the same time, she'd been careful to separate her private life from business. Just because she'd joked about erotic and exotic dreams and fantasies didn't mean those had been her actual dreams and fantasies. She'd never wanted to head into a jungle in search of Tarzan or seduce one of the world's richest men, but maybe her coworkers had believed that nonsense about her desire for a life of luxury.

Was it possible? What she'd considered good-natured fun had been taken as the truth? If so then why wouldn't everyone believe she was convinced she'd found a sugar daddy and was taking off for places unknown? After all, the same thing had happened to Amber Green.

Determined not to make herself sick contemplating the truth about Amber, she reluctantly turned toward Reeve. According to the nightstand clock, he'd been asleep for a couple of hours. He hadn't slept last night so logic said he wouldn't rouse for a while. What was he dreaming about, if anything? Thanks to the angle of his body, she couldn't tell whether he had an erection, but it wouldn't surprise her After all, he was a healthy young male with a helpless and relatively good-looking woman waiting for him to do whatever he wanted to.

Against all logic, her mind drifted in that direction. Upon waking, he'd free her legs and stroke her calves, knees, and thighs until her eyes glazed. As soon as she spread her muscleless legs, he'd slide into the space she'd made for him He'd check her receptivity and, finding her drenched and soft and swollen, he'd aim his cock at her waiting and willing hole. Sex would be hard and quick and silent with bodies twisting on the sheet and the dry desert breeze carrying away their cries. Maybe they'd come at the same time, although maybe one or the other would fall off the ledge first. Whenever the leader landed, he or she would help the other reach the crest.

She wanted to come before him so she could watch his loss of control. How empowering the sight of a sweating, pumping, grunting man was! Brought down to animal level, a man becomes primal and basic. Conversation, what there was of it, was crude and single-minded, his interests going no further than the end of his cock. How long could she keep him in her? If—

Movement from him stole her breath-snagging thoughts. For a moment she told herself he was still asleep and doing nothing more than changing position, but there was purpose to the way he stretched, and when his hand slid over her middle, she sensed energy in the touch. He didn't acknowledge her sigh, sent no message in intimate possession. It didn't matter; his heat became hers.

Then he sat up, his nude body turning from her as he stood. He walked away without looking at her, and she stared at the ceiling instead of studying his retreating ass. When he returned, he had on a pair of cutoff jeans but no shoes or shirt. His features were grim and became even more so when he glanced at the clock. It was nearing noon.

Not meeting her nervous gaze, he unhooked her ankles from the bed but kept the connection between them in place. Pulling her into a sitting position, he leaned over and threw her over his shoulder. Intent on keeping as much of her weight as possible off her hands, she gave little notice to where they were going until she realized he'd taken her to the rear of the house, where she hadn't been before.

When he straightened, she slid off him and took in her surroundings. They were in a room devoid of all warmth and personality. True, it had a dresser and a bed, if one could call that narrow mattress and high metal headboard and footboard a bed. Having seen a number of them at The Dungeon, she knew exactly what it was—a bondage prop.

The interior walls here, like the rest of the house, were concrete block, but where the other rooms had been painted in neutral but warm hues, these were gray. Metal rings had been attached to the walls at various heights.

This rear room was new and, she was willing to bet, constructed for one thing—to imprison.

Even more disconcerting, several video cameras had been set up. One was aimed at the bed, another toward one of the walls. From the looks of them, they could be detached in case someone wanted to carry them about, to provide a close-up of one body part or another.

Her mouth so dry she didn't try to talk, she stared at Reeve, but although he had to know she needed an explanation, he said nothing. She couldn't begin to read his expression.

Unwilling to give away any more than she already had, she turned her attention to her *prison*. There was a single long, narrow window near the ceiling through which just enough of the desert's sunlight entered. They'd come through the only door, and it locked from the outside.

Ropes spawned from her imagination circled her. Even with fear and disbelief warring for supremacy, she couldn't deny her body's reaction. For the first time in her life, she wasn't responding to the promise of multiple orgasms in exchange for a dose of well-paying bondage play. This was the real thing, danger and excitement rolled into one. Stealing a glance at Reeve, she concluded that she couldn't have asked for a more perfect *master* if she'd ordered him. Not only did he have the requisite size, strength, and dark stare, but every cell of his body shouted *masculine.*

He was male, she helpless female.

In her fantasy he'd take her to the edge of fantasy and thrills, to the limits of sexual experiences. She'd become putty in his hands, a shaking, sweating, begging whore willing to crawl for whatever sexual satisfaction he granted her.

Her knees nearly buckled, forcing her to concentrate on remaining erect. By the time she was relatively sure she wasn't going to collapse, much of the dangerous fantasy had faded to be replaced by the reality of an isolated prison where he could and would record everything he did to her.

For what purpose?

For who?

She took a backward step without knowing she was going to do so. Unfortunately, there wasn't enough play between her ankles to complete the movement. Off balance, she struggled to right herself. Instead, she all but tripped over her own foot and sprawled on the cool tile floor. Looking up, she saw him standing over her. He was huge, massive, all powerful, the beginning and end of her world.

Whimpering in terror and something else, she fought her arm restraints, but he'd given her less then two inches of play between her wrists and the rope around her waist. She fell forward onto her breasts.

Whimpering again, she struggled to roll over onto her side. Now her shoulder got in the way, and she wound up with her feet tucked under her, her ass in the air, her useless fingers clawing at nothing.

"What the hell are you doing?" he demanded, all but straddling her.

"Let me go! Goddamn you, let me go!"

"I can't." With that, he grabbed her around the waist and hauled her off the floor. Carrying her against his hip with her head hanging down, he strode over to the bed and all but threw her at it. "Don't move!"

Feeling too much like a chastised puppy, she rolled as best she could onto her side and watched as he walked over to the closest camera. After doing something with the equipment, he leaned down and looked through the viewfinder. She had no doubt that she filled the screen.

"This is me, Master X," he said. His voice sounded stilted as if he wasn't accustomed to talking to an audience. "I've been running a video of this room and its potential for several days now, both because I wanted to make sure everything was working properly and because—hell, because I wanted to give viewers something to look forward to."

He pushed a button and then another. There was a faint whirring sound followed by a replay of what he'd just said. Nodding, he pushed a button again.

"Sorry for the delay. Just making sure the audio and visual feeds are coming through. I apologize for the grainy quality of the picture you're seeing, but I have my reasons for hiding my slave's identity. Before I captured her, she was a bit of a public figure. My ultimate wish is for her to have value in another arena, one I hope certain individuals can give me access to. Because of the nature of the public arena she worked in, I've come to the conclusion that now isn't the time or place to reveal it. However, I'm a boastful man. I want viewers to see what a prize I have and to applaud my ability to work her. In order for that to happen, you, my audience, must have a clear view of everything. So if you will excuse me for several minutes, I'll get her properly prepared."

After turning off the camera, at least she assumed that's what he'd done, he walked over to her. Although she'd commanded herself not to, she tried to squirm away from him, but like when she was on the floor, she didn't get far. The only difference was that this time instead of picking her up and tossing her about, he sat on the bed and pulled her over to him.

Then, to her shock, he stroked first her clean but unkempt hair and then her shoulder. She could almost swear she heard him whisper, "I'm sorry."

The moment of closeness didn't last. His muscles suddenly tense, he rolled her onto her back and straddled her, his weight pressing down on her belly. Knowing it wouldn't do her any good, she put up no battle as he untied her right hand, hauled it over her head and fastened it to the metal headboard. When he was satisfied with its placement, he did the same to her left. Her arms weren't in danger of being pulled out of their sockets, which meant she could put up with the position for a long time, something he undoubtedly knew.

She saw the ball gag coming; she just couldn't do anything about it. Oh, she whipped her head away, but his fingers in her hair brought her back around. Although she clenched her teeth together when he pressed the red ball against her lips, his fingers pinching her nose so limited her ability to breathe that she instinctively opened her mouth. Then he lifted her head and tightened the straps at the back. As if that wasn't enough, he wrapped black tape around and around her mouth and the gag until it covered her from just beneath her nose to her chin.

When she spotted the hated blindfold, she thrashed her head

about, and if she could have bitten him she would have happily drawn blood. However, despite her desperate efforts, it didn't take long for him to close her in darkness, and as light faded, she slid into that nothing place where serenity lived. She'd stay there. No matter what he did to her, she'd refuse to come out, refuse to respond.

He stood up again and with his weight no longer pulling her onto her side, she settled onto her back and waited. She also *saw* herself as she had no doubt the camera did, a nearly faceless and naked woman secured to a bed and helpless to prevent whatever her captor decided to do to her.

"She is a beauty," Reeve was saying in that stilted tone she'd heard earlier. "After all my preparation, I wanted my first time with her to be as perfect as I could make it. I trust that whoever sees this will agree I chose well."

His voice seemed to be coming closer so maybe she shouldn't have been surprised when he rested his hand on her left breast. Just the same, her heart lurched. "I'm hoping it won't be long before you can see her lovely face, but as I already pointed out, I have my reasons for maintaining public anonymity." He closed his fingers around her nipple. "I'm a man who believes in putting all his cards on the table so I'm going to spell out my concerns. Although I've certainly paid enough for my personal anonymity, I'd be a fool to assume that money is all it takes. Until I have no doubt that this *adult* site is as private as I've been led to believe, I'm keeping both this location and my slave's identity to myself. The last thing I want or need is law enforcement at the door." A stretching sensation told her he was pulling up on her breast, undoubtedly for the camera's benefit.

"That concern aside, my goal remains the same—to be accepted by a segment of society I have a considerable amount in common with. I understand the need for a testing or preview process. I wouldn't be interested in joining an association such as yours if the only criteria were the financial ability to pay the dues, plus the necessary slave."

He was still pulling up on her nipple, making it difficult for her to concentrate on words vital to her understanding of what this was about. Concerned that he'd forgotten her while concentrating on his speech, she moaned and shifted as best as she could.

"Ah, the creature responds. I hope my audience will take note of her reactions. After all, they're key to my acceptance."

The pressure on her nipple let up a little. "I appreciate the guidelines I was sent," he continued. "Having a clear-cut standard before me allowed me to see how far I could and was required to go. I must say the boundaries are liberal enough to satisfy my darkest desires. Most likely this creature won't agree, but then her compliance isn't necessary or even desired, is it?"

Oh shit, what was he talking about, and to who? The sense that she'd become a nonentity, a faceless body, grew.

"I'm particularly fond of breast restraints. With that in mind, I selected a creature with large boobs because they show so well in bondage. I would have preferred natural boobs, but they're hard to come by. Be as that may, I assure you that this creature's are both sensitive and responsive."

When he released her nipple, the renewed blood flow caused her to catch her breath. Doubtless, the camera had picked up the sound, but who was listening? What was that he'd said about her breasts showing well in bondage? If only she could see what he had in mind she might be able to anticipate, to erect her defenses.

A snapping sound she knew all too well froze her. It was close enough to her ear that she had no doubt he was deliberately torturing her with it. "Silver clamps," he said. "It's a shame she won't be able to see how perfectly they contrast with her flawless flesh, but maybe it's better this way. She'll have no choice but to concentrate on sensation. See how she's holding her breath. She knows what's going to happen, and yet she doesn't. I intend to keep her off balance as much as possible because I'm convinced that the unknown has limitless possibilities when it comes to fully training a sex slave."

A sex slave? That couldn't be where this was heading, it couldn't!

She was still trying to convince herself of that when he pushed up on the underside of the breast he'd left alone so far. A deep wave of helpless anticipation caught hold, and when he fastened the clamp to her nipple, despite the sharp sting, she lifted her head toward her tormenter, offering her mouth to him. What did she care that her lips were covered by tape and her mouth forced open by the ball gag? The heavy silver now clinging to her nipple had accomplished its purpose. She was in a space she deeply understood and fed off. The difference this time was that role play had become reality. Maybe the only difference.

"I thought about starting off slow, gradually building upon her imprisonment while letting her know that the journey had just begun. But as I hope you will see in due course, this creature is no stranger to the world she's been thrust into. She has certain experiences and tolerances. In order to get past those elements, her education must proceed at a certain speed."

The way he was talking made her half believe that someone, or more than one someone, had entered the room, but she hoped he was simply talking for the camera's benefit.

His warm fingers on her other breast froze her thoughts. Froze a great deal. She knew what was going to happen, wanted and feared his next movement. He forced her to be patient by running the second clamp over her still-free nipple and from there to ever-widening circles that eventually encompassed her entire breast.

In her mind she saw every exacting detail of the restraint from the clamp itself with its broad, flat surface to the spring-loaded base that caused the clamp to slowly tighten when pulled on. She'd always liked the look of the large clover clamps because they contrasted with her pale flesh and made her think of medieval torture instruments. Fortunately, unlike something from the Middle Ages, modern clamps were incapable of inflicting real damage, not that looking at them would lead the uninformed to that conclusion.

"There," he said, his word coming at the instant the second clamp imprisoned her other nipple. "I confess to a deep love of the symbolism beneath what you're seeing. Although I've taken control of a small piece of this creature's body, I now rule her completely. She can't think beyond this seizure, can you, slave?" He punctuated his question by shaking the bases, causing a long and low electric charge to attack not just her breasts but her entire body.

She was lost in sensation, caught not by the restraints on her wrists and ankles but something more sensual. Determined not to make a sound, she gnawed on her gag. As she'd suspected, a chain led from one clamp to the other. It lay in the valley between her breasts and created its own heat.

"I've given considerable thought to whether I prefer wrapping my slave in miles of rope, leather, or metal." Picking up the chain, he drew her breasts together. There's something to be said for nothing but glimpses of flesh under proof of her utter imprisonment, perhaps a hip or shoulder left free to remind her of what she once took for granted."

Still holding onto the chain, he pressed down on her belly until she half believed he intended to weld her to the bed. Lost between the two sensations, she thrashed her head from side to side.

"On the other hand, I believe the female form, especially one as ripe as this one, deserves to be seen and admired. As I've demonstrated"—a quick tug on the chain—"a great deal of compliance can be attained with a minimum of restraint. I'm looking forward to discussing the relative merits of both approaches with masters of these arts—once I've been accepted for membership. In my public position, I anticipated and demanded that others defer to me, but I'm not so proud that I can't admit I'm a novice in the art of BDSM."

BDSM? Oh no!

"A novice who is more than eager to further my education. To bring people up to speed, I'm going to give a demonstration of certain aspects of the training techniques I intend to incorporate. If you'll give me a moment—"

He might still be talking but maybe not. Maybe he was doing this as part of a plan to test the limits of her sanity.

What did it matter that he'd released the chain now that he was lightly whipping her midsection. Not once did the thin stinging strands touch her breasts or crawl lower than her mons, and that was the hell of it. He could if he wanted, would when he was ready. And in the meantime, she quivered with every slap.

She'd been struck far harder than this; he had to know that. If she could only hold onto that piece of knowledge! But how could she when the kissing blows came one after another, close, so close to her pussy.

This was the magic part of what she did for a living, damn it! To her, being whipped was foreplay. Her nerves loved the stimulation, and although she'd never want *punishment* to draw blood, she could safely fantasize, pretend.

Don't go there. Damn it, don't!

Her warning wasn't strong or loud enough. Shaking, sweating, moaning in need, she strained to spread her legs and invite him in, but he'd lashed her ankles together, damn him. As to whether he'd deliberately placed her cunt out of reach to both of them or simply didn't know everything that took place deep inside her didn't matter.

"You're a pain slut, aren't you?" a rigger had asked once

after the day's session was over and she was standing in a cold shower, her skin glowing. "I've worked a lot of women, and I know. Most of them put up with whippings because the pay's good and it leads to certain rewards, but you get off on being hurt."

"Not being hurt," she'd thrown back at him. "Draw blood and I'll rip your lips off."

"What then?"

"The anticipation and risk. Leather or a cane on me and thinking about what it could become. Telling myself I can't do anything to stop the whipping and wondering how far it'll take me. My skin coming to life."

"Then you've got a hell of an imagination, right? Even with the cameras and crew around you can keep the fantasy going?"

"Yes," she'd told him. "Yes."

This wasn't fantasy, no contracted dom or rigger who understood that his job depended on never crossing a certain line. Instead, Reeve was in control, totally and for as long as he wanted. Her body, hell, her mind belonged to him. His arm was strong and the whip well made. He could keep after her until she no longer knew who she was—or cared. Until she'd become an extension of him and the training tool he wielded. Until she confessed that she sometimes came from pain and for him to *please* take her there.

A grunt from a masculine mouth penetrated her thoughts, but it wasn't until she felt his hand on the flesh he'd been abusing that she comprehended he was no longer striking her. Her own groan was primal, desperate, and despairing. *Don't stop,* she longed to beg him. *Don't stop!*

"I trust you don't mind the demonstration," Reeve was saying. "I wanted to give you an idea of the kind of whip play I anticipate indulging in." His fingers over her belly contracted and relaxed, contracted and relaxed. Thanks to the demo you sent me, I realize I'm far from reaching the limits of what's allowed.

What you just saw is my comfort zone. I want my slave to remain unmarked. Scars would, in my mind, diminish her value and make her less desirable to me."

Abruptly removing his hand from her belly, he unceremoniously shoved it as far between her legs as he could. Too late she ordered herself not to lift her buttocks off the ground in blatant invitation. What a slut she'd become, what a blind and mute and tethered whore!

His large, rough fingers headed for her hole. Too far gone for anything else, she bent her knees outward as far as she could and invited him in. She was suddenly grateful for the blindfold; otherwise, he'd see her for the animal she was. She couldn't tell which finger penetrated her first, bit into the gag when a second joined the first, cried when the ankle restraints prevented him from adding more. Along with her tears came hot anticipation. She was close, so damn close!

No! He wasn't withdrawing, was he? Despite her attempts to soothe herself with denial, not only wasn't his hand still between her legs, her lonely opening continued to weep.

"This is what I was after. Hopefully the light is strong enough that you can see the juice on my fingers. Take it from me, the slave's wet. Drenched. As those of you with more experience pointed out in the material you provide for potential members, key to the perfect sex slave is one with a powerful drive."

Using a rough strength that said he was finished with her, he straightened her knees and pressed her legs together. "There appear to be two schools of thought on this," he continued. "Given a slave with a high sex drive, how often should that drive be satisfied as opposed to teaching her patience? Her pleasure is hardly high on my list. In fact, I consider denying her part of the lessons she must endure. On the other hand, I don't want her so distracted by her needs that she can't attend to mine. I look forward to hearing the debate on this vital issue."

She didn't care who he was talking to. Only a few minutes

ago she couldn't imagine thinking that, but being whipped while tied and wearing the nipple clamps had taken her not into the nothing place she was so familiar with, but someplace just as all consuming. Maybe, she amended while he trailed his fingers over her upstretched arms, she wasn't in a place so much as a state of mind.

One created by her captor.

He was her captor, wasn't he? For the first time in her life her fondest and most deeply buried fantasy had morphed into reality. He was responsible for her silence and blindness. He spoke to people she hadn't known existed. This all-encompassing masculine presence went far beyond being dependent on him for food and water. He'd become her air. His hands and body would either please or punish, and whether she encouraged or fought made no difference.

Her world. For now, her everything.

"I'm excited by the possibilities," he was saying. "I'm not boasting when I say there aren't many challenges I haven't met, but as intriguing as creating and then running my own business was, the thrill's gone, which is why I divested myself of it."

His teeth raked over the underside of her upper arm, causing her to gasp and jerk. With nothing more than the strength in his hands, he forced her to lie still while he nibbled there.

"This excites the hell out of me," he said with his hands still demanding surrender. "To totally control another human being, a sexy woman at that—well, I don't have to tell any of you what a rush that is. I don't want to do it in a vacuum, not when I have peers—you."

Damn his seductive voice. Between that and the commanding message in his grip, she couldn't find her way out of the dark nothing he'd led her into. She'd drift for as long as he allowed, sink deep as the growling need in her pussy. She wouldn't, couldn't think anymore than she could free herself.

His. His.

10

"What is this bull, damn it? Look, sis, if you're listening to this, you'd better pick up. Otherwise I'm going to kick you into the next county. Seriously, call me. I don't like what's happening."

The message Hayley had left on Saree's cell phone ended, but there was another.

"I've been talking to those idiots you work with. Unlike them, I'm not buying that cock and bull about you running off with some rich stud. That message you left me doesn't sound like you, and this isn't how you operate. I'm going to go to the police. I don't have a choice. I don't know if they'll listen to me, but . . ."

"I told you," Saree said softly. "My sister and I have always watched each other's back."

"The cops won't do anything."

She sat curled on the narrow bed, her naked body looking small and vulnerable. He hoped she wouldn't figure out that he was in a recliner on the opposite side of the room because he didn't trust himself to get any closer.

"Because you've covered your tracks, that's what you're

saying, isn't it," she pushed. "I'm sure there's no sign of a forced entry at my place. Where's my car?"

"In your garage."

Her eyes widened. She picked at the length of leather running from her right ankle to the bed frame. "Who put it there?"

"Does it matter?"

"Yeah," she whispered after a brief silence. "It does."

Staring at her carried the risk of driving him crazy, not that he could bring himself to do anything else. Although he should be making sure the video feed had reached its intended destination and assure himself that traffic to said destination was limited to approved users, studying her was both easier and harder. After what he'd put her through, he was relieved to see she looked no more the worse for wear, but that wasn't all he was after. He needed to know she had the mental and emotional tools to survive him.

"What are you looking at?" she demanded. "You get off on seeing me like this?" She indicated the restraint.

The truth was that, yes, knowing she couldn't get away kicked his sex drive and something else up a number of notches. However, he wasn't about to give that away, at least he hoped to hell he didn't. "She isn't bluffing about calling the police?"

If Saree caught on that he was changing the subject, she gave no indication. "My sister doesn't cry wolf. If she says she's going to do something, you can take it to the bank." She shook her head, then pressed her fingers against her temple. "You're putting her through hell. From the tone of her voice, she's about a breath away from panic."

His first impulse was to tell Saree that that wasn't his problem, but a moment of looking into her pained eyes told him he'd be a fool if he did. He needed certain things from her, needed to build her into what it would take to get past The Slavers' walls, but quite possibly that wouldn't happen if she couldn't take her mind off her sister. Why the hell hadn't he thought about that?

Because to survive, you locked yourself away from everything that so much as whispered of family.

"You're going to call her," he said. "And when you do, you're going to keep one thing foremost in your mind."

She was watching him the way a cautious dog might study an unfamiliar human. *One thing*, her eyes probed.

"If I have the resources and manpower to return your car to your garage, I can silence your sister."

The sudden fear in her eyes along with her fingers now around her throat left no doubt that he'd made his point. What she didn't need to know was how much his tactic disgusted him.

"Talk to her?" she muttered. "Saying what?"

"That's up to you—whatever it takes to convince her that you don't need her butting in."

"What if she doesn't buy my explanation? My voice—she's going to pick up on my emotions."

"Not my problem." *The hell it isn't.* "Do what you need to." That said, he tossed her cell phone at her. If law enforcement got involved, he ran the risk of their being able to trace the call—yet another reason for Saree to do as he ordered.

Her hands shook as she punched the numbers. After completing the first video session, he'd removed her blindfold and gag and loosened her restraints but left her alone with her thoughts and emotions until he believed sexual energy no longer permeated her being. He probably shouldn't have given her back a measure of freedom so soon, but he'd wanted to see how thorough her recovery was—for his sake. He was a bastard, a damnable and trapped bastard.

"Sis? It's me." Saree's voice was strained. "No, don't, please don't cry." Her eyes accusing, she listened to whatever her sister was saying. Damn, he should have insisted she put the phone on speaker, but if he had, wouldn't Hayley be even more suspicious?

"I'm all right, let it go at that, I'm all right. No, I can't tell you where I am. It's, well, I'm not sure myself. I'm not alone, I just can't—no, no one is holding a gun to my head." Glaring, she picked at an ankle cuff. "It's going to be a hell of a story when it's over, but I've been sworn to secrecy. You don't want me to go back on my word, do you?"

Another silence had her frowning. "We're both adults, sis. I didn't try to live your life for you when you were getting to know Mazati. Trust me, that's all I can say, trust me."

The longer the sisters talked, the more the risk that Saree would blurt something so he pushed himself to his feet and stalked toward her with his hand outstretched.

"Don't do anything, not yet," she said. He reached for her but she spun away and fell onto the bed with the phone still clamped to her ear. "But if I haven't called back in two days, tell the police to look for the man who approached me at my last shoot."

Cursing under his breath, he rolled her onto her back and yanked the phone out of her hand. He punched End.

"What the hell was that?"

"What do you want? For me to sit there and wait for you to slit my throat?"

"You think that's what's going to happen?"

"I don't know anything except what you've done so far. Get off me!" She tried to knee him.

Damn but she was like heat lightning under him! Her small and surprisingly strong body was so tense he wondered if something might snap, but that wasn't all he felt. Laced up with taut muscles were the remnants of the sexual frustration he'd put her through. Whether via instinct or on purpose, her every move had a sensual quality to it, and she fit so well under him.

Not trusting his ability to ward off her body's impact, he slid off her, but instead of letting her sit up, he snagged her wrists and pinned her arms over her head. Sitting next to her and leaning over kept him in dangerous proximity with the form that had caused countless men to jack off, but then danger always reminded him that he was alive, that he hadn't destroyed his emotions after all.

He was alive today all right with a helpless and sexy woman at his command. Her eyes like burning coals dared him to press the limits, and his belief that her movements were designed to challenge and taunt grew with every breath she took. They both knew he could keep her like this as long as he wanted, but that didn't stop her from arching her back and rolling her hips. Her breasts, inches from his chest, begged to be touched and held, caressed and sucked.

"What the hell are you doing?" he demanded.

Don't you get it? At least that's what he read in those burning coals. Her silence chewed at him, he who could go days without speaking. What was going on inside that head of hers? Even more germane to the moment, what was her body saying to his?

Like he didn't know.

Driven by a hunger so deep he couldn't guess at its source, he brought her hands together so he could hold them with a single paw. Once he was certain the grip was going to hold, he spread his free hand over her throat. She instantly stopped struggling.

"What is it, Saree? Not so sure of yourself after all? Maybe you want to be punished, is that what this so-called fight has been about? You need to get off and being punished is a sure-fire way to make it happen."

"You bastard."

"Words? Is that all you have, words?"

She wanted to scream profanities at him. The urge was so strong that he felt it in her taut muscles and saw it in her hate-filled eyes. But was that really hate and rage or was something else at play?

Time to find out. For both of them.

Barely blinking, he began a journey from her throat down her lush body. Her eyes remained wide, her body still but ready. Although she might be able to free her hands, she wasn't trying. Neither had she aimed her free foot at his crotch. As he caressed the valley between her breasts and then her breasts themselves before journeying to her midsection and from there to her belly, her lips parted and the fire in her eyes darkened and began to speak of something else.

Damn but he loved seeing her like this. She was lost to her body's needs and demands, just like him. She'd become primal, elemental, breasts and cunt and arms and legs.

Her job required that her pussy always be shaved, and although his fingers noted the finest stubble, the newborn hairs did nothing to detract from the silken flesh. The pain of his swollen cock straining against his shorts made him curse the damnable garment, not that he was going to stop what he was doing long enough to get rid of it.

He loved these moments, loved them! Not only was she ripe and hot and he hot and horny, having absolute control over her was something he'd only mentally explored before.

She was under him, on his bed, tied to it, naked, struggling to breathe around her arousal with her eyes now searing his and the distance between her thighs widening. He smelled her excitement, the scent adding yet more to the size of his cock.

"Where's your fight, slave? Strip you of it, did I?"

Her silence answered his question; she wasn't fighting because she had no choice but to hand her body over to him. For a man who'd never thought he'd say the word *slave* and mean it, it felt right now. Along with the other reasons he'd taken this job was one he hadn't faced before—he wanted to control her.

No, he amended as he ran his fingers over her cunt, not want. He *was* controlling her. "Don't move," he commanded. "No matter what I do, you aren't to move."

The quick jerk of her head might not be compliance, not that it mattered because restraining her was an easy matter. In truth, he relished the idea of a no-holds-barred struggle with her. He might hold back a bit to make the fight more equal for as long as it entertained him to do so. Then when he was ready to kick things up another notch, he'd forcefully remind her of what he'd just called her, his slave.

His.

Trying not to give anything away took more concentration than he wanted, but for reasons he wasn't interested in examining, he needed her to believe he was totally in control as he forced her to the edge of sanity. Taking his time, he released her hands. When her fingers twitched, he pressed down on them. "What did I tell you?"

"Not to move."

"Then why did you?" He kept the pressure going, not enough to hurt her of course but firm enough that she'd have no doubt of his determination.

"I don't know."

"Master," he spat. "Call me Master."

Fire again danced in her eyes. That along with the way her legs had started to tremble left him with no doubt that he'd said what she'd wanted to hear. "I don't know why I didn't obey, Master."

Giving her an indulgent smile, he patted her fingers and then released her hands. The effort of not moving was being played out in her expressive features. She wanted to play her role and yet she didn't, same as him. She needed to be submissive as keenly as he needed to control. And it didn't matter that neither of them understood why.

"You're not going to let that happen again, are you?" he insisted. "Because you know the consequences if you do."

"I—I'll try."

"No!" Plastering on a stern look, he loomed over her. "Try

isn't good enough, slave. If you're going to please your master, you must put his demands first."

"I understand."

Did she? Did either of them?

Although he felt far from wise, he nodded solemnly. Then he straightened so he could look down at this creature who was willing to turn herself over to him. The shift in their relationship had happened so quickly, going from captor/captive to master/slave in a matter of minutes. Things could and probably would shift back, but as long as the same spell covered both of them, he'd embrace it.

He had no choice, not after a lifetime of wanting this and not knowing it.

"Your body is no longer yours," he heard himself say. "It exists to please me. In exchange for submitting to whatever I want, I'll keep food in your belly and chains on your body, you understand, don't you?"

"Yes, Master."

"You will worship me just as I worship your subservience. We'll feed off each other and find our own pleasure, won't we?"

"Yes, Master."

What he'd just said had been easy, but now things were going to change because even with the fantasy wrapped around him, he couldn't forget his task. "And you'll do whatever I order you to. Even if you don't understand and feel humiliated, you won't question. You'll feed off your fear and make it part of your performance."

She'd intertwined her fingers, but although she'd disobeyed him by moving, he didn't want to distract either of them from this vital lesson.

"Do you understand what I'm saying? I want you afraid."

"I—what do you want me to say?"

"Nothing. In fact, you aren't to say a word until I give you permission."

That didn't set well with her as witnessed by her narrowing eyes. Taking her expression as warning that she wasn't as deep into their *game* as he wanted her to be, he decided to test her limits. And although he told himself that the test was a vital part of their reason for being together, he knew different. He needed to see her struggle between her self-will and his.

"Sit up."

Confusion followed by disappointment rolled through her, and no wonder. Weren't her splayed legs proof of what she wanted? And what he did too.

"Do I have to punish you? Sit up, slave."

The grace with which she complied let him know she was testing him. Fine, he loved the challenge, which was why he didn't move so she was forced to rub her body against his. He waited until she was curled next to him with her free leg tucked under her and the other near the side of the bed. Her nudity in contrast to the multipurpose bracelets and anklets on her wrists and ankles gave rise to endless possibilities, and yet he wanted to introduce her to something new, to keep her as off balance as he felt.

He extracted a narrow key from his pocket, and he inserted it into the lock connecting the leather strip to her leg, unlocking it. "Go to the dresser," he continued. "There's rope in there. I want you to bring it to me."

She tensed as the ramifications of this latest order sunk in. Fascinated by thoughts of what it would take to melt her, he nevertheless grunted. Looking back over her shoulder at him, she crawled to the edge of the bed and slipped off it. He wasn't surprised to see her glance at the door, not that it would do her any good. Just the same, the thought of chasing her throughout the house and beyond quickened his breath.

Doing as he'd ordered didn't need to take as long as it did, making him wonder if she was trying to get him to punish her.

Then he noted that her hands were shaking as she dropped the soft white rope on the bed.

"Kiss it."

Not looking at him, she bent over and ran her lips along the length. Her movements were slow and languid, her body angled so he had a clear view of her flank. Giving into the challenge, he ran his hand over her buttocks and thigh. Maybe her quiver should have given him a sense of security, but all it told him was that she was as deep into whatever was happening as he was.

When he'd told her to get the rope, he'd had only a rudimentary idea of what he intended to do with it, but touching her flesh solidified his thoughts. He wanted to see that magnificent body encased in what he'd wrapped around it. Giving a silent thanks to the rigger and model he'd taken lessons from in preparation for this assignment, he picked up the rope, folded it in half, and draped it over the back of her neck. From there he crossed it between her breasts, then ordered her to turn with her back to him. Her eyes closing, she did as he commanded.

Imprisoning her arms behind her with her elbows bent at a right angle and her forearms resting against each other took considerable attention because he didn't want to compromise her circulation. In addition to strands that went around her upper arms and both under and over her breasts, all but immobilizing her upper body, he also lashed her forearms and wrists together before securing the whole with a final loop around her waist. Completing the complex tie called for her turning in circles as he worked. Although she'd opened her eyes by the time he'd finished, she didn't look at him. Good. It was time for her to exist as his possession and not a complex woman.

Stepping back, he studied his handiwork. The rigger had been adamant that ropes weren't to press on nerves or blood vessels, and from the looks of things, he'd managed that. The strand around her neck, although particularly arousing, didn't so much as touch her throat. From the waist down, she was as free as she was beautiful while the rest of her belonged fully and completely to him. The strands near her breasts caused her breasts to stick out more than usual. Pinching them between his fingers, he drew her toward him.

Her eyes were glazed over, her mouth open, nostrils flared. Feeding off her mood, he leaned over and took a nipple into his mouth. Not content with simply tasting her, he lightly closed his teeth over the firm nub before pulling back. Her spine arched, and she stepped toward him. Intrigued, he took a backward step while keeping his hold firm. Moaning low in that lovely throat, she matched his stride. Although he'd have loved to have seen how long he could have guided her this way, he couldn't hold this position for long. Reluctantly freeing her, he noted the saliva he'd left behind.

Thinking to show it to her, he reached out. Shaking her head, she leaned away.

Anger raced through him. She was his slave, damn it, his possession! How dare she think otherwise! "Stop it!" He punctuated his order by slapping first her wet breast and then the other. "Don't move, damn it, don't move!"

"Master! Master, please."

The words feeding his fantasy, he slapped her again. This time he didn't bother telling her why. She was no longer trying to get away, but unless he was the biggest fool in the county, she was trying to incur his wrath by whipping her body from side to side in a futile and beyond sexy attempt to protect those incredible breasts of hers

They battled. There was no other way of saying it. The more times his open palm connected with her full mounds, the more she hissed and growled. She'd arched her body again, which meant her breasts were front and center, challenges offered. He met them as he knew they both wanted until her milky flesh had turned red and her nipples were like rocks.

His clothes, his damnable clothes! What the hell had he put them on for?

The next time he reached out, it wasn't to continue punishing her. Instead, he wrapped his fingers around the rope over her breasts. Then, using his hold as a cowboy might handle a captured horse, he dragged her to the bed. "You asked for that," he threw at her. "You knew the consequences of fighting me and yet you did."

"Yes, Master."

"Why?"

"So you would punish me."

There. The words he'd known were in her spoken aloud. "Do you believe you've been punished enough?"

She took a deep and long breath. "No, Master."

"What more should I do to you to make sure you've learned your lesson?"

11

Saree had been asked that question any number of times, but it had always been rhetorical. This was different, excitingly different.

"These ropes," she began. "they aren't enough."

"You want more?"

What she desperately wanted was to be encased head to toe. Being rendered incapable of moving a single muscle was an incredible turn-on; just thinking about a crotch rope caused her crotch to weep in anticipation. "I do." She kept her head downcast.

"What else?"

"A whipping." Taken aback by the hungry eagerness in her voice, she swallowed. "Master, this worthless slave needs to feel your whips on her body. Only then will I learn everything I need to."

"What if I don't want to whip you?"

Was he tormenting her, denying her what she most needed? Maybe and yet maybe he was simply testing her. "You—I can't tell you what to do. All I can do is beg you to teach me your lessons."

"Maybe I don't have any."

"These ropes have a purpose. I know they do!"

"Perhaps I simply like the way they contain and contrast with your skin."

Although she could and perhaps should have thanked him for what she took as a compliment, she decided on a different tactic. Her gaze as submissive as she could make it, she dropped awkwardly to her knees and tried to suck his clothed cock into her mouth. He stood there with his knees locked and his hands fisted while she covered his shorts in saliva.

She was a wreck, a wretched, turned-on wreck! Being restrained always got her juices flowing, but what she felt now went beyond those familiar sensations. The difference was easy to determine—reality versus play. He'd known what he was doing when he tied her, making her wonder how many other sex slaves had felt his restraints on their bodies.

Sex slave? Yes, she had put that label on herself.

No way could she gnaw a hole in his shorts, but although she found it somewhat humiliating, she couldn't make herself stop any more than she could get back on her feet. She belonged on her knees before him, groveling for whatever tidbits of attention he granted her. As his captive, she'd become *his*. In her captivity she'd found something she'd been looking for for much of her life.

"Enough," he ordered. A hand gripped her hair and pulled her head back. Forced to release him, she stared up at the man she'd called Master.

"What do you want?" she managed.

"I'm not sure."

"Me," she encouraged. "You want me."

"That goes without saying, damn it." The tugging on her scalp increased. "Stand up. Did I give you permission to kneel?"

"No, Master."

"That's right, I didn't. Get up before I punish you."

He might consider whatever he had in mind to do punishment, but to her, it was a promise. Just the same, she tried to obey. Unfortunately, without use of her hands, she failed. Unlike when he'd used this hold to bring her to the bed, he didn't release her. Instead, he forced her up onto her toes.

She would have gladly widened her stance if he'd told her to. But with her mind cloudy and her body hot, the best she could do was order herself to anticipate.

So that's what he had in mind, was it? To work his hand between her legs.

"You're wet." Features grim, he ran his fingers along her pussy. "Did I give you permission to soak yourself?"

"No, Master."

"Then why did you?"

The longer he stroked her, the more intense the pressure there and deep in her belly became. If she hadn't been so wet, the friction would have been painful. As it was, the heat he'd created threatened to burst into flames. "I don't know. I'm sorry."

"You should be. This"—he slapped her labia—"belongs to me. It should do only what I give it permission to, do you understand?"

Cheeks flaming, she nodded. Even that small gesture made her dizzy. "I'm trying."

"Trying isn't enough. Yes, I am going to have to punish you."

If anyone had said that under different circumstances, she'd laugh at him, run, or fight back, but none of those options fit. "How?"

"However I want, get it! Spread your legs, now."

Suddenly trembling, she did as he'd ordered. Her simple and yet complex obedience added to the suspicion that they were entering a world neither had been in before. She might be mistaken about him of course, but years of exploring submission and mastery hinted she wasn't.

"Not good enough. Push your cunt toward me."

Guessing what was coming next made it easy to obey. She could only hope she didn't lose her mind before her *punishment* was over. She supposed she should be relieved because he wrapped his arm around her before the first blow struck her pussy. A shockwave of sensation shot through her. A second firm but not painful slap followed almost immediately.

A third, then four, followed by five. No matter that she tried to straighten, tried to close her legs against the fire-falls, they kept coming. Her sex fed off the relentless stimulation and forced sharp animal-like sounds from her.

"Stand straight," he ordered as he continued to pummel her. "Spread. More! Wide! Take your punishment, take it! You don't want to make me angry, do you?"

"No!" she gasped, although the thought of his anger being directed at her made her half wild with wanting.

"That's right, you don't. This cunt I've claimed is turning bright pink. It's also getting wetter. You love this, don't you?"

More slaps, a barrage of them raining on tissues that felt as if they might fly apart. Wise in the ways of a woman's sex, he peppered her from mons to ass.

"Answer me! You like this, don't you?"

"Yes!" she nearly howled. "Yes, Master, I do!"

"Of course you do." He punctuated each word with yet another blow, and when instinct again tried to close her legs, he redirected his palm to her inner thighs, stopping her. "Because you're a slut, a cunt. Tell me what you are."

Mindless. "A slut. I'm a slut."

"Yes, you are." His hot breath curled around her ear, making her shiver. "And this"—three rapid-fire blows—"makes you even more so, doesn't it?"

"Yes. Yes!"

"You want me to stop before you lose your mind." He pressed his hand against her heated core, forcing her back onto her toes. The pressure continued; she tried to rub herself against him. "And yet you don't because you're such a cunt."

"Yes, yes."

"How does that make you feel?"

"Master, please, I'm going to come."

"No, you aren't."

His harsh tone barely penetrated. What made an impact was that he was now running his sex-drenched hand over her cheek. Whimpering at the loss to her pussy, she tried to press herself against his cock.

"No!" Gripping her shoulders and shaking them, he backed away. "There'll be no pleasure for you until or if it pleases me to watch you come."

"Master, please." A volcano raged through her; nothing short of sex or plunging into an icy lake would silence it. "Anything. I'll do anything."

"Of course you will, my little slut. You have no pride left. Like a bitch in heat, only one thing matters to you."

He could call her anything he wanted; she didn't care. But even as she struggled to gather the courage to tell him that, the raw edge of her hunger blunted a little. A single touch from him would bring her to the brink again, maybe beyond.

"What do you want?" she asked in a low and hungry tone. "What do I have to do?"

"I haven't decided."

"Suck your cock? I can make you happy, Master."

"I should trust you? No chance you'd bite me?"

Maybe, if I was climaxing. "No, Master. You'd punish me if I did."

"Yes, I would." He closed his still-sticky hand around her throat. "Do you have any idea how much I love feeling your blood pulse? To know I have the power of life and death over you is nearly as good as sex." His hand tightened a little. Alert but not alarmed, she held still. "A question. Assuming that I truly have that much power, what are you willing to do to ensure I don't make good on my threat?"

"I—don't understand. What do you want?"

"Proof that you know I'm not bluffing. Your task, to keep from angering me. How do you go about that?"

She hadn't heard that tone from him before. It wasn't as stilted as when he was talking to the camera, but neither did it have the ring of honesty. A role he was playing? "By pleasing you."

"Hmm." Relaxing his hold on her throat, he closed his free hand over the elbow closest to him. "Wise words, slave. And how would you please me?"

A thousand images crowded her mind. Her bent over and anchored to a low post with her ass in the air. Her hog-tied at his feet. Her taking him deep into her throat while he whipped her buttocks. And most appealing, straddling him with his cock buried in her while they both laughed and kissed and nipped.

"Can I show you?"

"Perhaps."

"Thank you, Master. Thank you. First, I must get rid of your clothes."

When he nodded, she wasn't sure whether she was excited or overwhelmed. After all, she couldn't use her hands. Calling on all the resourcefulness at her disposal, she slipped to her knees, her face inches from his crotch. Freeing the button at his waist with just her teeth took concentration and effort. By the time she'd completed her task and tugged down the zipper, her mouth ached, and her pussy no longer commanded her full attention. Fortunately his hips were slim and his buttocks taut, which made sliding his shorts down relatively easy. By repeatedly changing her teeth-grip on his shorts, she got that snug fabric to follow his shorts' path while he did his part by pulling off his shirt. After he'd stepped out of the garments, she allowed herself her first true up-close look at his cock. Straight and strong with large, dark veins, it gave off a single and unde-niable message; worship me.

Yes, soon!

Although she hoped he'd again help her stand, he did noth-ing more than provide the necessary support for her to lean against. Grunting from the effort, she rested her head against his chest. "If Master would lie on the bed on his back, I will do the rest."

"And what would that *rest* be?"

"I would like to surprise Master, if he will allow me to."

By way of answer, he grabbed her hair and pulled her head back. His eyes became an incredible deep chocolate, his emo-tions adding to their depth. She both worshipped and feared that depth, and no matter how unsettled returning his stare made her, she refused to break the contact. She wanted to kiss him, needed to feel his mouth on hers.

And yet kissing spoke of a brand of trust and intimacy they couldn't possibly ever achieve.

When he released her, he did more than just let go of her hair. He also shoved her, causing her to stumble back. By the time she'd regained her balance, he was sitting on the bed and putting on a condom. Then planting his hands behind him, he studied her. Because she'd seen herself in countless bondage positions, she knew what he was seeing. And because a number of men had waxed carnal about how much studying a captive woman turned them on, she had little doubt of what was going on inside his mind.

Could he sense the invisible ropes between them? Did he understand that she could no more turn her back on what was happening than she could stop breathing?

"Relax." She swallowed. "Your slave lives to please you."

A quick shake of his head said he doubted that. Perhaps she should tell him she was simply following instinct and didn't know where this was going or how it would end, but it was safer to hide behind silence.

Caught in thoughts of how dependent she was on him, she climbed onto the bed, stood, and straddled him. He fell back, his hands on her hips. Looking down, she assured herself that cock and cunt were in alignment. Despite the strain to her thighs and calves, she didn't hurry her descent.

This moment was fantasy and truth. She'd crossed a line she'd never thought she would. After years of dancing at the edges of a fascinating and foreign lifestyle, she'd entered it, at least briefly. Doing so was taking her into a space she hadn't known existed, a space defined by one man's ultimate control over her. She willingly submitted to the ropes lacing and confining her upper body, but there was no guarantee he'd remove them. And even if he did, he might and probably would replace them with other restraints. There'd be no going home at the end of the day, no stopping at the grocery store or logging time at the gym, no working in her yard or talking to her sister. The activities she'd always taken for granted were now denied her.

Because that was what the man under her wanted.

Hot and shaking, she arched her back, her gaze now fixed on the wall instead of the man she intended to skewer herself on. With every inch of descent, a new shiver attacked her body.

Reeve's silence was as dense as her own, his hold on her unrelenting. When she guessed she was within three or four inches of her goal, he steadied his cock with one hand and guided the last of her descent. At the moment of contact a new and fleeting thought distracted her. There'd been nothing forceful about his role. In contrast to the way he'd bound her, he'd let her take the lead and control the tempo of their mating.

Ah yes, mating. Fucking. His cock relentlessly penetrating and filling her.

Unlike her earlier descent, there was nothing controlled or

graceful about the way her buttocks settled on his groin and her inner thighs scraped his hip bones. He'd bent his knees and splayed his hips, and as a result, she was fully impaled on him. Taking that knowledge with her, she started rocking forward and back. Feeling him move within her took her even deeper into the world they'd created. They weren't separate human beings. Maybe, in ways that defied explanation, they'd never be again.

This wasn't role playing or a game devised by two people who'd grown to trust each other. Insane or not, she'd willingly turned her cunt over to her captor at the same moment that she'd captured his cock.

When he lifted his head and stared at her, she ended her perusal of the wall and answered his gaze. Those were a cougar's eyes, a wolf's.

Time spun around her and took her back to a forgotten childhood memory. Her parents had taken Hayley and her to a wildlife preserve dedicated to the care and rehabilitation of predators. While her sister had been fascinated by the lions and tigers, she'd stood frozen before an enclosure holding a wolf with its broken hind leg in a cast. Although she'd been assured that the wolf would recover, the look in its eyes spoke of a profound loneliness.

Reeve was lonely, a loner who'd let down his barriers enough to allow her to venture where maybe no one ever had.

Shaken by what she'd just learned, she redoubled her efforts. Back and forth, back and forth, her pussy muscles clamping down on him, her thighs straining and relaxing only to do so over and over again. Her labored and loud breathing blended with his, and when he began lightly slapping her jiggling breasts, she howled her delight.

"You like this?" he demanded, raking his nails over her taut thighs.

"Yes, yes!"

Reaching behind her, he gripped her buttocks. "And this!"

"Yes!"

A slap, nails on her belly, fingers clamping around her hips and forcing her against him as he powered himself up and into her. "Fight me, slave! Show me how much you hate this."

"I can't. I can't!"

"What's this?" Capturing her nipples, he forced her down so her breasts now rested on his chest. Looping his arms around her, he held her in place. "You like not being able to move?"

"No." Although it would do no good, she tried to fight free. And as she suspected it would, struggling brought her within a breath of climaxing. "I can't—let me—"

"What's this?" Squeezing, he again drove his cock deep. "The slave is trying to order me?"

"No. No. I'm sorry, Master."

"As you should be." Leaning to the side while still holding her, he ran his teeth over her shoulder. "Take your punishment. Take it!"

"Yes, yes!"

Sweat from both their bodies threatened to seal them together; she loved the hard scent. In truth she loved everything about her body pressed against his. Although she managed a quivering action that allowed her pussy to sing and cry, it needed more—harder—if she was going to find the release she so badly needed.

"What's this, slave? You aren't strong enough to satisfy your master?"

"I'm sorry. So sorry. Please, let me try—"

"Try? It's time for results." That said, he shoved her upright. "Get off!"

Although she could barely comprehend what he'd just ordered her to do, the creature she'd become hurried to obey. As soon as the union between them was broken, he sat up, all but knocking her off the bed. Fortunately, he caught her, holding her in place while he planted his feet on the floor and stood. He didn't have to explain what he had in mind as he guided her to kneel at the edge of the bed with her back to him and her legs spread.

His hand through her ropes in back now, he pulled her upright and then forced her to lean forward until her cheek rested on the bed. "What's it going to be, slave? This or the night alone?"

"Master! You know what I want."

"I want to hear it."

"I need you to take me like this, from the rear."

"You won't fight?"

"No. Never." *Never?*

"Good." The word rolled slowly out of him as if he didn't want to say it. "As for why I'm doing it this way, I'm the master, not you. I don't do on the bottom."

She could have pointed out that having her pummel him while all he had to do was lie there and enjoy hardly made him subservient, but if he wanted to plow into her this way, it was fine with her. More than fine.

Leaving her with her head down, he spread her ass cheeks. "What a sight," he said as he drew her cunt lips apart. "So swollen. Hungry."

"Yes, Master."

"You're so dark in there, the ultimate mystery." He buried his thumb in her pussy. By turn he pushed even deeper and swept his finger about as if judging its contours. Mentally leaving her body, she stood beside him. Because of the way his hand was positioned, she could barely glimpse her external sex. Each time his thumb pressed against her inner core, she moaned and tried to lift her head. Her legs trembled, the smell of her arousal permeated her nostrils.

"You're so easy to control, slave. Your responsiveness is your greatest weakness; you can't deny that, can you?"

Despite the battle raging inside her, her cunt muscles closed down around him. "No, Master, I can't. Master, please, I need—"

"I know what you need"—he slapped her right buttock with his open palm—"better than you do. Don't you ever tell me what to do, do you understand?"

"Yes, yes."

"I figured that was what you'd say. And if I had no interest in fucking you, I'd spend hours forcing you to be patient. Your lessons will come, never doubt that. But the one thing you have to do now is please me. You're going to do that, aren't you?"

"Yes."

"And why is that?"

"Be—because it's what you commanded."

"Not good enough," he muttered, massaging her ass with his free hand. "Go into yourself for the truth. Why are you pleasing me?"

"Because it's what I want."

He didn't speak for just long enough that she sensed her answer meant a great deal to him. "We want the same thing."

"Do we?" she ventured. "Your thumb—surely you can't be content with that in me when it could be your cock."

"Content, no." On the tail of a low sigh, he pulled out. The sudden loss of all that warmth shook her, and although he hadn't given her permission, she sat up so she could look back at him. Watching her pensively, he wiped his thumb on her buttocks, then took hold of his cock, the message unmistakable. She responded by shoving her ass at him.

"An incredible sight, all that soft, white flesh waiting for me. You are patient aren't you, slave."

"If you wish me to be."

"Ah, a slave's proper answer, but is it what you want?"

"No, Master." She inched as close to the edge of the bed as she dared. "Master, I offer my cunt as my gift to you. Please take it, please."

Planting his hand on the small of her back, he forced her down again. Her vision started to blur so she closed her eyes and waited. Scant seconds later, he spread her labial lips and touched his cock to her opening. He grunted, perhaps in response to her unbidden gasp. When he grasped her around her hips and anchored her in place, she silently thanked him. The whisper-soft touch became an inch-deep penetration. And although she'd started trembling again, she willed herself to be patient.

He slipped in so smoothly that for a moment she wasn't sure. Then, although she readied herself for a fierce assault, he simply remained in place. Taken aback by his self-control, she stopped concentrating on her own battle. His hard and hot arousal buried in her said something about closeness, but she knew better than to read too much into the message.

There it was, that primal rolling strength charging throughout him. Caught off guard by the timing, she gasped. As the sound broke free, she fed off it. Reeve was power and possession. Something she'd been searching for her entire life.

More an extension of him than a separate human being, she offered her sex to him. He held her in place via the hand around her middle while the other clenched the ropes at her back and turned her into his mount, his animal. Head thrashing, she whined her desperate need. He kept plowing into her as if punishing her for something, and yet she fed off that power. Her head nearly bursting and her pussy in flames, she lost touch with reality. In her mind she became the slave he'd called her, not just a slave but willing feminine flesh under assault.

He kept coming at her, driving into her as if his life depended on fucking her, grunting and growling. Feeding off his energy, she screamed. Although her throat felt raw, she continued screaming. Otherwise everything that had backed up inside her might drive her insane. Despite her useless arms, she found a deep-seated strength. There was power in captivity, courage and joy.

One moment he'd pulled her up off the bed, the next, he'd flattened her onto it. It didn't matter. Only him on his way to explosion did. Her release was right there, less than a heartbeat away and yet just out of reach. The why didn't matter, and despite her screams, she loved the anticipation, the sweet pain of frustration.

Something shifted. It had no definition or form, no beginning. All she knew was that *it* had slammed into her. Feeling as if she'd been caught by a sneaker ocean wave, she let go. The wave pushed her up, then slammed her down, threw her skyward again and kept her there. Her climax became an endless downhill ski run with the wind tearing at her.

"Master, Master, thank you!"

12

"It's not working."

"What the hell do you mean?"

"It's me. I'm not as much of a bastard as I thought I was."

"So what are you saying?"

As little as possible. Restless, Reeve stepped outside, his cell phone at his ear. The moment he did, the afternoon's heat slammed into him. How the hell anyone survived living in the desert in the summer was beyond him. Oh yeah, there was AC but who wanted to spend months locked inside?

"I've been thinking about the trade-off," he told Agent J. Much as Reeve wanted to go back inside, he also didn't want to take a chance on Saree hearing. Just because he'd left her in the training room didn't mean she might not somehow pick up on what he was saying. Besides, thinking was marginally easier when he wasn't near her. "All our focus on shutting down The Slavers, we didn't adequately address the issue of what would happen to the woman we needed to get us in the door."

"You're doing it."

"Doing what?"

"Giving me that *we* shit. I've never met the subject. What is it? She's putting up more of a fight than we anticipated? Maybe having to put your hands all over her is asking too much of your cock? Damn it, Reeve. You said you could handle it."

Because I believed I could. "I was wrong," he admitted, his eyes on what he took to be a solitary buzzard high above. From where he was standing, it didn't look as if there was a single other living creature for miles. Maybe the buzzard was waiting for him to keel over from the heat.

"What do you mean, wrong? Damn it, Reeve, don't make me pull this out of you. Play that damn silent macho role with someone else. I need honest."

No arguing there, which whether he wanted to admit it or not was why he'd called J. One of the most complex operations The Clan had ever been involved in called for complete cooperation between the various players.

"She's getting to me." He forced the words. "Never saw it coming."

"Shit. Okay, back up here. You've been trying the techniques we agreed to, taking her through the same steps we know are being used on the women The Slavers have gotten their hands on, right?"

"Up to a point."

"What point?"

"I stopped at hurting her. I'm not going to put whip marks on her, I'm not." An image of Saree getting off on the whip play they'd indulged in floated through him.

"Reeve. Damn it, do you think I like this any better than you do? You know how many strategy meetings we had discussing this. But no matter how many ways we twisted things, it came down to believability. The Slavers are going to see right through an act. Fear and defeat can't be faked."

He knew that in spades because he'd been in on all of those strategy meetings. Back then, feeling the eyes of other agents on him and believing he was dead inside, he'd agreed that one woman would have to be at least temporarily sacrificed if others were going to be saved. There'd be counseling for her afterward of course, they'd all agreed. As for whether the counseling would help . . . *Find another subject,* he wanted to throw at J. "There has to be another way. The video feed made it into their site; we know that. What's so damn hard about locating the physical operation?"

"Because they're that good," J said, as Reeve knew he would. "Just because they roam the net for recruits doesn't mean they're going to open a real door. Damn, it's too late to change plans. Get that through your head and do your job. Go to confession or whatever you have to once it's over."

"What about you? No trouble facing yourself in the mirror knowing you had a hand in ruining Saree?"

J's silence lasted just long enough for the point to be made; this devil's decision hadn't been any easier on him. "She's not going to be in any worse shape than those we hope to save. Never forget, they can be salvaged, if we get there in time."

"Maybe."

"All right," J allowed. "Maybe. That's up to the shrinks."

"Yeah, it is. The thing is, we didn't have a hand in what's being done to those other women. We're the solution, not the problem—except with Saree."

For the second time, J didn't hurry his reply. Leaning against the door and sweating, Reeve wondered what Saree was doing. He'd untied her within moments of their explosive fucking and then watched as she half stumbled, half walked into the bathroom. As intriguing as the idea of joining her in the shower was, he'd been unable to summon up the energy to get off the bed.

When she finished, she'd returned to him. She'd made sure he saw her looking at the locked door before climbing onto the bed next to him. Only then had he given into the need for a drink of water and a pee. She was more asleep than awake by the time he'd finished. Knowing he wasn't in any better shape, he'd chained her foot to the bed before stretching out on the bed next to her. She hadn't touched him but then neither had she turned her back on him.

"Look, I didn't want to have to tell you this yet," J said. "You have enough of a job getting her prepared."

"Tell me what?"

"A certain video has shown up on the net."

"What are you talking about?"

Because he'd never professed to be a computer or Internet expert, Reeve missed some of the details of how a techno-geek member of The Clan had found the video that had recently been released to several underground sex sites. So far the geek hadn't had any luck tracking down the video's source, but one thing J was adamant about, the contents had shaken everyone who'd seen it.

"I've already sent it to your computer," he said. "Watch and then tell me you're turning your back on your part of our operation."

"Don't do this to me."

"I don't have a choice."

Reeve turned on his computer and went on the Internet but not before pouring himself a drink. He'd seen and participated in some things he knew would follow him to his grave, but that didn't mean he'd just sit back and calmly wait for the video to begin.

The quality was better than he expected, proof that expensive equipment had been used by someone who knew what they were doing. There was no slow pan across the opulent room furnished with leather recliners and heavy drapes. Instead, the first thing Reeve saw was four men with their faces in shadow, each with a naked woman kneeling at his feet. The men were all in recliners, drinks and cigars at hand. Because of the way the chairs had been grouped, each man could see what the others were doing. When the camera closed in on the women, he saw that they all had collars on their necks and S brands on their left hips. Unlike the men, no attempt had been made to hide their identities. Chains led from the collars to their *owners'* hands. The fact that they weren't restrained in any other way told Reeve they were intimidated—that and their trembling bodies and fear-filled eyes.

They were beautiful, at least they'd been back when they'd cared for their hair, worn makeup, and pampered their bodies. Every girl bore signs of having been whipped, ranging from red-laced backs to legs, even breasts. Looking too much like well-trained dogs, they sat on their haunches with their hands resting on their thighs as they looked up at their masters. Although the men seldom paid them any attention, the girls' gazes remained locked on those they believed would punish them when and if it occurred to them to do so.

As for why the men were otherwise occupied—

Pushing PAUSE, Reeve took a deep and hopefully calming breath. A fifth woman who'd been in the process of crawling on hands and knees from one man to the other was frozen in midcrawl. A few strands of dank hair had fallen over her face, but he could still make out her features.

The dead woman whose body had shown up a few days before he'd captured Saree.

Hating everything with a cock, himself included, he forced himself to hit PLAY. The woman wore both handcuffs and ankle restraints designed for visual appeal as much as practicality. The metal around her slender wrists and ankles was at least twice as wide as necessary and included large, serious-looking locks. As for the chains binding her limbs together, unless he didn't know what he was looking at, they were gold. Nice touch, unless you were on the receiving end.

Like the docile pet-women, she'd been fitted with a collar to which a good five feet of chain had been fixed. He'd already seen one man hand the chain to the man on his left.

The final touch to her captivity, or maybe it had been the first, consisted of an O-ring gag. The damnable thing wasn't going anywhere as witnessed by the elaborate leather harnessing around her head. The ring itself had been shoved deep into her mouth, keeping it open. Thanks to the O's generous size, the average man would have no trouble fitting his cock inside it. That done, all he'd have to do was sit back and relax while she struggled to suck him. She'd already enticed one man to climax and was making her way to the second so she could repeat her earlier success.

She'd been crying as witnessed by the dried tear tracks on her cheeks, and her eyes had a defeated look he'd never be able to forget. She too had been whipped, on her back and buttocks and maybe elsewhere.

But she was alive. Back then, damn it, she'd been alive!

The moment Reeve walked in the room, Saree knew something had changed in him. The complex man she'd had sex with had disappeared. In his place was the near robot she'd briefly believed him to be earlier. No, she amended as he stared at her, he wasn't a robot after all. And complexity was there all right, only it was different from what he'd revealed before.

Despite what had taken place between them, they weren't equals because of her restraint and lack of clothes. Yet that wasn't what kept her silent. Making no attempt to hide her scrutiny, she stared as he locked the door behind him, folded his arms across his chest, and stared down at her.

"What happened earlier isn't going to be repeated." His voice held no warmth. "My task is to train you. That's what I intend to do."

Although she tried to prepare herself for whatever he had in mind, he only continued to stare at her. Both unnerved and turned on by everything he represented, she willed herself not to move. After what seemed like a vast stretch of time, he stalked over to the dresser and selected several items. She spotted more of the short leather straps that he'd fastened to her wrist and ankle cuffs earlier.

Why are you doing this? There was something between us, I know it.

He was on her before she knew what he'd intended, easily knocking her back before forcing her onto her back. Instinct took over, and she fought his hold on her arms, but of course he won. Deceptively quiet clicking sounds told her what her muscles already knew; he'd cuffed her hands in front.

When he lifted his weight off her, she turned onto her side in preparation for sitting up. He reached for her free leg.

"No!" she yelled, and aimed her bare foot at his crotch. The blow missed its mark but connected with his inner thigh. Taking a deep breath, he clamped a hand around her calf. Pain marched up her leg. By the time she realized he'd driven his thumb into her calf, he'd fastened leather to the anklet. Using the leather as his anchor, he forced her leg close to the one already fastened to the bed. She sobbed when she heard yet another click, didn't have to see her legs to understand that he'd hobbled her.

"You don't have to do this," she snapped. "Don't you understand, I wanted what happened between us."

"I don't."

Liar. You can't mean—Stifling the words that would make her sound even more vulnerable than she was, she forced her thoughts off herself and onto him. Shorts again masked what made him a man, but he couldn't completely hide the look in his eyes. *Something* had happened while they'd been apart, and all she could do was wait for him to reveal whatever it was. In the meantime—in the meantime, what did he intend to do with her?

"You suck cock," he said. "I've seen you do it."

Did he expect her to respond? Suddenly something she'd long enjoyed and saw as yet another element of job security seemed shameful.

"That's what you're going to do to me, now, the way I tell you to."

Since he'd seen her at work, he surely knew she'd been told that or versions of that particular line any number of times, and that although she'd usually pretended to put up resistance, in truth she'd loved the act.

Leaning over, he freed her from the bed but left the hobbles in place. "Follow me," he ordered. That said, he headed toward the door. After a numb moment, she slid off the bed. Forced to shuffle, she was torn between anger at him for putting her through this and wondering if she deserved her treatment.

Was that it? He might have wanted sex as much as she had, but in the aftermath, he'd come face to face with how many other men there'd been. As a result, had she become less than human to him, a piece of garbage who needed to be taught her place?

He sat down in an overstuffed chair, his long legs splaying out as he rested on his spine. "Not like that, slave. On your hands and knees."

"Don't call me a slave! Not after what—"

"What happened? I took advantage of what you've always given away. What man wouldn't?"

"There wasn't anything—"

"On your knees, now."

Stopped from trying to ask if there was still something, anything, between them, she did as he'd ordered. Kneeling before Reeve was different from those times when such behavior had been part of a scene. Always before, she'd been secretly amused. Now she felt, what, less than human? Ashamed?

"Crawl to me."

Doing so with limited use of her legs was awkward and ungraceful. She who knew how to present her body as something sensual for the camera was now inching forward like a worm. It might not have been that way if she could make herself believe the sight of her in all her subservient nudity was turning him on, but he'd only glanced at her before turning his attention to the wall behind her.

His expression, so complex, emotions determined to stay hidden but breaking through anyway. When she was so close she could rest her head on his knees, she stopped and settled onto her buttocks, waited. She continued to study his expression.

She'd sometimes seen that look in the eyes of would-be models. They'd come to The Dungeon full of curiosity about public sex and interest in the considerable paycheck only to discover they weren't cut out for S and M. Reality set in as soon as the first ropes went around them: they didn't want to be doing this, wanted out, now!

That's what she saw in Reeve, not the fear element but the reluctance and regret.

"You don't have to do this," she said.

"The hell I don't."

"You're serious? You truly believe you have no choice but to do what you are doing to me?"

For a moment she thought he was going to strike her. Instead, he rested his head on the back of the chair. His eyes closed to slits. "Lives are at stake. At least one has already been lost."

Shocked, she rested her hands on his knee. Instead of responding to the touch, he rubbed his eyes. The wrong words and he'd slam a door between them that might never unlock, but if she didn't try to reach past his barriers, they'd never have anything. Even worse, she might never know freedom.

"You feel responsible for that life, do you?" she ventured.

"Who is it? Can you at least tell me that?"

"Not her name because it'll mean either too much or nothing to you."

"I might have known her?" A woman. At least she now knew that.

"Maybe."

Maybe. What deep pit of a nightmare had she fallen into? The world she'd always lived in didn't have room for the murder of someone she considered her friend. In the wake of her parents' death, her quota of bad things happening to good people had been met. "How did she die?"

"Beaten. Strangled."

Appalled by the thought of so much violence, she snatched her hands from his knee so she could protect her vulnerable throat. She was still trying to put the pieces together when he opened his eyes, straightened, looked down at her as if he'd never seen her.

"What?" she asked.

"Don't speak, all right. There's—yeah, I don't have a goddamn choice. You have to view this."

Had she ever seen anyone look as tortured as he did right now? Scared and hurting for him, she snagged his left hand and turned it so she could kiss the back. Briefly, the barest touch, and yet she'd always remember the way his just-kissed skin felt as he rubbed it against her cheek.

Then he reached into his pocket for the key, took hold of her hands, and freed them. Leaning over, he did the same to her ankles. And yet although something had once again changed in their relationship, she knew better than to tell herself they'd become equals. Taking that to heart, she followed him into the dining room where a laptop was set up on the table. He pulled up a chair next to the one already in front of the laptop. "Sit down."

She did so, trying less than successfully not to think about how the sleek wood felt on her bare ass. Not trusting herself to keep her hands off him, she tucked them between her legs. After turning on the computer, he sat down and together they watched it power up. Another kind of power had taken up residence in her simply because he was sitting so close. If learning what he intended to show her wasn't so important, she'd, what, throw herself at him? Beg him to fuck her?

Probably.

"This was sent to me earlier today. I'm sure my colleagues never thought I'd show it to you, but they aren't here. I have to play it my way. If it backfires . . ."

Although she was accustomed to bondage videos, no way could she have prepared for what she was looking at; bottom line, this was no staged presentation. Not only didn't the *actors* know how to work with the camera, the faceless men were hardly worthy of what the word *dom* signified. They were all past their prime, their bodies mushy, muscles nearly nonexistent. They muttered instead of speaking clearly. One thing about them, however, was so real that just the thought made it nearly impossible for her to swallow. They were arrogant, filled with the confidence born of money.

In contrast, their slaves were young and beautiful women, especially the one engaged in servicing the men. The lack of makeup, unkempt hair, bruises, especially the S brands, said more clearly than any words that none of them had gone into this willingly.

Except for an occasional order or oath from one of the men, there was only silence. The poor creature moving from man to man had been crying, and on the few occasions when she looked at the camera, Saree was nearly undone by her air of defeat.

"You're going to take me there," she made herself say. "That's what this is about, getting me ready to become one of them."

"Pretty much."

"Pretty much." He should have left her hands tied because she wasn't sure she could keep from punching him. "Can't you do any better than that?"

He seemed to consider that. "The woman doing all the work? It might have been the last thing she ever did."

What was it about momentous announcements that took them a while to sink in? It was like that now. Oh, she heard the words all right. She just couldn't put them together until she'd silently repeated them several times. Then more time passed while she tried to work saliva back into her mouth. "She's dead?"

"Yeah."

"She was the one you were talking about, the one who'd been beaten—"

"Yeah."

The video was still playing, and although she hated doing so, Saree returned her attention to it. If that tired, dirty, and scared woman had indeed been killed, the least Saree could do was acknowledge her as a living, breathing human being. Murdered. She'd been murdered. Probably by one of those men.

Much as she needed to ask how Reeve or more precisely his coworkers had gotten hold of the video, she couldn't bring herself to do so. Hating those damnable arrogant men as she couldn't remember having ever hated before, she ordered herself to study them. She had to understand how any so-called human being could—

"No!"

"No what?" Reeve insisted.

But she couldn't respond because she couldn't take her eyes off, not the men, but one of the silent and still women.

Reeve paused the video. "What are you seeing?"

Lifting a shaky finger, she pointed at a petite redhead with large, high, natural breasts. "Amber. Amber Green."

"You know her?"

"Yes." As horrified as she was by the sight of Amber with a brand and minus the mischievous sparkle in her eyes, she was also deeply impacted by the leather cuff circling her own wrist. "She, ah, she worked for The Dungeon. She left to—everyone thought she'd quit because she'd found a sugar daddy. Where is she? Damn it, where is she?"

"I don't know."

Reeve's tone pulled her attention off Amber. He looked defeated and trapped, an expression that shouldn't have been on someone who wielded so much power over her. "Is she still alive? Please, can you tell me that?"

"No, I can't." Standing, he stalked to the far end of the room only to whirl and stride back. "All right, all right, Amber lived—lives locally, does she? If the two of you worked together, she must be from the L.A. area."

"Born and bred. She loved to go into the mountains for the skiing, and when she had enough free time, she'd fly to Vegas, but she said she'd never leave Southern California no matter how bad the air quality got." The way Reeve kept staring at her made her even more self-conscious.

"When did you last see her?"

Think. This is important. "Six weeks maybe. I don't think it's been two months. Why?"

"Because since then she's been incorporated into The Slavers."

"The Slavers?"

He shook his head. "Doesn't matter."

"The hell it doesn't! All the models, we joked about why did it have to be Amber who'd found someone to support her instead of one of us. But we were wrong, weren't we? She's in hell." Saying the last exhausted her.

Instead of agreeing or telling her she was being melodramatic, he turned his attention back to the video. He didn't start it running again but brought his face close to the screen while he traced Amber's cowed outline. "Did she say anything before she disappeared?"

Think. Think. "About who the man might have been, no. But before she left she talked a lot about this club she'd found." At that, Reeve swung his attention to her, his intense gaze demanding she mine her memory for everything she could.

It wasn't much, at least she didn't think it was, but he hung onto every word as she told him about one of the last conversations she and Amber had. Although Amber hadn't told many people at The Dungeon this, she'd confided in Saree. Despite the all-American looks that had belied her strong sex drive and thus made her a favorite with members, beneath that pert nose, wide green eyes, and flawless flesh beat the heart of a submissive.

"She wanted an owner. Not games playing, but the real thing. She wanted to be owned by someone she didn't quite trust, if you know what I mean."

"I'm trying."

"All right." Placing her feet on the chair, she hugged her knees. "Danger turned her on. At the same time, she wanted to be pampered. Scared and worshipped. That's what she said one time."

"What about this club she talked about? What was it?"

"For BDSM play." *Or had it been play after all?* "She wanted me to go to it with her, but I never did."

"Why not?"

"It didn't sound like my thing. Besides it doesn't matter. Just finding Amber does."

"If she's alive."

Even with the air-conditioning going, the desert's impact had seeped into the rooms, but suddenly Saree felt cold. She nodded. Funny how quickly things could change. Oh, her body still responded to Reeve's, but sexual attraction was no longer predominant. Now she wanted to work with him toward a single goal, saving Amber and those other women from the death one of them had suffered.

No, not a death. Murder.

Think. Think.

"The club—I'm trying to remember if she told me what it was called. I know it was in Hollywood because I joked that I'd go there only if she threw in one of those maps of where the stars live."

"Hollywood." Going by his tone, she'd have thought she'd given him what he'd asked for for Christmas.

"Yes." Needing to distance herself from Reeve's impact, she closed her eyes. In her mind she saw herself and Amber in the oversized shower that was part of The Dungeon complex. They'd worked together on some shoot and were getting rid of sweat and other body fluids, joking, discussing high heels and terrible traffic. At some point Amber had caressed Saree's breast. Then just as Saree was wondering if Amber was coming on to her, the younger woman had said that masters preferred their slaves to have real breasts.

"Maybe that's why I'm a hit at Segun, because of my natural boobs," Amber had said.

Opening her eyes, Saree grabbed Reeve's forearm. "Segun. That's what it's called."

"You're certain?"

"Positive. I asked about the name and she said it meant conqueror. It was her favorite place to go. In fact—why the hell didn't I think of this before—she said that if she had her way, she'd move there."

"Shit."

"I thought she was joking. Oh God, I thought she was joking."

* * *

"Yeah," Reeve admitted to the voice on the other end of his cell phone. "I showed her the video. That's how she was able to identify one of the slaves."

Saree hadn't moved since she'd given him the name that just might be the biggest break they'd had so far. Despite her relaxed look, he sensed her tension. So much had changed today, so damn much.

At the moment he was speaking to Agent B, so called because B was second in command at The Clan. B not only knew where most of the important bodies in the United States were buried, he could also make decisions without bothering with a damn committee. True to form, he didn't ask a lot of questions. Neither did he give any indication whether he approved or disapproved of what Reeve had done. What mattered to him was whether Saree had given them anything they could run with.

"I'll get someone on it," B said no more than five minutes after the two of them had started talking. "As soon as I know about Segun I'll call you back. In the meantime, keep her on ice."

Ice. Fire was more like it.

13

Reeve's phone rang an hour later, saving him from the impact of Saree's presence. Like him, she'd said little during that hour. Right or wrong, he'd let her view the rest of the video, and when she was done, she'd curled up on a couch in the living room and stared out the window. Her eyes had taken on a haunted look that dug into him. No wonder; after all, she had to be asking herself what in the hell she'd been sucked into and what she would have to do to be free again.

Unfortunately, he didn't have the answer.

"Segun gives underground new meaning," B said by way of greeting. "Not going to find it in the yellow pages, and they're really saving on advertising."

"What is it?" As if he didn't know.

"Before I tell you, do you want her to hear this?"

That surprised him. After everything The Clan had gone through setting up Saree's abduction, training, and use, had they changed their minds?

"Yeah," he said. "I do."

"Because?"

"We owe her. You're going to tell me that taking advantage of her memory might have resulted in a breakthrough. Learning about Segun is a hell of a lot more productive than throwing dirty movies onto the net and hoping they landed in the right place." Although Saree hadn't moved, he noted new tension in her body. No doubt about it, she was listening to his every word.

"It's looking like it."

That's all it took for him to punch the speakerphone. "What did you learn?"

"Segun's a sex club, but it's a hell of a lot more than that. Anyone who gets in the front door is going to find vanilla BDSM, the whole role-playing thing with slaves and masters getting into their acts for their and the audience's kicks."

Still slumped forward, Saree began rubbing her arms. Damn but she looked seductive as hell nearly lost in the large couch. He was going to have to either order her to put on some clothes or fuck her until neither of them could think.

"I've never considered BDSM vanilla sex," he told B.

"It is compared to what rumors say goes on in the back rooms."

Saree's head came up; she stared at him. "Go on," he managed.

"First, clarification. I'm not going to reveal our source on this beyond saying he isn't someone more than a half percent of the population would want to have anything to do with, but when he tells me something, I believe him. When you're amoral and don't give a damn who knows it, you speak the truth. He could and probably should be locked up, but so far law enforcement has found him to have enough value as an underground snitch to allow him to remain on the outside. His involvement with Segun isn't as intimate as he would like it to be, he's a fringe player."

"But he is involved. He's not just saying what pops into his head?"

"Right. He's been in the back rooms."

At that Saree's eyes widened, and she shook her head as if trying to free herself from what she'd just heard. For someone who believed he'd made his peace with the world's underbelly, Reeve suddenly felt the same way.

"To save you from asking, according to our source, there's no *play* to the back rooms," B continued. "No consent, boundaries, safe words, bouncers."

"What is it?" Reeve asked. "White slavery?"

"Our informant wouldn't go that far. He probably will in time; he's that much of a bastard. He took great pride in describing the private area where the rough, good stuff takes place. Membership's pricey, a hundred thousand."

Reeve whistled. "Eliminates a hell of a lot of people."

"And opens doors for those who believe money and power are the same."

He'd been caught up in what he was learning. Now, however, he forced himself to look ahead in time. "Keep going," he ordered the man he really wasn't in a position to order. "You've already talked to A about this, right?"

"Right. Your instinct was correct, Reeve. This is the *in* to The Slavers we've been looking for. I'd bet my life on it."

"So turn what you know over to the cops and let them close down the goddamn place."

B grunted. "*Great* idea. That way the real players will go underground. We'll never flush them out; you know it. Damn it, Reeve, don't force me to say it. Nothing has changed except for our focus. It's no longer going to be aimed at casting a net via the Internet. Now we concentrate on Segun."

We? Not likely. "The hell we will. Damn it, she's safe as long as all those bastards have is the video of me playing with her. Someone takes her into Segun and she could get killed."

"Not if whoever gets her in there does his job. Something else you need to know—know, not curse about. As we're speaking, one of our men is updating Saree's Web site."

"What?"

"By morning it's going to say that she's decided to come out about her commitment to BDSM as a lifestyle. Not only that, she's found someone to help her experience it and can hardly wait to hook up with others who feel the same way. This way when she shows up at Segun, the logic's there."

"Hell."

"Look, this isn't what any of us want to do. If women's lives weren't at stake, we wouldn't, but we honestly don't believe we have a choice."

"People always have a choice."

"Don't give me that again, Reeve. Unless you've been watching the news over the past twenty-four hours you don't know this, but a woman was just kidnapped at Manhattan Beach. Grabbed off a path while she was jogging and thrown into a van that was later found abandoned. Her clothes were in it, no prints. She's a college sophomore, just twenty years old, a gymnast and model, a beautiful girl."

Saree, the color bleached from her cheeks, was rocking back and forth.

"Reeve, damn it, if we felt we had a choice, we wouldn't have done what we just did."

"Which is?"

"The video you took of her? A copy of it is being linked to her Web site. It's a two-way link."

He'd done a number of things in his life he was still trying to justify like kidnapping a drug lord's son to flush the father into the open. The drug lord was in prison for the rest of his life, but the son had been so traumatized that he'd needed lengthy therapy. What he'd just heard was in the same category. "In other words, that so-called private site I sent the video to can trace it to Saree McKeon, porn model?"

"Yes."

"Why?" *Why the hell?*

"She's our ticket. Whoever shows up at the front door of Segun with her in tow isn't going to stay there long. He's going to be let in all the way."

"Whoever? It's my mug on that video."

B didn't say anything.

"What if I refuse?"

A short silence. "Then let her go. Take her back to her place, walk away."

"I fucking can't!"

"That's what we hoped you'd say."

Saree had never seen so much trapped fury in another human being. As Reeve paced and talked, paced and talked, she found herself thinking not about how trapped she was but the reasons for what he was going through. Why had he kidnapped her in the first place if he hadn't wanted to follow through on this complex, dangerous, and still incomprehensible plan? The answer might be as simple as his not liking anyone telling him what to do and their not involving him in every step of the scheme, but that didn't strike her as the whole story.

He couldn't just release her and expect her to pick up the threads of her life, and she supposed she should be grateful to him for that. True, it didn't take a rocket scientist to figure out that she'd become what, a sitting duck, a beyond-public figure. Whoever these Slavers were, they all but had the key to her front door now. They'd seen her in true bondage. If they wanted her—

The Slavers had just kidnapped an innocent college student, had already imprisoned Amber Green, killed at least one woman. Although she was far from flattered, she'd be a fool not to put it together that getting their hands on her would be a major power trip for them. Not only that, once she was under their command, they'd do whatever they needed to do to her in order to learn who was trying to stop their despicable operation.

Life as she'd always known it was over! As long as The Slavers existed, she was in danger. Thanks to Reeve and whomever the hell he was involved with.

A college co-ed, Amber Green, other terrified and helpless women.

Her head pounding, she stood and stared out the window. This time she saw not the seemingly lifeless and yet vibrant desert but the room where those men had exerted power and control over their sex slaves. She wasn't one of them, yet.

But she might be the slaves' only chance of regaining their freedom.

But only if she played the role she'd been chosen for.

A sound turned her around. Reeve had folded the flip phone, ending the conversation. "How can you face yourself?" she demanded. "Playing with my life, it doesn't bother you?"

"It isn't what I want."

"Don't try to tell me you didn't get off on treating me like your personal bondage toy. Is that why you agreed to this damnable assignment? It gave you an excuse to indulge in your sick—"

"Sick? It's how you earn your living."

Don't go there. "That's play, fantasy. This other thing is life and death. You're going to do it, aren't you? Take me to Segun."

His silence said it all, and she wasn't going to let his trapped expressions get to her—she wasn't. Neither was she going to reveal the decision she'd just made. Let him believe she was fighting him the whole way, because that would make her performance more believable. Whomever he worked with were successful, resourceful, and committed. Once she and Reeve were in the inner sanctum, his colleagues or whatever they were called would storm in like a SWAT team, free the women, and arrest those responsible for their being forced into slavery.

That was the only way she'd ever get her life back.

Ever get away from him.

Even as the thought ran through her, his body called to her. He was clothed, protected, while nudity was becoming a way of life for her, that and the straps circling her wrists and ankles. How could she possibly be drawn to the man who'd destroyed the life she loved?

Because he'd started to take her into a world she'd long suspected she'd love even more.

Head high and shoulders back, she faced him. She had two choices: to fight him with every bit of strength at her command—and lose—or *force* him to take her to Segun. The end result would undoubtedly be the same, but if she opposed him, she'd only delay the rescue and salvation of those who depended on her, while challenging him with her body could result in her own victory. She'd test his self-control while mining his treatment of her for as much pleasure as she could get.

Whichever course she chose, one thing was vital. Keeping her emotional distance from him.

"I hate you. I want you to know how much I loathe you."

"Get in line."

"There is no line here, Reeve, just you and me. Are you man enough to do what *they* want you to? Can you wrap a rope around my neck and haul me into Segun? Make them believe you own me? I don't think so."

"What are you doing?"

"Fighting for my life."

A shake of his head sent his rich hair moving. "You don't know what it means to fight for your life, Saree. You can't begin to guess."

"And you do?" She picked at the leather around her left wrist. "You aren't wearing this, I am."

His fingers became fists, and he again shook his head. Those things plus the emotion dancing in his expressive eyes warned of his inner battle. Her words angered him, which was what she needed, but he was too much of a civilized human being to lash out at her.

Fine. She'd force his hand.

A single step. Her arm uplifted and cocked, then firing. Her palm colliding with his cheek. His head snapped to the side. Before he could straighten, she struck him again. "Goddamn bastard! Playing God with my life, how dare you!"

Clamping down on her shoulders, he spun her away from him, igniting a war within herself. She wanted to be manhandled and she didn't. She wanted to face tomorrow with this man and desperately wanted back the life he'd torn her from.

Wrenching her arms up behind her was so impossibly easy for him that she wondered why she bothered to struggle. And when he shoved her toward the room she'd been imprisoned in, she was tempted to hurry the pace. Instead, she hissed and cursed and tried to kick back at him.

All too soon the harsh walls surrounded her. In the half second before he tossed her facedown on the bed, her attention locked on the steel rings that had been imbedded in those walls.

Straddling her buttocks ensured that she'd remain where he wanted her while he wrapped rope just above her elbows, the tie so snug that her arms nearly touched. When he'd secured her, he got off and shoved her higher onto the bed so he could once more hook her ankles together. That done, he stepped away from the bed. She rolled onto her side. He was unfastening his shorts.

"Two simple ties, Saree. Is that all it's going to take to break you?"

"Is that what it takes for you to feel like a man?"

"Speak like that around a true master and you'll be beaten."

She had no doubt that he was right, but she'd been through

so much since he'd walked into her life and the journey was far from over. Did he really expect her to bow down before him? Did she want to?

A headache began raging as she struggled to face her conflicted emotions. She wanted Reeve dead. At the same time, she'd never felt more alive than she did at this moment. The ties hadn't broken her. Instead, they'd taken her into a place that was both familiar and new, a space ruled by touch and heat.

"Is this how I'll be when you force me through that door at Segun?" she asked. "Will you allow me to speak or gag me?"

He touched the side of her mouth. Instead of jerking away, she leaned toward him. "A gag then," he said, "but not now. I want to hear you moan."

"In pain?"

"No. Because you want this." His hand trailed from her cheek to her chin and from there to her throat. "Because you need to be treated like this." A whispery touch ignited her collarbone; a fire began in the valley between her breasts. "Keep your mouth shut and they'll accept you as the perfect slave. You're so easy, so hot." He demonstrated by pulling her to her feet and trailing his forefinger over the swell of her right breast.

Trembling and even hotter than he could imagine, she pressed her thighs together. "Don't, don't."

"What? Touch you?" He treated her left breast to the same light caress. "Whatever you do, don't lie. I can see right through it."

Although he was right about her transparency, she tried to deny the truth by shaking her head. His expression hardened until she could no longer guess at what he was thinking. His size intimidated her, but that was nothing compared to how he could turn her inside out with his knowledge of her needs. What had brought them together and why was their relationship continuing? As long as his hands were on her, she couldn't remember.

"Pleasure and pain. That's what speaks to you. And what will be your undoing." He gave her belly a sharp slap. "Don't move. I have more to tell you but not until you're in the place I need you to be."

Confused, she watched as he went to the dresser. When he returned, he was carrying the nipple clamps he'd used on her earlier. At least she thought it was the same pair. Instinct sent a message to retreat to her legs, but she forgot it the instant the leather between her ankles tightened. "Don't, please."

Her pathetic attempt at stopping the inevitable died when he closed his hand around the back of her neck and forced her head down. Concentrating on not losing her balance, she was slow to comprehend that he'd positioned the metal clips over her nipple. "Enjoy," he said as the metal settled against her flesh.

A gasp became a garbled groan of pleasure/pain when he did the same to her other breast. He didn't allow her to straighten until he'd made sure the grip was secure. Apparently he wanted her to study his handiwork. Otherwise why would he have lifted the chain between the two clamps? "An amendment. It's no longer just two ropes ensuring that your world doesn't extend beyond me. Do you have any idea how appealing The Slavers are going to find you?"

"You're not going to really turn me over to them, are you?" The pressure on her nipples made concentrating on anything else difficult, but it wasn't pain she felt. Something else lived in her; that something settled hot and ready and alive in her pussy.

Still holding the chain, he ran the knuckles of his other hand over her cheek. "I'm well trained. You might not yet be the kind of slave I need you to be, but I know and understand my role in this world we're going to be entering. And, I don't feel."

She couldn't believe that, couldn't! Or was the truth that she didn't want to believe he was a robot?

This time when he left her, the thought of trying to get away never entered her mind. She existed where the ropes circled her elbows, where leather imprisoned her legs, where clamps made her nipples burn. And her poor hungry cunt, mostly she existed there.

Reeve, back again. Taking digital pictures. Telling her to straighten so her breasts stuck out and once she'd done that to lean over so the chains dragged on her breasts and everything dangled.

Alive. So out-of-control alive.

After dropping the camera on the bed, he hauled her backward over to the dresser where he pulled out a short, multistrand whip. Switching his hold to the back of her head, he forced her so far over that she would have fallen if not for his hold on her hair.

He beat her ass, heated it, took her down into that awesome place where the world revolved around nerve endings. Not hard, nothing cruel, teasing and testing, pleasure snaking through her sex. "Please, oh please. Yes, do me. Do me."

"Pain slut?" He punctuated each word with another pleasure-blow. "You get off on pain?"

On feeling alive.

"I asked you a question." Sting after sting after sting. "Is that why you do what you do for a living, because you crave this, not the sex but this?"

Yelping in reaction to something that came quick and hard, she fought, not him so much as the red-rimmed cave she'd fallen into.

"What about it, slave? Your secret's out? You have needs most people will never understand. Maybe those needs scare you but you can't do anything about it because the impulse is so strong."

"I hate you. Hate you."

He responded by dropping the whip and lighting into her with the palm of his hand. Energy bloomed throughout her ass, crept between her legs, flooded her pussy. Better, damn it, better! His flesh against hers, his heat joining with hers. Drooling, she slumped in his grip. Her world began and ended with her buttocks and what he was doing to them and yet there was more, a fire in her cunt. She wanted to beg him to stop, needed to thank him, didn't dare do either so pushed her ass at him.

The pressure at the back of her head ended only to be replaced by a lifting sensation in her arms. By putting all of what scant ability to concentrate she had into the effort, she gathered that he'd grabbed the rope around her elbows and was using that to pull her arms away from her body. Anchored. Plain and simple, she remained anchored.

But something changed.

No more slapping her, instead rubbing the flesh he'd been abusing. Gentle and possessive at the same time, caressing and firm, all-encompassing. Whether blood pooling in her head or being totally under a man's control was responsible didn't matter. All she knew was that every fiber in her wanted to be here, being manhandled. She might curse or even fight but beneath that was a sense of rightness that blocked out everything else.

"It's going to happen," he said as he slid his thumb into her crack. "Not pulling off the greatest acting job the world has ever seen, but you, living as my sex slave."

"What—what are you saying?"

"This." Ah, how incredible his thumb felt on her damp folds! "You're the real thing, Saree. A true submissive. Maybe scared of your nature but helpless to do anything about it." Penetration! Just enough to have her silently begging for more. "I keep you like this and we'll get in there."

"Keep?" Too far gone to give a damn that she was drooling, she fought the restraints that prevented her from spreading her legs enough to grant him full access to her sex. "What do you mean, keep?"

"Frustrated and off balance, willing to do anything for a climax."

She'd been sexually teased before; being denied release was a popular theme in what she did for a living, but the end had always been the same—a climax and often many more than one. What was he saying, that he intended to keep her on the edge?

"No, damn it, no!"

"No choice. Otherwise, they'll know you're faking. Having you restrained and near the breaking point's our only chance of being believed."

"No, please!"

He jerked her upright. "Don't. Don't beg."

"How can I help it?" she all but blubbered. "You'll tease me, won't you. Drive me crazy."

His answer came by way of a cold stare.

She was losing it, would have clawed him until he bled if she could. "What are you going to do after you're done with whatever the hell you intend to do with me?" she demanded. "Jack off?"

"Probably."

"And deny me the right to do the same thing."

"Yeah."

"Bastard, bastard, bastard."

"That too."

14

Saree hadn't spoken a reasoned word to him for two days. Although that was how things had to be, Reeve wished to hell he had memories of more than her curses and begging. One thing he had to hand to her, she knew what was expected of her tonight. She'd glowered at him when he'd been preparing her for her performance, but not once in the five days since he'd let her know he intended to keep her sexually frustrated had she tried to break free.

One other thing he had to hand to her, she'd held it together during the brief conversation he'd allowed her to have with her sister. Hayley had left a furious and frantic message on Saree's cell phone shortly after the update on Saree's Web site had been posted. In a nutshell, Saree had an hour in which to call. Otherwise, Hayley was going to the police because no way did she believe her kid sister had dropped out of sight to embrace life as a sex slave. He hadn't said much to Saree about how to handle the conversation, in part because Hayley would see through a rehearsed speech and in part because he figured Saree would tell him to drop dead.

Saree's voice was choked with tears as she told her sister she'd made what was probably the biggest decision of her life. If things came out as she prayed they would, lives would be saved, but if something went wrong—like Hayley bringing in the police—people, her included, might die. By the time the sisters said good-bye, they were both crying.

He understood that tears were a great release, not that he'd had much experience in that department—none since he'd learned that not all parents were capable of love or had an ounce of humanity in them. If he'd broken down when that lesson was hammered home—

Too bad Saree hadn't cried more than that one time. If she had, maybe she wouldn't be strung so tight. Of course, given the nearly nonstop sexual teasing he'd forced on her, he was a damn fool to think that anything short of an explosive climax would right her world.

She wore a slender but sturdy metal collar; a long, solid silver chain hung from it. Because he wasn't sure how long he'd be presenting her as his bondage toy, he'd wanted to use a restraint that, although effective and erotic, wouldn't put undue strain on her body. He'd come up with a combination of cuffs and a three-foot-long wooden bar. The cuffs, longer than standard, anchored her arms in front while the bar went behind her back and in front of her elbows, forcing her to arch her back and display her lush breasts. The flexible leather ankle restraints had been replaced by harsh metal and a chain that dragged on the ground. Overkill, yes, but erotic as hell.

After too many damn hours spent caressing and pushing that body, the last thing he needed was to have her naked, but he had a point to make—one that said he didn't give a damn who saw how he handled his slave He hadn't gagged her until they were within a mile of Segun, and as he'd pressed the cloth into her mouth, he'd informed her that he intended for it to stay in place the whole evening. That way she wouldn't have to worry about saying the right thing.

She smelled alive, hot and hungry. Even with the shower she'd taken this afternoon, her body gave out the essence of a woman in sexual hell. Either that or he was picking up on his own body's messages.

It was going to work. It had to!

As he pulled into the gravel parking lot behind the large but unremarkable building his invitation had assured him was Segun's, he forced air deep into his lungs. The invitation had come to Saree's in-box from one of those free e-mail providers. The message had been deceptively simple, but Clan members, Agent B among them, had been convinced that their work had paid off.

Dearest Saree, or should we say, her owner. We're delighted to see you're embracing what gives us the ultimate in pleasure and satisfaction. Perhaps Slave Saree is already learning her new role and no assistance, guidance, encouragement, or information sharing is needed or wanted. But if you, her owner, are interested in a local association consisting of like-minded gentlemen, we invite you to bring her to a location of our choice on Friday night. We promise complete freedom of expression for those in positions of power and utter subservience for those who have had liberty stripped from them.

The accompanying map had directed him to Segun.

Reeve turned off the engine and opened the driver's door. Although Clan members wanted a recording of what took place tonight, wearing a wire was too dangerous. He was in this alone, he and the woman he'd vowed to protect even as he took her down a road that was changing both of them.

Sensing a presence to his left, he turned. A short, stocky man was stepping out from behind a black SUV. "Good evening," he said. "May I have your name, sir?"

"Reeve Robinson."

"Ah, and are you alone?"

"I was told to bring my property."

"Told?"

"Look, I'm used to giving orders, not taking them. Am or am I not going to meet, shall we say, a certain class of individuals? If not, I'm taking my property elsewhere."

To his relief, the man chuckled. "We've been researching you, Reeve. And to save you from having to ask, all we needed was your face on the video you made in order to identify you. You're successful, quite successful. And I'm not surprised by your response, because with success comes a sense of entitlement."

"Call it what you want." Reeve shrugged, then looked around. "This location is secure?"

"Absolutely. After all, what are we except a group dedicated to a pleasurable experience?"

"Not pleasurable for all participants."

A hearty laugh caused Reeve to wince. "Anything that takes place beyond the front door is consensual, otherwise we'd be breaking the law. However, I dare say you're right. But would you have it otherwise?"

"You already know the answer to that. Look, I have no intention of standing out here when—"

"Yes, yes." For the first time, the man's gaze left Reeve as he glanced at the car. "Let's get her in the light where we can see her."

Drawing comparisons between what the man had just said and ranchers at a livestock auction, Reeve nevertheless opened the back door. "Get out," he ordered.

Slow and so graceful that she deserved an award for it, Saree extended her legs. He grimaced when she placed her bare feet on the gravel but made no attempt to help her. The other man stared at her chained ankles.

"No attitude, slave," Reeve snapped. "You know what happened the last time you attempted that."

A strained grunt followed his comment. Then, a long moment later, her head and shoulders emerged. Spotting the chain dangling from her collar, he snatched it and jerked. She grunted again, and he felt her effort as she scooted her buttocks to the end of the seat. Thanks to the wooden bar, she had to exit sideways, a nearly impossible task for someone denied use of her arms. Finally, her movements slow and reluctant, she straightened. That accomplished, she brushed her breasts against Reeve. The touch caused a hot current to arc through him.

"Marvelous," the man breathed. "A truly special creature. Highly sexual I see."

"Keeping her like that, I've learned, benefits me in many ways. She's mine, only mine."

"For tonight."

"We'll see."

They should have talked about this, Saree thought as two pairs of male eyes raked over her restrained, silent, and turned-on body. Instead of Reeve touching and touching and touching her until she'd thought she'd go insane, they should have rehearsed their roles. But no, he'd obviously decided that all he needed from her was her body.

Well he had that, all right.

Hayley, I don't know what's going to happen. I might—I might be in over my head.

Not that she could do anything about it.

"They're waiting for you," the newcomer said. "Nice touch with the restraints, especially the gag. Hate all that blubbering. I also like the leg irons; she's not going anywhere."

Shrugging, Reeve gave her breast a possessive pat. "Necessary, I'm afraid. When push came to shove, it turned out that she isn't as into our *relationship* as I am. Oh, she's hot for me, but that's only animal instinct. Until I'm certain she's put her old life behind her—"

"Keep her like she is. It's a hell of a lot more entertaining and challenging."

When Reeve frowned, the man shrugged and started toward the building. Reeve's hold on her chain tightened, forcing her to take a step. If she could have run, she would have fled.

No, she couldn't. Not with Amber and other innocent women in there. *Sis, it's worth the danger. I swear it is—I think.*

Gravel ground into her feet. Between that and the heavy chain between her ankles, she could barely shuffle, but at least the inner heat was backing off a bit. When they were leaving the desert house, Reeve had picked her up and carried her, but he wouldn't do that now. Neither would he demonstrate the slightest amount of sympathy for his *possession.*

"Did you tell her where you were going tonight?" the man asked conversationally. "You don't have to answer if you don't want to, I'm just curious."

"Why do you think she's gagged?" Reeve shrugged life-weary shoulders. "I did something that in retrospect I shouldn't have—I showed her the e-mail. You've seen it, have you?"

"Of course."

"I wanted to see her reaction. Good as it was, I now believe that keeping her in the dark would have been better. She can't protest what she doesn't know is going to happen."

"She can't know what goes on in here because you don't."

If Reeve was uneasy, he gave no sign. "To some extent. Just as you researched me, I did the same."

"We expected nothing less. And for the record, I'm confident you won't be disappointed. Indulgence is indeed the operant word."

Thank goodness, they'd reached the nondescript metal door,

but how was she going to manage that single step? And once she was inside, how would she survive what she saw and experienced and participated in?

The deceptively light banter continued while the newcomer rapped out a series of taps on the metal. With each sound, her heartbeat kicked up until her chest hurt. All too soon, the door opened, not that she could see anything in the unlit interior. Trying not to look at Reeve was nearly impossible, but if anyone guessed how complex their relationship was, both their lives might be in jeopardy.

The heavyset man started to step inside, then stopped. He nodded at her feet. "Got a bit of a problem here."

"The hell I do." With that, Reeve grabbed both ends of the wood behind Saree's back and hauled her toward him. Shaking his head as if the inconvenience was all her fault, he hoisted her inside. "Last bit of help you're going to get. Now, get your ass in here."

Reeve was to her left, the other man to her right and slightly behind her. As a consequence, she doubted Reeve saw the stranger grab and squeeze her buttocks. Much as she hated it, her body responded to the intimate touch.

"We keep the entryway unoccupied," the man said, still pinching. "It's kind of a buffer zone. In case you don't know, this place is called Segun, the conqueror. Men like you and me, we're the conquerors. As for the conquered—"

"Where are they?"

Thank goodness, the man had stopped manhandling her. Now if only she could relax enough to take in her surroundings.

"We'll get to that. First, perspective."

"Not necessary."

"What?"

Folding his arms, Reeve looked down at the shorter man. "As I said earlier, I've done my research. I'm a cautious man.

That's part of why I'm successful—cautious and shall we say arrogant. Segun exists so participants can engage in a number of practices that go under the umbrella term of BDSM. You already pointed out that as long as everyone involved approves of those practices, they're legal. Adult activity, nothing more or less." Reeve had spoken the last sentence in a slow and measured tone, and his eyes never left the other man. "At least that's what outsiders believe, isn't it?"

"You tell me."

A shake of the head was followed by a quick and dismissive glance at her. "You didn't invite me and my slave here to play games. What's the second layer?"

The second layer, as Reeve called it, was eventually revealed, but not before they'd spent some time in a large room lit with low-wattage red lights. The space was broken into a number of what seemed like cubicles, somewhat like an office, but that's where the resemblance ended. No attempt at sound baffling had been attempted, and even with the hard rock music loud enough to shake the walls, Saree heard occasional cries, grunts, curses, and of course laughter. As far as she could tell, each cubicle was occupied. Instead of the flimsy portable walls seen in offices, these were solid, reaching nearly to the ceiling. They had to be because of the use they were being put to.

Jeffrey, as the heavyset man introduced himself, took great pleasure in taking Reeve, and as a consequence her, around to each space. She witnessed women in various forms of bondage doing everything from being whipped to servicing their so-called masters. Someone who'd never witnessed anything like this would have been appalled, but although her senses were on overload, she saw beneath the surface. True, one woman was anchored to a wall via chains that held her arms out from her ripe body and a cord woven into her long hair, but even as she writhed and begged the man she called Lord to stop lashing her midsection and thighs with a thin whip, her false nails caught the light and her artificial lashes fluttered like a drunken butterfly. Her skin had been oiled, her muff was newly shorn, her pedicure immaculate.

The slaves came in all sizes and physical conditions from a nearly cadaverous woman who looked to be in her midforties to one who couldn't have been more than eighteen and was built like a wrestler. Saree even spotted two men in bondage, one who was busily servicing his mistress without use of his arms. The other sniveled as his nude mistress gyrated in front of his tethered body.

From the moment she'd known where they were going, she'd wondered if the air of saturated sex would be her undoing. After days of being kept on the edge of sexual insanity, could she handle watching people fuck? She now had her answer, a resounding yes. There was nothing erotic about what she was seeing, certainly nothing that came close to what she provided for The Dungeon's paying members. Where was the slow buildup, the heat and power?

"That's what I came here for?" Reeve demanded, his voice heavy with distain. "I can get this in any number of cheap BDSM clubs."

"I trust you noticed the doms checking out your property." Jeffrey ran his nail over her throat. "You have prime stock here; they're jealous."

"Tell them to get their own prize. Look, if this is the best you've got, I'm leaving."

If she hadn't been keeping her eye on Jeffrey, she would have missed his knowing nod. "No, this isn't the best we've got. Far from it. I simply wanted you to get an idea of what law enforcement sees when they come in here. That's why we've stayed in business as long as we have. The so-called moral majority might turn up their noses at what goes on, but no laws are being broken. Consenting adults, you know."

"Your point is?"

Up until now, there'd been something unassuming about Jeffrey. Even with the way he'd copped a feel, he'd treated Reeve with the utmost respect. However, that changed with nothing more than the way he folded his arms over his chest. "My point, there are video cameras in use all over here."

"I figured as much."

"With a select group of men watching those consenting adults."

"Watching me and my property, that's what you're saying, isn't it?"

Jeffrey nodded. "The two of you have been on camera since just before you pulled into the parking lot. You'll be pleased to learn that you've officially passed your first test. If you're interested, it's time to experience what the invitation you received was really about."

No, she didn't want this! Forget everything she'd said about wanting to rescue Amber and the others!

"Before we do," Reeve drew out his words, "what did the first test consist of?"

"Behavior. We were looking at the relationship between you and your property, the kind of communication you have going."

"And?"

"And there isn't any. She's desperately hot but not looking to you for any kind of protection 'cause she knows it isn't there. Your hand on her chain tells her what to do when. She could be a dog you're taking for a walk for all you care."

"Oh, I care." He shot a glance in her direction. "I'm a man who appreciates the finer things. The pathetic creatures in here can't hold a candle to her."

"Then I can take that to mean you're ready to go where the candles burn bright?"

If Jeffrey hadn't just said what he had about people watching them, she would have slipped to Reeve's side. Instead she gazed up at Reeve, her expression hopefully that of a well-trained dog waiting for her next order.

"I've been ready since we got here," Reeve said. The slight tension on the chain telegraphed something she didn't understand.

Jeffrey laughed. "Something tells me you're going to get along with the men you're about to meet. Money indeed breeds arrogance."

"Call it what you want. I just don't like having my time wasted."

Nearby, a woman started gasping. Recognizing the unmistakable sound of a climax, Saree struggled to hide her reaction. Even if the scenes here did nothing for her, she wanted to share that woman's experience. However, after making sure Reeve—and she—were following him, Jeffrey headed toward the rear of the building. The pace was faster than while they'd been studying the various activities, forcing her to concentrate on her progress. Just the same, she caught the look on several doms' faces as she passed them. They wanted her, chains and gag included.

15

Jeffrey led them to a short hall with three doors on the left. The first two were marked as restrooms and the last was labeled MAINTENANCE. Jeffrey stopped in front of the third door, and after looking around to assure himself that no one else was around, he slipped a key into the lock. The door swung open. "Step in and then wait for it to close. When it does, the light'll come on."

Try as she did, she couldn't force her legs to follow Reeve into the dark space until he reached back and grabbed her hair. "She knows something's up," he said to Jeffrey. "One thing about this slave, she doesn't like the unknown."

"You could beat that out of her."

"I could and maybe I will, but she's no good to me with all the life sucked out of her." He released her hair but only so he could run his hand under her breast. More primitive heat plowed into her.

When muted overhead lighting came on, she discovered that they were in a space about five feet wide and twice as long with another door at the far end. She could no longer hear the loud music let alone any human sounds.

"What the hell—" Reeve exclaimed.

"Relax," Jeffrey told him. "You haven't been kidnapped, far from it. I've no doubt that you'll appreciate the effort we've put in to ensure that only those we want to know about the rest of this operation actually do. The sound-deadening properties are excellent, aren't they?"

"Yeah."

Tension radiated out from Reeve. To Jeffrey, Reeve's hand on Saree's breast probably came across as domination plain and simple, but she understood—or hoped she understood—that he was communicating with her on another level. *Stay calm. I'm here.*

She wanted to believe him

She also wanted him, plain and simple.

Again Jeffrey led the way. Another key opened the second barrier, and she found herself looking down at a well-lit flight of stairs. "It's a different world down there," Jeffrey said. "I'm certain you'll appreciate the effort that was taken to separate what you're about to see from the, shall we say, tawdry quality of where we've been. After all, men of means such as ourselves deserve the best—in both our trappings and possessions." He stared at Saree as he said the last.

"We'll see." After releasing her breast, Reeve positioned her in front of him so she was sandwiched between the two men. Reeve kept his hands on her arms to steady her. The chain between her ankles was barely long enough to allow her to take the stairs on her own, and Jeffrey watched her every move with an amused and aroused expression. When had she last worn clothes or felt free?

Sis, sis, hang with me, please. I really need to know you've got my back.

She was shaking by the time she'd tackled the last step. She'd also learned that this wasn't the only way into the underground space they'd just entered. According to Jeffrey, another door at the back of Segun labeled SERVICE led to a second set of stairs, designed so those who had a right to come here didn't have to parade past the players on the main floor. "I wanted you to see what we offer the public," Jeffrey explained to Reeve. "That way you can make your comparisons between a membership that can be bought for a couple hundred dollars and one available only to a discriminating and wealthy few."

"Point taken."

They were at yet another door. For some reason this one unnerved her more than those that had come before. Unable to stop herself, she slipped closer to Reeve. Jeffrey took note.

"We like seeing that in a slave. She might be scared to death of her master, but she's also aware of how dependent she is on him. If you don't mind, how did you prepare her for tonight?"

"I told her to behave herself or she'd get punished. I couldn't say more because I didn't know. I still don't."

"Oh, I believe you do. At least you have a fair inkling. It goes without saying that whatever you see, hear, and experience goes no farther than these walls."

"You're right. It goes without saying."

If Jeffery was bothered by Reeve's sharp reply, he gave no indication. Reeve's body was giving out a heat that Saree hadn't noticed before, proof that he was as tense as she was? They should have discussed this ahead of time, developed a plan.

But if they had, whomever they were about to see might sense it.

Trembling despite the heat she was absorbing from the man whom Jeffrey—and soon others—saw as her master, she battled the nearly overwhelming urge to fight her bonds. Jeffrey seemed to be making a show of unlocking and then opening the door. In contrast to the ear-splitting music upstairs, soft instrumental music speaking of refinement reached out to embrace her. Refinement in a world of masters and slaves?

The lighting had a blue hue, not cheap but subtle. And as her eyes became accustomed to it, she began making sense of what she was about to enter. The floor was richly carpeted in off-white. The room, maybe thirty by thirty feet, had been arranged with several groupings. Closest to her were a number of leather recliners angled so whoever was in them could carry on a conversation. At the moment only two were occupied by men she didn't have the courage to study.

Beyond that and to the right was an alcove of sorts designed for one thing—bondage. It had been furnished with a cage so low to the ground that whoever was in it would have to stay on her hands and knees. The cage was occupied by someone curled into a tight and unmoving ball.

A number of rings and hooks dangled from the ceiling, and one wall of the alcove was well stocked with bondage devices ranging from collars and chains to an assortment of metal locking devices.

To the left was another area designed for the pleasure of those in charge. There was a bed with metal framing designed to anchor arms and legs. Several comfortable chairs, obviously for viewing, had been placed around the bed. Nearby was something the uninformed might mistake for an elaborate sawhorse, but she understood the difference—and purpose. A slave could be forced to straddle the sawhorse. Once there, her legs would be anchored to the ground while her arms were cuffed overhead. Immobilized, she'd have no way of escaping while what she was forced to sit on began vibrating. Operated by electricity, the sawhorse could tease and then torture a helpless pussy into endless climaxes until pleasure became intolerable.

"Reeve, it's good to meet you," one of the two sitting men said. "I was beginning to wonder if you were a figment of my imagination."

He was surrounded by shadow as was the older, heavyset man to his right. Just the same, she had no doubt that their gazes were locked on her. Even when she'd done a live shoot watched by thousands, she hadn't felt as exposed as she did now. If only she could move her hands, she'd at least cover her crotch. And yet despite her unease, the hunger Reeve had placed in her growled. She was a body, a vessel, ripe and empty.

"I believe in being cautious," Reeve said. "That's why I didn't immediately respond to the invitation. Research, you know. Only two? I was under the impression I was going to be allowed to observe your *association*."

"It's going to happen; however, it isn't the only thing tonight is about. Please, sit down."

Reeve took an inordinate amount of time deciding which chair to take, finally choosing one that allowed him to look at both men without more than the slightest move of his head. Of course he left her standing center stage.

"Prime," the man who hadn't spoken yet said. "Absolutely prime. I've seen the video you took of the two of you and was already familiar with her from her work at The Dungeon, but the camera didn't do her justice."

"Which is why I went after her. Come here, slave. I want you close."

Not so he could protect her, she acknowledged when he ordered her to kneel before him, but so he could slip off his shoe and rub his foot over her belly. Just the same, the contact helped. He was a known commodity, capable of tenderness, her *partner* for lack of another term. He was also responsible for her wet and clenching pussy.

"You haven't had her long," the first man said. "Just the same, her training appears to be coming along."

"I'm making strides. Before we go any further, I want to know who I'm talking to."

The first man introduced himself as Paul and his companion

as Ty, which might or might not be the truth. Although they were sitting, both men appeared to be taller than Jeffrey, who'd taken his own seat. Dressed in expensive slacks and crisp collared shirts, they looked as if they'd just come out of a business meeting. Under other circumstances, she might have been flattered to be included in the exclusive gathering. However, her helpless nudity made a joke of that notion.

"We've taken a calculated risk by inviting you here," Paul told Reeve. "You're an interesting man, public and private at the same time. In short, we don't really know who you are."

"I'm not a cop if that's what you're getting at."

"We know that. We're just not sure who you are."

"Someone who highly values his privacy." For all the attention he was giving her, she could be a stuffed animal. At the same time, his toes against her midsection calmed and centered her. "As do you. You know of my special interests—" He ran his foot between her breasts. "Interests I believe you share with me. There's a large and provincial segment of society that considers us criminals. Instead of granting us the freedom to indulge in our *hobbies,* they'd like to see us castrated and locked up."

"True."

"What they fail to comprehend is that although civilization has progressed a great deal since Neanderthals, two givens remain. The strong prevail and sex drives will always be primitive. This"—Shoving against her chest, Reeve knocked her back so her legs were under her and her body impossibly arched. Without use of her arms, she couldn't move—"is a prime example. I'm not going to apologize for my animal nature, and I don't believe the three of you ever would either."

"Indeed, indeed," Ty agreed. "And when one of the strong is able to get his hands on a fine example of the weak"—getting to his feet, Ty planted himself near her head—"then his superiority must be acknowledged and rewarded by the weak." Leaning down, he gripped the rod behind her back and righted her. His next move was to slide the rod out of the crook of her elbows. Her shoulders caught fire. "I've no doubt that you'll see what I'm about to do as circumventing your rights of ownership. However, before we can go further with our possible association with you, we need to be assured that she is indeed your possession."

"Are you asking my permission to question her?"

"After a fashion." Wrapping Saree's leash around his hand, Ty tugged, forcing her to strain toward him. Behind her gag, she silently begged Reeve to come to her defense. "You can leave any time you want if you object to what's about to take place. She just won't be coming with you."

Reeve sat upright. "Go on."

"Quite plainly, she's our bargaining chip. You're a wealthy man and, as such, powerful. Despite our research of you, it's possible that your motivation for responding to our invitation isn't a simple matter of wanting to hook up with kindred souls. It could be—a desire to blackmail us perhaps."

"Let's see if I have this straight," Reeve said. "You want to explore the possibility that she and I are partners in, what should I call it, our scheme to extort you."

"Reeve, none of us in this *association* wants this aspect of our nature to become public knowledge so, yes, we are vulnerable. However, determining the truth is a simple matter, a short test. Our relationship with our possessions is both complex and simple. Anyone who joins our association must have the same relationship with his possession. I'll demonstrate in a moment but first—"

Ty's hand snaked out to grab the chains between her wrists. An instant later he'd hauled Saree to her feet and was dragging her over to the nearby alcove with the cage and bondage equipment. Reaching up, he pulled down a hook attached to a cable and slipped her chain through the hook. As soon as he had, the hook started to retract, forcing her arms up over her head. It stopped when she was on her toes. A few feet away, whoever was in the cage lifted her head.

Instead of coming to her rescue, Reeve remained seated. He looked more curious than alarmed.

"Despite the progress you've made in her education, she needs to become accustomed to being under someone else's control," Ty explained. "Feels different, doesn't it, slave? You believe you know what to expect from your master, but you don't know what the hell I might do."

The way he stared at her, he obviously expected an answer, so she shook her head.

"You're about to be interviewed. I suggest you answer promptly and honestly, do you understand?"

This time she nodded. Fear and something else kept her in the moment. She felt alive, so terribly alive.

"At least she's a quick study," Ty told Reeve. "Captivity sometimes turns a bitch stupid. When that happens, she's useless. First order of business, making it possible for her to respond."

Ty was probably a hair over six feet tall. Despite the belly that lopped over his belt, his arms were well-muscled and his chest thick, probably the result of hours spent in a private gym. He wasn't as strong as Reeve, but given the situation she was in, that didn't matter, did it?

Besides, there it was, that gathering of energy between her legs at the thought of being at a man's mercy. She supposed she should have been alarmed when Ty drew out a knife, but he had no reason to harm her—at least not now. He easily dispensed with her gag, even massaged the sides of her mouth.

"I trust you noticed that, gentlemen. She made no attempt to bite me, proof that the veneer of civilization hasn't been stripped from her. Either that or her master has broken her of that impulse. Which is it, slave? Has he beaten you?"

"Yes." Talking felt unnatural.

"Hmm. For biting?"

"No."

"His reasons were?"

This wasn't a simple question any more than the situation was simple. "Master? Do I have permission to answer?"

Her question obviously impressed the three men, who exchanged nods. There wasn't enough light there to bring everything into focus, but then nothing really mattered except for her up-forced arms and the men who shared the room with her.

"Answer," Reeve finally said. "And if your responses displease me, I'll punish you later."

Jeffrey laughed. "The slave needs to understand how essential honesty is. I suggest an example of the consequences of lying."

"I agree," Paul chimed in. "And since its my slave who prompted the issue, I suggest we make that clear to our guest and his property."

16

Even before Paul walked over to the cage, Saree had guessed what he was talking about. She wanted time to stop. Hell, she wanted to go back to before Reeve had stormed her world. But that wasn't going to happen. And she couldn't prevent whatever was going to happen next so only turned and watched. Paul unlocked the metal door, snapped his finger, and stepped back. After several seconds, a slight brunette crawled out. She made no attempt to get to her feet but cowered as low to the ground as she could. Saree wasn't sure but she might have seen her on the video Reeve had made her watch. She wore a brand.

"Reeve," Paul said. "Because you were so good as to share your training techniques with us via your video, I have no doubt that you insist on absolute honesty from your slave, right?"

"Right."

"And if you caught her in a lie—"

"She'd be punished."

"A punishment designed to teach her the error of her ways while providing you with pleasure and entertainment, right?"

Reeve grinned. "I don't need to remind you that the creature I brought here just recently became my possession. I'm still refining my mythology."

"Which is one of the most pleasant aspects of slave ownership, as I'm about to demonstrate." Paul stepped toward the cowering woman, then kicked her in the side, knocking her off balance much as Reeve had done to Saree a little while ago. As the woman fell sideways, Saree saw that she was wearing a crotch rope. Tight strands hugged her belly in front, pulled down by the strands stretched over her cunt before being tied to the rope belt in back. Other than that she was free. Or was she?

"I allowed her to sleep at my feet after servicing me the other night," Paul explained. "Instead of waiting for her orders in the morning, she slipped off the bed as I was waking up. I asked what she was doing. She said she was afraid she was taking up too much room, but she hates taking me in the ass, don't you?"

The poor naked woman tried to curl into a ball the way she'd been in the cage. *Answer him,* Saree silently begged.

"Don't you?" He kicked her again.

"Master, please."

"Don't you!" A third kick.

"Yes," she whimpered.

"There. What the hell was so hard about being truthful?"

"Because—because you punished me for admitting that earlier."

Smiling a little, Paul shrugged. "True, true. Kind of puts you in a bind, doesn't it? Either you're in trouble for telling the truth or for trying to get away with a lie. The point it, punishment for lying is far worse."

What was she hearing, a ticking clock? The longer the horrid scene went on, the more Saree feared the outcome.

"Tell us, slave," Paul went on. "What were the consequences for lying?"

"You—you forced your cock into my ass three times that day. And when you weren't doing that, you made me wear a plug there."

"And are you wearing one now?"

"Yes." Saree could barely hear her.

"Hmm. And when do you anticipate that *corrective device* to be removed?"

"I don't know, Master."

"But you'd love to have it gone, wouldn't you?"

"Ye—if it pleases you, Master."

"Ah, progress is being made." Paul turned toward Reeve. "The point being made here is that the longer she's a slave the less important her will becomes. She learns to put her master's wishes first, foremost, and always because the consequences if she doesn't can be terrible. Can't they, slave?"

For too long the slave didn't answer, making Saree wonder if she was thinking about the death of the woman whose body had turned up on the side of the freeway. "I wish to please you, Master. That's all that matters."

"So you say, but that too is a lie. And how do I know that?" Grabbing the woman by her hair, Paul yanked her to her feet. She made no effort to free herself but stood with her arms dangling at her sides and her head downcast. Saree couldn't be sure but didn't think she was crying, proof she knew how hopeless her situations was?

A thought rocked Saree, one she'd never once considered during her fantasies about being the pampered possession of a powerful man. Quite possibly slavery in its rawest form destroyed one's will. If that was the case, what was the point of a golden cage and a collar made of spun silver?

Distracted by a soft moan, Saree clamped down on her

thought. Paul must have ordered his slave to lean over because she was bent low with her hands on her knees and her buttocks offered to him. Although Saree couldn't see his hands, she knew Paul was doing something to the butt plug.

"Just as I thought." Paul slapped the woman's buttocks. "A piece of information I withheld from you, slave. When I inserted this, I made sure that a red mark I'd made on it was at the rear. It's now off to the side, proof that you tampered with my work."

"I'm sorry, sorry."

"Are you ever going to learn!" He yanked her upright. "This is my ass, not yours. I do what I want to it when I want." Forcing her elbows together, he herded her over to one of the walls. Saree fought a cry when she realized he'd chosen cuffs that were connected via a metal bar some two inches wide and maybe four inches long. She clenched her teeth while Paul locked the woman's slender wrists behind her in the harsh restraints. Unlike cuffs made with chain, these allowed absolutely no movement.

"What's the point of this?" Reeve asked, sounding bored. "Your treatment of your slave is none of my concern."

"The point"—Paul hauled the woman back to the cage—"is the issue of honesty, and proven methods for ensuring that nothing is held back."

Already tense and wary, Saree became even more so. Despite what she and Reeve had just witnessed, this wasn't about Paul's slave. Instead, the scene had been choreographed for her and Reeve.

Speaking as if he were training an unruly puppy, Paul ordered his slave back into the cage. Although she struggled to comply, the metal cuffs made her awkward. Finally an impatient Paul crouched beside her and shoved her into the small confinement. "My point," he said to Reeve as he stood, "is one shared by other members of our association or fellowship. A number of signs indicate that you would be a good fit. However, an equal number or even more considerations prompted tonight's meeting. Before we truly open our doors to you, we need assurance that our trust is warranted."

"That cuts both ways."

"True. However, you are on our turf, your position more vulnerable than ours." Walking over to Saree, Paul forced his hand between her legs. "She certainly is vulnerable, and if we can believe the effort you went to getting possession of her, she's one of, if not *the,* most valuable commodity you own. You don't want to jeopardize that, do you?"

Even with the distraction of those knowing fingers on her flesh, Saree locked her gaze on Reeve; it was important for the others to believe he had so much control over her. For his part, Reeve's knuckles whitened as he gripped the chair arm. "I'd never touch your slave without permission," he bit out. "I expect the same consideration."

"I'm not going to fuck her. But I'm going to ask her some questions and want to make sure I have her full attention and will hear the absolute truth. Have you given her a new name now that her old life no longer exists?"

"Hasn't been a need. There's just the two of us."

"My suggestion, don't. That way she gets the message that you don't consider her a human being." With his free hand, Paul spread her labial lips and slid two surprisingly soft fingers inside her. "Wet," he announced. "What is it, slave? Being handled this way turns you on?"

Her throat felt rough. "No, sir. I mean, I've been, he hasn't—"

Paul's fingers dove deeper, forcing her to strain against her ankle cuffs. "He's been teasing you? Keeping you on the edge."

Act, damn it. Much as you hate it, do this right. "Master." She addressed Reeve. "May I have permission to answer him?"

Something, approval maybe, flickered in Reeve's eyes. "Go ahead."

She made a show of swallowing. "My master—I recently displeased him. He has been punishing me by bringing me close but not allowing me to climax."

"A sometimes vital training tool." The invading fingers were in constant movement, and, unable to stop herself, she pushed her pelvis at him. "So," Paul continued, "how did you displease him?"

Why had she said what she had? Now she was going to have to lie and somehow get away with it. "We—he fucked me. I came before he did."

Reeve's head nod was so slight that she doubted the others had seen.

"And for that crime, he's been forcing you through the wringer, has he?"

"Yes, sir."

"Which can be delightful to observe," Ty said, "as long as the master isn't subjected to the same frustration."

Jeffrey chuckled. "How right you are. Paul, are you going to get to the point or are we going to have to sit here and watch her dance on your paw?"

Paul's answering laugh lacked warmth. "A bit of both. She indeed is sweet in there. If I didn't know it, I'd never guess you were well used." He withdrew his fingers, but instead of leaving her, he closed his thumb and forefinger over her clit. Trapped and on fire, she rose higher onto her toes and then stood as still as possible. He couldn't squeeze—please, he couldn't! "I have no doubt that you're furious," he told Reeve. "If someone took these liberties with my possession, I'd be entertaining cutting off his nuts. I hope this part of the evening's interview won't take long since it's going to be hard for her to concentrate. To that end, I must insist you say nothing while I ask her a number of questions."

Reeve seemed to be considering the proposal that had been

put to him. How could he waste time like that while it was all she could do not to scream. If only she could kick Paul! It might be worth the punishment she had no doubt would follow.

"Ask your questions," Reeve finally said. "I won't speak unless you cross over the line."

"What do you think?" Paul asked the others. "Can we live with that?"

Identical nods served as their answers. Then to her relief and disappointment, Paul released her clit. "Slippery little sucker," he explained. "I don't want to risk giving myself a cramp—or kicking you into subspace when I need you to concentrate. The questions won't last long, but I'm going to first do something to ensure you won't linger over your replies."

No, damn it! He had her all but trussed up like a side of beef! He didn't need to bring out those nipple clamps, he didn't! But he did and of course she couldn't do anything about it as first one and then the other metal jaw closed around her flesh. The chain between them was more than long enough for hanging weights, which, going by the lead weights he held in his palm, he had every intention of doing.

"Effective," Reeve said. He'd settled back in his chair and appeared more curious than concerned. "And for the record, her breasts are satisfyingly sensitive in spite of the surgery that was done to them."

You don't give a damn what he does to me! As long—

"All right." Paul nodded as if pleased with himself. "That didn't take long." He held up a weight. "Satisfy me with your response and I won't place it on you. Leave doubt in my mind and—well, you don't need me to spell out the consequences."

"Yes, sir."

"Respectful. And the lowered lashes—if I hadn't seen your videos, I'd believe that a few short days with your master has turned you into the ideal slave. But not only are you beautiful, you're an experienced actress. In your own words, tell us how you came to be living with this man."

The pressure on her breasts was working its magic on her pussy, the mix of pain and pleasure flowing into one. How she loved this! Loved and feared her helplessness in the wake of her body's demands.

Stumbling over the words because she couldn't concentrate fully, she did her best to detail what had happened the night she'd agreed to have dinner on Reeve's boat. When Paul brought the weight closer to the chain, she hurried to add that they'd had sex before he'd drugged and kidnapped her. No, she insisted, she hadn't wanted his leather and ropes on her.

"I find that hard to believe." Watching her intently, Paul hooked the small piece of lead in place. Gasping, she stared at what he'd done. "You get off on bondage. Hell, you make your living doing just that. Maybe this is even better. No longer having to pay taxes and pretend—"

"No! What you saw—that was my job. My job. I love my freedom."

"Do you?"

"My sister," she blurted, desperate to get him to believe her, "doesn't know what happened to me, where I am. She's frantic. She's the only family I have and I'd never put her through this." Eyes burning, she glared at Reeve. "I hate him. Hate him!"

Another weight materialized. "But you call him master."

"I have to. Otherwise he'll punish me."

"As I'm doing?"

"I just want to survive, to live."

"Even if you spend the rest of your life as his possession? Is it worth it?"

Careful. Don't say the wrong thing. Her attention split between Reeve and Paul, she fought the hot pleasure/pain that had clamped hold of her. "I don't want to die. He—he's—at least he isn't cruel. His cock—even though I don't want it, I love the feel of it inside me."

"So maybe you're thinking the trade-off might be worth it? Being his slave means you get what you want, at least some of the time."

"I don't know. I never imagined—never thought this—what do you want me to say?"

"Maybe nothing." Paul patted her breast, causing a ripple of sensation to run through her. Moaning, she pressed her thighs together. "Ah, I think we're getting at something here." He patted her other breast, forcing her to arch her back. "A bitch in transition. Leaving one existence and entering another." He swung toward Reeve. "You ever want to sell her, let me know."

"Sell? Maybe you'll take her from me."

"Always thinking, aren't you?"

"Just facing facts, or should I say a matter of at least three against one."

"We don't operate that way, unless there's no other option. Reeve, until we know what we're operating with, we'd be foolish to attempt double-crossing you in any way, wouldn't we?"

"You tell me."

"We'd prefer you tell us," Ty broke in. "If the tables were turned, wouldn't you be suspicious if someone you were investigating appears not to have existed prior to when he started his business? Your social security number—which we obtained from a mostly legitimate source—that particular number was never issued. How do you account for that?"

"I don't. That's your issue."

If the men were surprised by Reeve's answer, they gave no indication. "We have access to a couple of the most professional private investigative agencies in the country and neither of them came up with the college you graduated from."

"Because I didn't."

"A self-made man? One so intelligent he had no need for the institute of higher education?"

"It appears that way, doesn't it."

The questioning continued with all three men demanding to know about various aspects of Reeve's background, but he refused to answer any of the questions. He wouldn't say where he was born or raised, who his parents were, or whether he had any siblings. Every refusal was punctuated with a simple comment. He was an intensely private individual and determined to keep it that way, which he could thanks to the resources available to those with the money to pay for them. Because he'd sold his company, he was no longer a member of the business community. He paid his taxes but under what social security number he refused to say, and as long as he continued to do so, the government had no interest in him. As a result, he spent his time and money as he saw fit and indulged in what he called his personal interests, currently taking a human being and molding her into what he wanted.

"As I said—" Giving an impatient sigh, he stood. "You can either accept or reject what I'm willing to reveal about myself. And unless you pull a gun on me and use it, my property and I are leaving, now."

The seemingly simple act of standing snagged her attention. Yes, being restrained had made it hard for her to concentrate on the details of what he'd been telling or rather not telling the others, but how had she forgotten how damnably masculine he was?

After presenting Paul with a stare that caused the other man to move aside, Reeve removed the clips from her breasts. Before renewed blood circulation could make her cry out, he expertly massaged her nipples. Then he triggered whatever had forced her arms over her head. In a few seconds she was able to lower them to her side. Despite her gratitude, however, she knew better than to let that distract her from her role as Reeve's possession.

"I'm sorry things didn't work out to our mutual advantage," Reeve said to the trio. "I believe we would have found common ground. But I'm not willing to give up my anonymity and you're unwilling to take me at face value."

Jeffrey stood. "Don't be so sure things won't work out. You are intrigued by what we have to offer, aren't you?"

"Which is?"

"A common interest in the ownership of beautiful female flesh *and* more experience in training that flesh than you have. You want her obedient without being broken, don't you—spirited and devoted at the same time."

Reeve cocked his head.

"We can and are willing to aid in your education."

"In exchange for what?"

A appreciative smile touched Jeffrey's thin mouth. "Spoken like a man of wealth who's learned that everyone wants a piece of the pie. Perhaps we're interested in how you managed to bury your childhood so we can do the same ourselves."

"It can be done, if the reason is strong enough."

17

Even once they were back at the desert house and sitting in the living room, Saree was still trying to wrap her mind around the fact that those men had let them go. She shivered as the air-conditioned air hit her, then, folding her hands in front of her naked cunt, studied Reeve. He still turned her on; maybe she should accept that as a permanent condition. He'd removed her restraints once they were several miles from Segun, but except for telling her that he was impressed by how well she'd held herself together, he hadn't said much. Back then she'd had no interest in breaking the silence, but that was no longer true.

"What you said," she began, "about being able to bury parts of your life if the reason is strong enough. It sounded—were you really talking about your childhood?"

He didn't answer, but because she'd learned to read his eyes, he didn't need to. "You were. That's where the whole secrecy thing began, your childhood."

"Let it go."

He held all the power so she'd be well advised to do just

that, but how could she when this might be her only chance to break through the mystery surrounding him. "What was it? You got into trouble, maybe wound up in juvenile detention, and decided you needed to close the door to that chapter in your life if you were going to make something of yourself? That was the only way you could get banks to finance your business?"

"There was no business."

Too much. Damn it, too much.

He was walking around the expensively furnished room, not because he was interested in the contents but because he didn't know what to do with his energy. She felt the same way, no wonder given what she'd been through tonight. And given who she shared the space with. This man who'd locked a collar around her neck had become her world.

Casting aside all caution, she positioned herself in front of him. Nude and nearly a foot shorter than he, she had to be crazy to think she could stop him. But she had to try. "Thank you," she whispered.

He stood a few feet away, big and strong and everything. "For what?"

"Paul wanted to put me in a cage the same as he had his slave. I know he did. You could have let him."

Dark emotions rolled through Reeve. She willed herself to wait them out. "No, I couldn't."

She'd already known that but wanted to hear the explanation from him, so she took his hand and placed it at her throat. Yes, the current, still there, still dangerous and heady. "I fascinated them. Letting us leave together was the last thing they wanted to do."

"But they did because we all know there's going to be a next time."

"I don't want to talk about that."

"You have to. Amber—"

"I know! Amber." Her hold on him tightened. "Don't you think that makes me sick? Not just Amber but the others as well. Imagining them in cages or—it's a nightmare."

"Yeah, it is."

What was that look in his eyes? Could it possibly be he felt as trapped as she did? "Why won't you say anything about your childhood?" she asked the stranger who'd taken over her world. "After everything you know about me, the way you're using me to get close to those disgusting men—I deserve something."

His fingertips began stroking her throat.

"You know I do," she pressed instead of putting safe distance between them. "You ripped me from my life and all I get is this?" She covered his hand with hers.

"My father was a monster, Saree. Less than human. I wanted nothing to do with him. Fortunately, I found a man who could make that happen."

Feeling as if she'd been punched in the gut, she stumbled over to the nearest chair and slumped into it. "A monster."

"I'm not going to speak his name because that's a vow I intend to keep for as long as I live. After he murdered my mother, he hunted down her brother and parents and did the same to them. Then he killed the first policeman who tried to stop him."

Reeve paced, stopped, and then paced some more as he spun out a nightmarish tale of a man who believed he had the power of life and death over people. Reeve had been twelve years old when his father destroyed so much. Although Reeve didn't spell it out, because his eyes took on a hunted look that tore at her, she had no doubt that the twelve-year-old he'd once been had seen some of the victims of the monster's rage. Reeve believed he would have died the day his mother did if he hadn't been with friends. He'd been taken into protective custody until his father was arrested and then taken to a foster home, but the authorities had decided he couldn't stay there because according to jailhouse rumors, his father was trying to have him killed so he couldn't testify about years of physical and emotional abuse. The authorities' solution had been to get him into a witness protection program. He'd surfaced only long enough to answer a day's worth of questions about what life with a dictator had been like.

The media frenzy had nearly done him in, and although he'd hated leaving familiar surroundings and his newly widowed aunt who loved him, he believed he owed his sanity to the man who'd buried his old identity. Not only did that middle-aged refined and determined man build a life for him in a different state, he'd arranged for therapy and would have financed his college education if that's what Reeve had wanted. When Reeve told him that sitting in a classroom for the next four years would be like being in prison, the man had presented Reeve with an option.

Reeve would become the youngest member of The Clan

"Have I regretted it?" Reeve said. "Sometimes, like now, yes. But I believe I've accomplished a lot of good, maybe enough to make up for what my old man did."

Saree couldn't say how long she'd been sitting there listening to him talk while a lifetime's worth of emotions were born and died and were reborn in Reeve's eyes. All she knew was she'd never felt closer to another human being. She wanted him. Hell yes, she needed his body molded to hers and their hearts beating like racehorses, but this went far deeper than sex.

He was no longer just her captor, her *master*, the man who'd taken her deep into her own heart and emotions where the truth of her lay. Tonight at least, he'd become her everything.

Reeve had remained on his feet while telling her what he had, but suddenly it was as if the air had escaped him. Slumping into a chair, he rested his head against the back. A moment later his breathing slowed and deepened, making her wonder if he'd fallen asleep. Not long ago she would have pondered whether she could grab the keys and escape, but she couldn't leave him now.

"Tired," he muttered. "So damn tired."

"Get some sleep."

He opened his eyes but didn't lift his head. "Without making sure you're still here when I wake up?"

"I will be."

He was turning her words around in his mind; she saw the task in every line of his body.

"Believe me," she said. She could have brought up Amber and the other slaves, but this was no longer about them.

He wanted to ask her why she'd made this decision, but to her relief, he didn't. Gathering what remained of her strength, she forced herself to stand. "I'm going to get a shower, and then I'm going to bed. Morning—everything can wait until then."

"Not everything."

You want to have sex? Do either of us have the energy?

"What about your sister?"

Hayley. Until tonight the most important person in her life. "What about her?"

"Call her."

It was incredible what two words could do. Although she was still exhausted, she found the strength to face him. "What am I going to tell her, Reeve? What will you allow me to say?"

"Everything."

Two minutes later she was listening to the phone ring at the small house and studio Hayley and Mazati lived in. Hayley's jewelry-making business had become so successful that they'd been talking about moving into a larger place, but house hunting had taken a backseat to simply being together. It was Friday night, wasn't it? Maybe they were chasing each other around the rooms.

Someone picked up a receiver. There was a brief pause. "Saree?" Hayley breathed.

"Sis!" And then she was crying. "I'm sorry," she said when she trusted herself to speak. "I didn't mean to break down. You're all right?"

"Me? What about you?"

I don't know. That's the hell and wonder of it, I don't know how I am. Mindful of but not constrained by Reeve's presence, she again told her sister that she was all right. "I'm in the middle of something," she added. "I can't tell you everything now but hopefully soon."

"Of your own free will?"

She closed her eyes, went deep into herself for the truth. "Yes."

"Are you certain? What you told me about being involved in something important—what something? And that BS about you embracing BDSM that's on your Web site, you know I'll never buy that."

"You should. I've changed. Or maybe I should say I've learned some things about myself that I never expected." Not bothering to hide any part of her naked body from Reeve, she slid her free hand between her legs. "I don't know why I always said I'd never let any man really put a collar on me. There are aspects of—there's something about—hell, part of me wants to turn everything over to a man and let him do what he wants to me."

"You're serious, aren't you."

"Yeah, I am. That's separate from what I'm committed to accomplishing, and yet I don't think I would have ever learned what I have about myself if it wasn't for that."

"I'm not sure I follow you. What is this thing you're going to accomplish? So far you haven't told me squat."

Although she gathered her thoughts so she could answer her sister, in truth, the words were for Reeve's sake. And hers. As briefly and superficially as possible, she told her sister about

The Slavers. Although she didn't spell out the minute details of what had taken place that night, neither did she leave out anything essential.

"Call the police," Hayley insisted. "Those bastards *have* to be stopped!"

"I agree. But the police can't accomplish what we have been able to. They can't infiltrate the organization. And their approach and technique could jeopardize the lives of the women those bastards have kidnapped. This man—he's a member of another organization, a private and powerful one. They're determined. They know what they're doing."

"I don't give a damn about that. What about you?"

"I'm a tough bird, sis. I wouldn't have survived in this business if I wasn't."

"But this is different. Not only are those *Slavers* monsters, you're changing. You just admitted that everything you always believed about yourself is being turned on end. That's what I'm worried about—you."

Saree closed her eyes against the hot burn of tears. "That's how I felt when you met Mazati. The way he treated you at first . . ."

"Bondage. Consuming me."

"Yes."

"The same is happening to you now, isn't it," Hayley whispered.

18

Reeve hadn't heard Hayley's side of the conversation, but he didn't need to; Saree's expression and body language had filled in the blanks. Instead of asking if she wanted to talk about it afterward, he reminded her that she'd wanted to take a shower. Much as he longed to join her, he remained where he was.

And much as he wanted his brain to lay fallow, it refused. True, every time it surfaced, he managed to dodge the question of how he felt about her, but that didn't stop him from worrying about her.

What damnable determined fools he and The Clan had been when they'd sucked her into their vendetta against The Slavers! Reasoning that as a *player* in the BDSM scene, she'd have the resources to weather whatever was thrown at her had been more than insanity! He'd taken her to some of the worst of the world's underbelly tonight, and she'd have to live with that memory for the rest of her life—the same as he lived with what his father was.

He'd told her about the monster!

Only one man had known about the nightmare that had

compelled him to change his identity, and that man, one of The Clan's founders, had died three years ago. At Howard Capron's funeral, he'd stood over the casket and silently thanked Howard for making it possible for him to bury his past.

But tonight he'd dug up that past and dumped it in the lap of a woman who already had too much to handle.

Not asking himself what, if anything, he had in mind, he planted his leaden legs under him and plodded into the bathroom. She hadn't closed the door, and steam floated out to warm his cheeks. He couldn't hear the water running. Instead of pushing in as he would have done as recently as this morning, he leaned against the wall and waited.

A few minutes later, she stepped out. This woman he'd recently met knew about his past—her, no one else. Her hair looked towel-dried, shining and clinging to her shoulders. She wore an oversized towel, prompting him to ponder when he'd last seen her wearing anything. Strange. Even with his cock hard and heavy, he didn't want her naked right now. Everything felt unreal to him, not a dream but not of this world either.

Stopping, she looked at him, just looked.

His mind churned with what he might say, but nothing seemed right so he simply returned her honest gaze until she cocked her head. As she did, she winced. "What's wrong?" he asked.

"Stiff neck."

Because of the positions he'd forced on her. "I'll give you a massage," he heard himself say.

Her mouth opened. She licked her upper lip, then closed her mouth. "I'd like that."

With that, she led the way into the master bedroom where he'd slept while she'd been confined to the room he wished he never had to enter again. The towel still flattening her incredible breasts, she sat on the edge of the king-size bed. "I try to get a couple of massages a week," she said without looking at him, which should have made things easier but didn't. "Between that and stretching and weight lifting, I'm able to keep the old body going."

It occurred to him that she wasn't fishing for a compliment. Instead, she was nervous and using words to get her through it. In contrast, he still couldn't think of a damn thing to say. Action. Action had always served him. That in mind, he opened the nightstand dresser where he'd seen several containers of personal lubrication. Only when he'd selected one and was opening it did he face what she must be thinking.

"Not that. I just—I didn't want my hands to be too rough."

"I appreciate that." Her mouth twitched. "I found some body lotion in the bathroom and used it after my shower. Still . . . do you know what you're doing?"

He wasn't sure he'd known anything since the first moment he'd seen her. Not wanting to tell her that, he shrugged. "I figure you'll tell me what feels good."

"That would be a change after—we're really doing this, aren't we?"

He poured a little lotion in the palm of his hand, then rubbed his hands together. "Yeah, we are."

"Do you want to talk about it?"

"No."

"Me either." Pulling her hair away from the back of her neck, she leaned forward. "It's mostly on the left side; the muscle's tight and sore."

Sore. Sore called for a light touch, right? Crawling onto the bed behind her, he ran his moistened hands all over her neck. He wasn't sure but thought he noted a difference between her left and right side, the left putting him in mind of a taut bowstring. Thinking she probably didn't want too much pressure on that spot, he gave everything from the nape of her neck to her shoulder blades and out to the end of her shoulders equal consideration. His fingers knew her body, boy, did they. But unless he'd forgotten more than he thought he had, he hadn't touched her here before. Her skin was like silk all right, so soft that he wondered if he might puncture it if he pressed too hard, but beneath that she was all muscle and bone.

Although he occasionally had to switch positions to keep his legs from falling asleep, he more than half believed he could do this as long as his mind remained in neutral. She no longer held onto where one end of the towel was tucked under another. Instead, her hands rested on her legs, making him wonder if she'd bother with retrieving the towel if it came loose.

He wanted the towel gone. At the same time, he was glad it remained in place.

She sighed, a long, slow, deep sound, and her body slumped. His cock, to say nothing of the rest of him, might be on the kind of primitive high alert he'd weathered as an adolescent, but she was falling sleep.

"Lie down," he suggested. "On your stomach."

"You don't have—"

"Yeah, I do."

After another sigh, she gathered herself enough to comply. Now she was on her belly with her head on a pillow and her hands on either side of the pillow, those going-on-forever legs stretched out on the spread. Still not thinking any more than absolutely necessary, he replenished his supply of personal lubricant and began transferring it from his hands to her calves. Recalling how ticklish the back of the knees could be, he avoided that area. He also kept his hands off her thighs because they were too damn close to another part of her anatomy, but unless something drastic like an earthquake happened, it was only a matter of time before his fingers asked her flesh if she wanted to take things to the next level.

Her sighs made him think of innocence and trust, of his mother and childhood. Other things had triggered those memories, and he'd always run from them, but he didn't tonight. Instead, he brought his mother back to life, listened to her voice, told her how much he loved her.

And when she'd said the same in reply, he wished her peace and brought his attention back to Saree.

His slave.

What a joke that had been.

"Hmm. Nice."

His hands were no longer on her calves. Neither had he given her ankles and feet more than a few seconds of attention. Instead, his fingers had covered her thighs after all, and somehow her towel no longer covered the sweet swell of her buttocks.

Slow and steady, steady and purposeful. No thinking beyond those well-muscled thighs and the ass that could make an adolescent boy come just from spotting it at a distance. More lubricant found its way not onto his hands this time, but directly onto her. Droplets and dribbles stretched from the base of her spine to her knees. She lifted her head, but he didn't think she could see, not that her flesh wasn't telling her everything.

"Whose lotion is that?" she asked.

"The owner of this place is a bachelor. Maybe he has sleepovers."

"Good thing he had a lot." Her head dropped back onto the pillow. Her movements had disturbed her hair, and he brushed several damp strands off her cheeks. He'd loved her hair from the first time he'd seen it. No expert in such things, he couldn't tell whether the color was all her own, but the thick length sure as hell was. If he'd had any inkling how to braid, he'd be tempted to gather everything into a loose rope in the middle, but she probably didn't want lubricant in it.

Bemused and confused by where his thoughts were taking him, he tucked them back into whatever cubbyhole they'd been

slumbering in and went to work spreading the drops and dribbles over every inch of her lower body not in contact with the
coverlet. Having an all-consuming task was good. It kept him
from rooting around in his mind and his libido under control,
barely.

Why hadn't she seen this side of Reeve before, Saree pondered as her legs opened so he could reach her inner thighs. He
might not have a master masseuse's touch, but she'd never felt
more alive. She wasn't on fire. Oh, sensuality and sexuality were
there, humming like a distant high tension wire, but as long as
she didn't touch the wire, she could keep it under control. At
odd and unpredictable moments she ached to touch, but each
time she was able to clamp down on the impulse.

She wanted sex. She also wanted to drift in whatever slow
and easy river he'd taken her to. Frightening things had happened tonight. She'd committed to try to accomplish the impossible. But that commitment, like the shore, remained out of
her grasp, and she had neither the will nor the energy to swim
for them.

Reeve's hands were on her waist, buttocks, the join between
ass and thighs, over her thighs, easy along the back of her
knees. Floating was good, as easy as his fingertips. There was
just the two of them in a desert home owned by a sexually ac-
tive bachelor. Night was for hawks and owls and whatever ro-
dents thrived in the arid land—and for a man and a woman.

It kept coming back to that, didn't it—him and her. And as
long as he massaged her, and she hugged the pillow, morning
wouldn't come. No plans. No danger or risk. No questions about
the future. Just them.

A sudden shiver pulled her back to the moment. When a second wave followed in the wake of the first, she went in search
of the source. There. Again. His mouth lightly touching the

small of her back. "My God," she whispered, and tried to turn over.

"No." Gently but firmly, he pressed her shoulders against the bed. "You're mine, remember. I do whatever I want to you."

"Not ropes. I don't want that."

"Neither do I, this time. And neither of us trying to take what happens into the future."

"All right." And yet although she didn't want to think beyond this moment, it would eventually happen. The next stroke of lips down the base of her spine forced a whimper out of her. Clutching the bedspread, she acknowledged the flood of wet heat that seemed to claim her from the waist down. "Oh God."

"Gets to you, does it?"

"Of course." She spoke into the pillow, imagined him crouched over her vulnerable and helpless body.

He ran the side of his thumb from where his lips had been to her crack. After a momentary pause, he slid his finger between the soft mounds. Still gripping the spread, she ground her pelvis into the mattress. Sweat slickened the sides of her neck, and not moaning called for all the strength at her command.

"I thought—after all the times—it doesn't get old?"

All the times. Fighting tears, she planted her elbows under her so she could lift her upper body off the bed. "Don't bring up the past, please. I don't want what I've done and been to be part of tonight."

She thought—feared—he'd insist she was asking too much of him, but the longer his silence drew out, the more she dared to hope. Besides, there was this heat, this soft and fluid heat stripping her muscles and lowering her back onto the bed.

"I don't want that either," he muttered. Then he placed his hands on either side of her buttocks and slid his damp tongue along her crack, and she whimpered like a puppy. His tongue, his bold and knowledgeable tongue, tested her as she'd never been tested, delving deep, depositing moisture along the base of her buttocks, running lightly over her spinal column.

She stopped trying to silence her sounds, gave up trying to keep from thrashing her head. Instead she listened to her cries of surrender.

Change. From gentle to sharp. With each nip he took of her buttocks, she wondered if she might crack and splinter. Wise in her body's ways, she knew she was experiencing a series of mini-climaxes. None were earth-shattering, but they kept coming, kept her off balance. Now his hands were over the back of her thighs, holding her in place and giving him something to brace against. What had happened to her relaxed state? True, she kept sinking back into nothing every time he paused, but then he'd rake his teeth over her flesh and everything would kick back into high gear.

More change.

Caught between alarm and anticipation, she didn't breathe while he slid lower and stretched out next to her. With her head turned from him, he became a fantasy man, her intimate desires come true, nothing connected to reality. Then he began nibbling her thighs, and when he wasn't doing that, he licked the back of her knees, and she was certain she'd cracked into a million pieces.

"Reeve, Reeve, Reeve," some breathless stranger chanted.

"Not Reeve. Master." He raked his fingers from her waist to her calves. "Call me Master."

"Master. Oh shit, Master!"

"Down. Quiet. You're my toy tonight, do you understand?" A light slap of her ass cheek punctuated his command. "My possession."

"Yes. Oh yes."

No longer shattering. Instead she melted and melted and

melted some more as he bent her knee and began sucking on her toes. The bed would have to absorb and hold her because no way was she capable of gathering a single muscle. Shiver after shiver after shiver rolled through her. How could she dissolve and shudder at the same time? Did it matter?

His lips closed around one toe after another. At the same time, he stroked and kneaded her calf and his elbow pressed against her tailbone, and she was more him than a separate human being.

"You're killing me. You know that, don't you?"

He lifted his head. "Do I?"

"You have to. My God, I—"

"You've been *killed* before. What makes this time different?"

Damn him for bringing up her history again! Hurt and angry, she tried to straighten her knee only to have him grip her ankle and press her leg against his midsection. "I asked you not to bring up my past. If you can't handle—"

"You're the only thing I'm interested in handling, slave. I want you tamed. Shivering and hungry and licking my feet while you beg me to fuck you."

Excited by the image he'd just drawn, she turned toward him. "You think you can make me beg?"

"I don't know, but I'm sure as hell going to try."

Before she could put the words together to challenge him to live up to his promise, he'd released her foot and placed her leg back on the bed. That done, he spread her legs and ran his nails up one inner thigh, over her sex, down the other thigh.

And she screamed. No ladylike moan or sigh this time but a scream and a squall, primal hunger turning her voice rough. "My turn!" she managed. "Damn it, my turn!"

"No." Placing his hands on her ass cheeks, he pulled them apart. "You're my slave and this is how I want it. Do you understand? I'll play with you for as long as I want."

Until I'm insane?

"Understand!" He slapped her buttocks.

"Yes, Master, yes."

"Good. Because I need this to be right for you, different from every—forget I said that. You're incredible. So beautiful." Her rear hole was hardly beautiful, but if that's what he wanted to say, she'd take the words into her.

With her legs widely spread, he had no trouble running a finger into her offered opening. Caught by him, she squirmed, whimpered, and waited.

"Relax, slave. Loosen your muscles. Remember who this ass belongs to and that your owner has every right to it."

"I'm trying."

"I know you are, my pet." His finger dove deeper, held her. "And I appreciate the effort. Now, listen to me. Listen and obey. You'll do that, won't you?"

Subservience swept over her, wrapped itself around her limbs, bound them together. "Yes, Master."

"There aren't any bounds this time. Do you know why that is?"

A different pressure tore her mind from the question. Two fingers were now in her. The second, a middle finger she thought, had invaded her pussy. "Relax, relax," he chanted when her cunt muscles closed down on him. "You can do that because your master tells you to and it's what you want, isn't it?"

"Yes."

"Good. Now relax. Float. Don't rush."

How strange it was to be told to float instead of having sex thrown at her. Maybe she should tell him, thank him, but as his *slave,* her role was to respond to his commands, not initiate conversation.

Without him telling her to, she lifted her pelvis and increased his access to her. His finger in her remained a quiet warmth, not so much an invasion as a welcome visitor. Much of the time her muscles remained slack and equally quiet, but occasionally and without warning, a spasm caused her to clench him. When that happened, he waited her out while whispering for her to relax, and when she'd done as he'd ordered, he rewarded her by sliding both fingers deeper in their respective caves.

"I'm going to leave you now," he said, his voice like a breeze on a still pond. "I want you to wait a minute and then turn over onto your back. You can do that, can't you?"

Leave? Where are you going? "Y—es."

"Good." His fingers made a slow retreat that nearly had her begging, and yet when she was empty, a strange peacefulness slid over her. She nearly boasted that she'd mastered the art of relaxation but settled for listening to her body's messages. Sexually she was on alert; that was a given. But she could be patient.

And if he was gone too long, she might fall asleep.

How long had she been heeding her inner whispering? Although she couldn't come up with the answer, she gathered her strength and rolled onto her back, not trying to take her towel with her. Somehow she'd wound up mostly sideways on the bed with her legs dangling over the edge. Instead of correcting things, she looked around. There weren't any lights on, but Reeve must have gone into the bathroom because a sliver of light oozed out of it to define the bed and furniture. She loved expensive bedding, especially silk, but she was on the quilted covering so didn't know what kind of sheets she'd find. Maybe, if she was here long enough, she'd learn.

What was ahead of them? Would she and Reeve be welcomed back to The Slavers? If not, how could she possibly find the women she was committed to help, and if the answer was yes, did Reeve have a plan?

The sound of bare feet on carpet freed her from unwanted thoughts. Reeve, naked, was coming out of the bathroom. Because he'd left the light on, he was backlit, a shadow among shadows. Twisting to the side a little, she watched his slow but sure approach.

Instead of climbing onto the bed next to her, he knelt on the floor between her dangling feet where she could no longer see him. Gripping her legs, he pulled her toward him until her buttocks were near the edge. With no pillow under her head, she stared at the ceiling.

And waited.

"Are you still relaxed? Easy in your skin?"

Because his breath slid over her belly, relaxed was hardly the label she'd put on herself. Still she nodded.

"I don't think so, not entirely anyway." That said, he spread his hands over her belly and pressed down so she felt sandwiched between him and the bed. Her searching fingers found his hair; she held on. "You're tense."

"You—know why."

"Because your pussy is in front of me and you don't know what I'm going to do?"

"Yes."

"What do you want me to do?"

"Fuck me," she said with her eyes closed, and her fingers threatening to cramp. "I need you to fuck me."

"Can you be patient?"

"I'll try, Master."

"Then that's what I want you to do, try. But I'm not going to make it easy for you because there are things I need and want." With that, he spread her legs and slid into the V he'd made for himself. His fingers inched lower and lower on her mons, approaching what she had scant control over.

He was a butterfly, a faint breeze. By turn his fingers and breath teased her labia and danced over her clit. Then just as the touches eased her toward the edge, he pulled back, quieted. During those times, his fingertips put her in mind of a tiny feather. There was just enough contact that she couldn't dismiss it.

He stirred, hands and breath on the move again, but now he'd left her sex and was concentrating on her inner thighs. His fingers walked over silken, living flesh while she tugged on his hair and tried to bury her nails in his shoulders. All the same time, she moved her hips and shoulders and stared at the ceiling and made keening sounds.

"Cover your breasts," he ordered. "Make them feel good."

They already did, but the moment she cupped them, they throbbed. Head thrashing, she fought the assault on her thighs by kneading and lightly pinching her breasts. A molten river flowed up from her legs to embrace her untouched cunt. She swam in dark heat, floated somewhere, drifted within inches of a climax only to pull back because once she'd fallen over the edge, she might stay there until insanity owned her.

Another change, fingers now under her buttocks. Lifting her so his mouth could close in on her pussy.

Reality tore through her with a firebrand's strength. No matter how fiercely she squeezed her nipples, her mind remained locked on the tongue dancing over her labial lips and dipping into her for a drink of her flowing juices. He wasn't immune; his grip on her ass and quick, deep breathing gave him away. But he wasn't the one under assault, yet.

"Let me, let me—your turn," she got out. "I want to—do you."

"Not tonight." He didn't bother lifting his head. "Tonight's about my learning everything I can about you."

Hadn't he already stripped her naked in every way there was? Maybe not, she amended as he went back to work. When he ran his tongue over her shaved mons and from there to her pussy, she dug into the sides of her breasts. He flicked, barely flicked her clit, and then went back to drinking of her offering. After another flick, he sucked a labial lip into his mouth, and she nearly drew blood on herself. Pain stood between her and experiencing everything he was doing to her so she released her breasts and covered the hands on her buttocks with her own.

"Killing me. You're killing me."

"Not going to happen, Saree. I don't want you dead." He stopped, licked, then licked again, on the space between her cunt and ass this time.

"Don't don't don't."

"Quiet. Quiet." He mouthed her other outer lip. "Tell me what you're feeling. That's all. An explanation."

Oh shit, his teeth brushing her clit. "Killing," she blurted even though he was gone before she could get the word out. "You're killing me."

"That, or bringing you to life?"

Another teeth stroke. Another lift of her buttocks off the bed and rapid breathing as if she were in labor. "Life. Oh shit, life!"

Much as she wanted to know what he was thinking and feeling, she couldn't form the necessary words to ask. A core requirement in what she did for a living called for her to climax for the camera. For their part, those whose job it was to make that happen practically manhandled her clit. In contrast to relentless mechanical or human assaults on her most sensitive organ, Reeve was gentle. She jumped every time he breathed on or touched her clit, but for the first time in so long she couldn't remember, her trigger wasn't being overloaded.

Was it possible? He understood that she didn't want an explosion wrenched out of her?

That instead she needed to be handled as if her sexuality was a fragile thing?

Digging her elbows into the bed, she pushed herself closer to him. Much more and she'd be in danger of falling off, but that was all right because he was there to protect and stop her. Losing herself in the wonder of having turned her body and maybe more over to the man she should fear most in life, she stroked her sides, breasts, belly. He continued to feather her sex with kisses, to lightly stroke her inner thighs and the join between pelvis and leg. He knew how to keep the pressure firm so he wasn't tickling her, and yet his fingers felt like silk running over her flesh. She whimpered and called out sounds without meaning.

And sometimes she laced her fingers through his and they held hands before one or the other retreated from what might be the most intimate gesture of all.

His hands now rested on her belly, holding her in place, pushing down with pressure that demanded acknowledgment. "What?" she whispered.

"If you could fuck any way you want, what would be your first choice?"

"I love it all."

"But when the choice is yours, what is it?"

The answer, to her surprise, came easily. "Man on top. Nothing fancy. Basic missionary, that's it, basic and uncomplicated."

"With or without ropes?"

"Without." She didn't have to think before saying the word. "Sex. Just sex."

Silent again, he pushed her back onto the bed. He kept pushing until now her head was near the edge. "What—"

"Hush, slave. Don't speak, just experience."

Of course. After all, this was moment by moment, breath by breath, nothing choreographed or planned. She'd never imagined his hands could be so gentle or that she'd trust him this much. He knew her ticklish spots, the places with a direct connection to her pussy, even areas that needed nothing more than a light pressure. He circled an ear with his fingernail, covered the pulse at her temple, and held it there for a long time as if checking her heart rate. Then he rested his thumb in the hollow of her throat, gently reminding her that greater pressure would cut off her ability to breathe, and still she trusted him.

The insides of her elbows, back of her knees, chin, hip bones, wrists and between her fingers, armpits, the ladder of her ribs—all those places and more absorbed his touch. As he worked her, she ping-ponged between sensations, always off balance and yet accepting. Wondering. Questioning. Rocking her hips from side to side and grinding her buttocks into the coverlet. Lifting her ass off the bed and him sliding a couple of pillows under her.

Although he'd crawled onto the bed and positioned himself between her splayed legs, her head was so far back that her view of him was now limited to the shoulders up. He became not just big but huge, massive, and masterful.

"Missionary did you say?" Sliding closer, he positioned his cock at her entrance. "Why?"

Hurry, please! "I don't know."

There he was, tall and strong and over her, his hands gripping her hips and lifting her up. Mouth hanging open, she let herself melt from the waist down. Her fingers found his forearms, and she raked the tanned flesh.

Then his silken cock head kissed her core. "Oh God, God," she whispered.

He gathered himself, pushed even farther forward, the movement sleek and controlled. Instead of the raging waterfall of need she expected, she kept on melting, drifting off into nothing behind her now-closed eyes.

"Damn. Damn." His voice was as low and slow as hers had been. "You're killing me."

She was boneless, nerveless, stripped of all muscle. He was in her. With every breath she took, her body absorbed even more of him. Her pussy was both her power and weakness, master and slave. And much as she wanted to ask if he felt the same—whether there were times when he feared the power of what lay between a woman's legs—it would have to wait.

Filling up, expanding, legs starting to tremble, knees bent and feet pushing into the bedding, head sliding yet closer to the edge. When she opened her eyes, she saw only the ceiling and the lighting fixture hanging from it. It seemed to be moving but maybe the movement came from her. And him.

There. Suddenly so deep into her that his balls pressed against her. She was gripping his wrists, no longer scratching, hoping she hadn't drawn blood. If she relaxed her hold, she might slide onto the floor—if his hold on her hips didn't keep her in place and they weren't anchored to each other.

Mewling sounds rolled out of her, not the harsh, hungry cries that had wrenched free when her clit was under assault, but soft and low and sleepy. That was her, that contented woman with the blood running into her brain and her body still drifting?

He started moving, not thrusting yet but something soft and sleepy, a kind of quest, questions being asked maybe. *Yes,* she responded by tightening her pelvic floor muscles. *Yes, I want you here.*

Why, he seemed to ask during a long, slow push. *Why do you want me?*

I don't know. The intensity of what we've shared, yes. But more than that. Closeness. Barriers breached. Intimacy sought.

There, stronger but still building, a promise and threat of what he was capable of. Wise in the way of the male body and maybe mind, she knew he'd crossed over a line. He might speak. He might even say words that reached her heart, but he was all about himself now, primitive and demanding.

She wanted demanding and primitive—primitive was essential. And yet she continued to float, to ooze, to simply be. Even as she rolled her head from side to side and the pressure on her shoulders built, she remained disconnected from fucking and being fucked. It didn't matter how many objects and organs had filled her because it had never been like this, her turning herself without reservation over to a man and trusting him to put her back together when he was done.

A warm and languid twitching rolled over and into and through her cunt. Fascinated, she gathered up what brain fragments she could find and molded them into the semblance of a question. The twitching came from deep inside, from a place beyond where Reeve's cock reached and yet was dependent on it. She could distinguish between a climax triggered by her clit and one her G-spot lay claim to, but this was neither of those. Similar. Incredible. All-consuming. And yet different.

It built, warmed, and spread, burning her throat and stealing her muscles. She wasn't floating so much as flying now, gasping at the quick assent. Then as she pondered whether she might be turning inside out, the deep shivers smoothed. And in their wake came something familiar, her clit overloading and spraying electricity over everything.

She knew this electricity, its quick and delicious heat. Mindful of how quickly it could come and go, she mounted it, pressed her body tight around it, rode it. Her nails dove into his wrists as if she were trying to draw the blood out of him.

"Killing me," he snapped. "Killing me."

No, it was he who'd laid wreck to the old her.

19

"Official cause of death—broken neck."

"From being thrown out of a vehicle?"

"No. According to the autopsy, she was already dead when they dumped her along the side of the freeway. Going by the bruising, someone did it with his hands."

Reeve had heard and seen a lot of things in his life that would make most people sick so he'd anticipated something like this, but it still hit him hard.

"You needed to know that," the voice on the other end of the line said. "Looks can be deceptive. As long as they know what they're doing, a pampered CEO could have the strength for—"

"I get it. You're warning me not to trust anyone, which I've already figured out."

"I'm sure you have. Reeve, you're not going to want me to spell it out, but I'm going to anyway. It's different for you this time. You're personally involved."

I can deal with it, he wanted to say but didn't. He'd placed his call to The Clan headquarters because they needed to know that The Slavers wanted to see him and Saree again, tonight. The conversation with agent B was supposed to be about plans and logistics, not him being psychoanalyzed.

"Are you listening to me?" B asked. "She's gotten under your skin."

"Call it an unavoidable by-product of the working conditions. As we speak, I'm forwarding the e-mail that came to her in-box to you. Maybe the computer geeks can trace it, maybe they can't. What matters is that we're not going back to Segun's. Whoever wrote the e-mail called Segun a transfer site and said they're looking forward to showing off their private quarters."

"Wait. Yeah. It just came in." B paused. "This is it. I know it is." He sounded excited. "You're going to be walking in the front door tonight."

"That's what I got out of it. And we both know what that means."

"Yeah. Time to spring the trap."

"But how?" Despite his best efforts, his thoughts went to the woman watching TV in the living room. "I don't know where they're taking us. Hell, I wouldn't be surprised if they made us wear blindfolds. You can't spring a trap if you don't know where the prey is."

"We'll track you."

"How?"

"GPS."

Holding onto his temper, Reeve pointed out a simple fact. Although the geeks at The Clan had perfected a GPS tracking device that was no bigger than a AA battery, given how thoroughly he'd been patted down before going into Segun, it would be found. And although he wanted Saree dressed tonight, she too would be searched. "Bottom line," he said, "I'm not taking her there unless I know you're going to be busting in the doors before the night's over, and you can't promise that. I'm not risking her neck, got it?"

"You can't pull the plug at this date, you can't! Do that and you're through here."

Eyes closed, Reeve shook his head. So years of giving The Clan everything he had to give didn't count for crap. The only thing that mattered to those who ran the organization was shutting down The Slavers. In exchange for once again risking his life, he'd be allowed to remain part of the only sense of belonging he'd known since his father's rampage. And if he rebelled, he'd be cast aside—unless someone decided he had too much insider knowledge and needed to be silenced.

Like he didn't already know that.

"If I didn't have the balls for this, I wouldn't have signed up for the gig," he pointed out. "And you wouldn't have selected me if you couldn't trust me. I'm a pro. As such, I'm making sure all bases are covered, number one being that Saree and I get out of there alive. I wouldn't be any use to you if that wasn't my priority, and you know it."

"Yeah, I do. Maybe I shouldn't have questioned your professionalism, but something's happening with you that hasn't before."

"Which is?"

"Falling in love with the subject."

"Love? Where the hell did you come up with that?"

"I'm not an idiot."

No, B was far from stupid, but he was way off base on this one. Love, whatever that was, came after a man and a woman got to know each other. Once they'd spent time in each other's company, time doing ordinary things, they might slide into something deeper—not that he could speak from personal experience. Just because he'd handled every inch of Saree's body and fucked her, just because he'd given her a massage didn't mean—

"That new GPS, could it be hidden in a collar?"

"A collar. Shit, I don't know why not. Look, let the geeks work on it this morning. I'll have it expressed out to you this afternoon. Reeve, now you're sounding like the agent I know. Keep your head pointed in that direction, and we'll put those bastards behind bars."

If only it was that easy.

Saree ran her fingers over the leather collar Reeve had just fastened around her neck. It wasn't as wide as the one she'd worn earlier, but it was a little thicker, hopefully not noticeably so. Knowing that what was in it represented their only link with the outside world scared her, but even more unnerving was the unknown they'd be walking into in a few hours.

Ever since the e-mail from The Slavers had shown up she'd been able to think of little else, which in a strange way was a relief because otherwise she'd continue replaying the last time she and Reeve had had sex, the lingering yet explosive quality.

"I want to call my sister," she said. When he started to speak, she held up her hand. "I'm not going to give away anything. I know her. If she believed calling the cops would increase my chances of staying alive, she'd do it no matter if I yelled at her not to."

"What about you? Don't you care about staying alive?"

"Of course I do." Damn him for sitting across from her without his shirt on while she wore one of his. His scent on the fabric plus knowing it had caressed his skin—"But I can't turn my back on the most important thing, freeing my friend and the other women."

"What are you going to talk to Hayley about?"

"Girl stuff," she snapped. "Things a man can't possibly understand."

He frowned, then shrugged. "Go ahead. I trust you."

He trusts me, does he, she mused as she picked her cell phone off the coffee table and walked into the room she'd been confined to when she first came here. Telling herself she didn't care what he thought, she closed the door behind her. Only, now that she didn't have to look at him, her self-defenses fell away. Ever since the best massage she'd ever had had turned into something incredible and impossible, she'd spent her time trying to pull herself back together. The core problem, she determined, was that although she knew how to deal with men manhandling her, she was a babe in the woods when it came to handling lovemaking.

Yes, that's what it had been, not fucking or even sex but that mystical and romantic thing called lovemaking.

Well, it had been a mistake. A huge one on her part. He'd been messing with her body and mind, maybe so she'd go through with this insane and dangerous plan of theirs. And she'd bought into the mystical and magical, briefly turned her back on the reality of their relationship.

"No," she told her sister a few seconds later. "I'm not crying. Close to it but not there."

"What's wrong?"

"Nothing." *Everything.*

"Don't give me that crap. If you're in danger—"

"I'm not," she lied. "I've just been messing up my mind." She drew in a deep breath that failed to calm her. "That's why I called. I don't need advice, at least I don't think I do. What I need you to do is listen to me. I'd love to have you tell me that I don't know what I'm ranting about, but I'm afraid you can't."

"To quote Dad, that's clear as mud."

Her father. Dead before his time. "I'm sorry. All right, you know how I pay the bills."

"Go on."

This was so hard to get out. "Maybe—maybe if Mom and Dad were still alive, I wouldn't have taken off in the direction I did. But you said you weren't embarrassed, and they weren't here to keep me in line."

"You always said why shouldn't you make good money doing what you loved doing?"

"Yeah, I did." *Stupid, stupid!* "But most people don't think of it that way, especially men."

"I'm missing something here. The majority of your fans are men."

"Ones with overdoses of kink in their systems. But what about decent men, the kind who are looking for someone to marry and raise their children?"

"Is that what this is about? You've fallen in love with whomever you're with?"

"No! Of course not!"

"Protesting a little loud there, kid. All right, this hypothetical decent man who's after a brood mare, he's got your thinking all turned around, hasn't he?"

"Sis, I've been ridden hard and put away wet by more men than I can count." Standing in this room made for bondage was getting to her, yet she sank onto the bed and closed her eyes. "There isn't a part of my anatomy that hasn't gone out over the Internet."

"I can't argue that."

"I'm soiled property. Overused."

For the first time, Hayley didn't immediately reply, and when she finally did, her voice was low and soft, a touch across the miles. "Don't put yourself down, not after all this time. All those conversations we've had about free will and doing what feels good—I bought into them as much as you did."

"Not quite as much. You didn't make your living the way I did."

"You're using the past tense. Have you quit your job?"

Her *job* was part of a world she could barely remember. "No. I don't know. Until—until he and I have done something, nothing else matters."

"It's dangerous, isn't it?"

"I can't talk about it. I promised—"

"I'm not your nosy neighbor. I'm your sister. All right, forget I said that. I never could pull things out of you if you didn't want. Like when our folks died and you didn't cry, I knew you were as torn apart as I was, but you bottled it all up inside. Then you threw yourself into porn, and I figured that was your brand of therapy."

"So that's why you didn't try to talk me out of it, because you figured it was cheaper than paying for a shrink?"

"Oh hell, I don't know. Hon, until Mazati came into my life, until he did the bondage thing with me and everything started revolving around him, I didn't understand what you got from being tied up. The truth is, I didn't want to think too much about what you were doing. But there's something about it, like I've given up control and turned it over to someone sexy and mysterious. That's a hell of a turn-on."

"It is," she agreed, not sure how the conversation had taken the direction it had, "for those who get off on it. As for others . . ."

"Like whomever you're with?"

She could have told Hayley about how Reeve had imprisoned her and turned her love of bondage to his advantage, but that would mean revealing more than she'd promised him she would. "He hasn't said anything, but I know he doesn't embrace that scene. How could he?" *He's all about risking his life to save others.* "Look, I have to go. I just—just needed to talk."

"I'm glad you called, but did you figure anything out?"

Yes, she silently answered. *I'm not good enough for him.*

20

Except for the collar and chain, Saree was free. She was also dressed, albeit in a skirt that barely covered her ass and a plunging blouse, items he'd found in the master bedroom. They'd debated her doing her hair and putting on makeup but had nixed that idea because they didn't want anyone thinking she enjoyed what was happening to her.

As per their instructions, Reeve had driven to Segun after dark and they'd waited out in the parking lot until a black SUV with tinted windows rolled up. Two men they hadn't seen before had ordered them into the backseat. There'd been no inside door handles, and they were still putting on their seat belts when a partition between the front and backseats slid into place, blocking out the world. The trip to wherever they were going had taken the better part of an hour, much of it on a road with countless turns. Saree couldn't be sure but thought the air had a salty tang to it.

Reeve hadn't spoken to her the whole time, not that a *slave* would expect a *master* to carry on a conversation, but after enduring his moody silence for more than twenty-four hours, she'd give anything to know what was going on inside him. Of course then she'd be expected to do the same in return. The SUV eased to a stop, the engine a low hum. Both front doors opened. Suddenly everything seemed to stop for her. *This* was really going to happen. If only she knew what that entailed, if only she had confidence in the tracking device imbedded in her collar.

The door on her side opened, and a long male arm reached in. Snagging her hair, he hauled her out before switching his hold to the chain dangling nearly to her knees. The sound of male voices, one of them Reeve's, told her that he too had been let out.

"Smoothly done," Reeve said as he and the other man walked around the front of the vehicle to where she and her handler waited. "I take it this isn't the first time you've transferred people."

"It's among our many talents," the strangely young-looking man with him said. "Top of the list, ensuring the safety of our bosses."

"Thanks for the warning. Nice place."

Looking in the direction Reeve was, she took in a house nearly large enough to qualify as a mansion. It was on a slight rise, and the circular driveway they were on curved below and in front of it. Going by the sounds and smells, she guessed it overlooked the ocean. Her mind boggled at the thought of how much this piece of real estate cost. Although the mansion was well lit, the horizon was dark, proof that they were far from the city. She couldn't say whether they were north or south of the L.A. area. She hoped that those tracking the GPS knew.

If Reeve was impressed by the building, he gave no indication. Instead, he held out his hand, the gesture plainly saying he wanted responsibility for her turned over to him. She relaxed a little when he was holding her chain, but only a little. Mentally reaching out to him, she sensed nothing in return. This was business for him, only business.

"They're waiting for you," the man who'd gotten her out of the car said. "We'll be back when and if we get word that you're ready to leave."

"If?"

"You never know. Plans change."

When the two men headed back toward the SUV, Saree wondered if she would have stood in place forever if Reeve hadn't tugged on the chain. Mindful that they were surely being watched, she clasped her hands in front of her and tailed after Reeve with her head downcast. He didn't so much as acknowledge her presence.

Although the front of the house was already bright, another light, powerful enough to illuminate the whole area, came on the moment they reached the bottom step. Reeve's grip on her chain tightened.

"Welcome," someone said from inside the opening. "I trust you had a pleasant ride."

"A bit over the top with regards to security, but that's a fine vehicle. Great suspension."

"And lousy gas mileage. Come on in, Reeve. The bar's open."

Stairs, four of them—made, she thought, from granite. Then there was the door that had to be fifteen feet high and so solid it could probably survive dynamite. Once inside, she found herself in a wide entryway with a number of impressive seascapes on the wall. The oils had been done in pastels, peaceful colors at odds with her pounding heart. Recognizing the speaker as Paul, her mind immediately went to her last glimpse of the man's caged slave. Would she see her here, and would she be in another cage?

"What's this?" Paul indicated her. "Clothes on a slave?"

"If it suits me, yes. Besides, if someone is denied all modesty, after a while there's nothing left to take away."

"Whatever. We have a full house tonight, and the booze is flowing. You a whiskey man?"

"Within limits. I don't believe in doing anything that might blunt my mental faculties."

"Suit yourself. Follow me."

When Paul turned his back on them, Reeve fell in line behind him. She had no choice but to do the same, aching for any sign from him, the slightest indication that he was thinking about her. When it didn't come, she clenched her teeth. After this nightmare was over, she'd let him know what he could do with his indifference!

Or would she?

Reeve stopped, causing her to nearly run into him. Mindful of her role, she kept her eyes downcast instead of trying to see around him. Music from an incredible stereo system drifted out to her. The air was fresh, making her wonder if windows were open, and the dense, lush carpet was off-white.

"So, what do you think?" Paul asked.

"Who's your interior decorator? Nice furniture."

"We think so."

A light jerk on the chain let her know she was expected to stand beside him. Only then did she risk looking around. They were in a massive living room occupied by a number of men. Floor-to-ceiling windows looked out over a cliff to the ocean below. A rock fireplace took up the better part of one wall. Like the carpet, much of the furniture was white, although there were several dark brown leather recliners and couches. The bar was to her right, a chess table to her left. If she didn't know better she'd conclude this was the home of a man with exquisite tastes and refinement. The women crouched in a corner made a lie of that.

From what she could tell—she didn't want to stare and risk angering someone—they were waiting for their orders. Naked and wearing collars, they put her in mind of dogs who might but might not be let out to exercise. Because they were in a part of the room with little illumination, she couldn't tell whether they sported bruises or whip marks. Despite the terrible lessons to be learned in their cowed demeanor, the peaceful instrumental and mind-stealing view lulled her.

Someone asked Reeve how he liked his whiskey. Then someone else said that they'd be turning on the big-screen TV soon so they could watch a particular news program. Once that was over, everyone was expected to participate in a bidding. "The rules are pretty simple," said a fifty-something man dressed all in black. "The slaves will each perform a little act they've been working on. If it's something you're interested in having performed on you, you place a bid. The proceeds go for a good cause."

That caused several of the maybe dozen lounging men to laugh.

"The reason for the levity," the man in black said, "is that we employ a lobbyist whose function is to monitor and deal with any bills in opposition with our policies and bylaws. We're particularly cognizant of anything the so-called moral majority or religious conservatives might try to ram down lawmakers' throats."

"What kind of opening bid are we talking about?" Reeve asked as he accepted a glass with whiskey over ice.

"Depends on how much we feel we'll be asking of our lobbyist in the foreseeable future. Right now except for a lackluster attempt to find a way to verify the ages of those who access adult Web sites, it's pretty quiet. To keep us from getting bored, we *asked* our slaves to come up with activities calling for two slaves and one master. Since yours was unable to participate in the rehearsals, we were debating how she could participate just before you arrived."

Reeve gave her a dismissive glance. "I'd say it depends on what the activities are. She does have a fair amount of acting experience, something I'm sure you're all aware of."

"Indeed, indeed. And that's why we anticipate that any bidding she's part of will be vigorous. A master can bid on his own slave, but he seldom does because the opportunities to enjoy other slaves is limited."

She was going to be sick, damn it! If that disgusting man with the too-white capped teeth and surprisingly big hands didn't shut up, she'd either vomit all over his shoes or attack him. Expecting to see the other women looking as disgusted as she was, she stared at them. Not a single emotion played in their expressions. Didn't they care what happened to them or were they afraid to give away anything?

Someone must have shown Reeve where he could sit because he was heading toward a large leather chair not far from the women. With his hands around her chain, she had no choice but to trail along. Settling into the chair, he jerked down on her chain, and she sank to her knees. He sipped on his drink as the man to his right said he'd been looking forward to seeing her in the flesh after months of *taking in her charms* on his monitor. For the first time, she was grateful because she was expected to keep her head down and her mouth closed.

"I prefer her without the false nails," Reeve said, "which is why I ordered her to remove them. Takes away a possible weapon. She's rather plain without makeup, but those boobs always at attention make up for it."

Why did energy continue to arc from him to her? Damn it, she should absolutely hate his every word. She did, but that didn't stop her from feeling his tense heat. As for the source of his tension—

"Saree?"

The question was so soft that she wasn't sure she'd heard it. Just the same, she looked in the direction she thought it had come from. As far as she could tell, none of the women had moved. Only one stared at her instead of the floor.

Amber! She was thinner than when she'd last seen her, and her hair was longer and lifeless. She wore no makeup, and her shoulders slumped instead of the proud breast-out stance Saree was accustomed to. Most chilling, Amber's eyes no longer danced with mischief. Instead she reminded Saree of a lost and frightened child.

Not giving herself time to think, Saree yanked the chain from Reeve's hand and scrambled over to Amber. Throwing her arms around the slight form, she held her tight. "My God, you're alive! You're really alive!"

"Don't, please," Amber begged but didn't try to break free. "They'll hurt—"

"What is this?" a male voice demanded.

"Damn it, slave!" Powerful hands yanked her arms off Amber. A moment later she was hauled to her feet and spun around. Reeve's fury-filled eyes bore down on her. She'd never seen him look like that, never. "What the hell are you trying—"

"My friend." Despite her shock, she tried to pull free. "That's my friend! Let me—"

"No! Damn it, no!" Reeve slapped her cheek. She tried to straighten only to have him strike the other cheek.

"Hit her again. Make her understand who is her master."

"You call that a trained slave? If she were mine, I'd beat her into unconsciousness."

When Reeve wrenched both arms up behind her and forced her to lean over, she half believed he was going to do what someone had just suggested. Instead, his body as taut as tightly strung wire, he kept the pressure going so she couldn't straighten. He'd positioned her so she faced the obviously terrified slaves.

Amber, who'd rejoined them, was crying, and yet a new energy pulsed around her. Seeing someone from her old life had pulled her out of her lethargy.

"I'm sorry, gentlemen," Reeve said in a smooth and controlled tone. "I must ask all of you to remember what it was like before your possessions were well trained. Believe me, she'll be punished."

"That goes without saying. The question is, what's the most effective technique?"

"She's my slave. I'll determine that."

"Not here you won't," the man who'd wanted Reeve to continue hitting her insisted.

Why had she given away that she and Amber knew each other? If only she'd held onto her self-control, done whatever she needed to do in order to stall for time so whomever Reeve was depending on could get here. Instead—

"Slave, who is she to you?" the man who'd just spoken demanded.

Before she could decide what, if anything, to say, a crying Amber spoke up. "We worked together," she managed. "At The Dungeon. She was—we were friends."

"Were you? So you wouldn't want anything bad to happen to her, would you?"

Although she couldn't see anything except the floor, Saree knew the man had forced Amber to stand close to her because she could now smell Amber's fear. "No, Master," Amber whimpered. "I'm sorry. I shouldn't have—"

"No, you shouldn't. What are the rules?"

"That—that whoever I was before I belonged to you no longer exists."

"What else?"

"That I live to please you, and if I don't, you will punish me."

"Do you believe you deserve punishment?"

Silence weighed the air. Hating Reeve nearly as much as she hated herself for putting Amber through this, Saree again tried to straighten. Reeve held her in place just long enough for her to understand that her strength was no match for his, then jerked her upright. The middle-aged man in black had an oversized hand around Amber's throat. Instead of trying to free herself, Amber stood with her hands hanging at her sides, trembling.

"I asked you a question!" the man who seemed to be Amber's master asked her. "Do you deserve to be punished?"

Amber's eyes all but rolled back in her head. "If—if it so pleases you, yes, Master."

"And what form should that punishment take?"

"Not now, Elton," Paul insisted. "We agreed ahead of time about tonight's agenda. If you're dead set on playing mind games with your slave, do it when the two of you are alone."

Elton's hand tightened on Amber's throat, causing her mouth to gape as she tried to breathe. "You wouldn't be saying that if it were your bitch. Like we've always said, there's no time like the present for bringing a pet into line. What do you think, Reeve? Do you agree with me that both slaves are equally guilty of disobedience?"

Because Reeve was standing behind her with his fingers still digging into her wrists, she couldn't see his expression, and she knew better than to move a muscle without his approval. They'd come here knowing their individual roles. Unfortunately, she'd jeopardized a great deal, maybe their lives, by hugging Amber, and now she'd do whatever it took to assume her role again— unless it was too late.

How long would it take The Clan members to find this place and storm the walls if that's what they were going to do? And why hadn't she asked?

"I'm not sure that the disobedience is equally distributed," Reeve said. "Truth is, much as I'm loathe to admit this, my slave made the first move. Yours simply reacted to the attention thrust on her."

"Interesting." Elton traced the tendon at the side of Amber's neck. "I would expect you to repeat what you said earlier, something about your slave being little more than a just-roped filly. It takes a man to face facts the way you have."

"I have no choice, not if I want to be accepted here. Which I do."

"Then what lengths are you willing to go to in order to obtain that acceptance?"

The way Elton had worded things, an outsider might think he was asking a workman how he was going to address a problem with a project.

"That's a loaded question," Reeve said, his voice expressionless. "One I can't answer because I don't yet know what acceptance entails. I refuse to overcommit. Neither do I want to appear as if I don't take the situation seriously."

Elton snorted. "You should have been a politician. Talk about not saying a damn thing. All right, examples. Slave?" He spun Amber toward him. "You know what I insist on in the way of behavior and have both experienced and observed my training methods. I want you to tell this so-called slave what happened when I first took possession of you."

Saree expected Amber to be so frightened that she couldn't speak. Instead, Amber lifted her head and stared at her. Her eyes were all but lifeless; only the smallest spark of the life-loving woman she'd once been remained. "I was home, in bed. I'd been at a club earlier where you approached me about exploring our mutual interest in domination and submission, but I'd said no." She spoke in a monotone.

"And why was that?"

Amber swallowed. "I was interested in someone else."

"Someone younger with a larger cock?"

Another swallow. "Yes."

"Go on. You were in bed. What happened then?"

Elton's fingers remained on Amber's throat while she described how she'd woken up as a gag was being thrust into her mouth. She'd fought but not for long because Elton had choked her into unconsciousness. When she came to, her wrists and ankles had been tied together and her limbs secured in a hog tie. Elton had wrapped her in something and carried her out of her apartment as if she were a package he'd decided to take delivery of in the middle of the night; Amber suspected that he'd bribed the night guard to look the other way.

Her emersion into her new life had begun with sensory deprivation and isolation that had gone on for about a week, although it could have been less or more because she'd lost track of time. She'd seen no one except Elton, who provided her with what little food she was allowed to eat and insisted she exercise inside the closet-sized cage she never left. A bucket served as her toilet. She wasn't allowed a shower or clothes, and rope, chains, or leather always constricted her in one way or another. He barely spoke except to order her to spread her legs or open her mouth for him.

By the time he'd taken her from her cage to a shower, she was so grateful that she'd offered him her ass without being asked.

Then the true punishment had begun.

"Master had me sleep on the floor by his bed. A chain leading from my collar to a metal ring in the floor kept me there. He'd beat me as soon as he woke up and again before going to bed. Sometimes—sometimes he tied me spread-eagle to the wall and take a whip to me."

"And why did I do that?"

"You—you ordered me not to ask. That because I belonged to you; you had a right to do whatever you wanted to me."

"And what else?"

"You were teaching me how to be your slave." Despite the

awful words, Amber still showed no emotion. She also didn't seem to have noticed that Elton was no longer touching her throat. "I—I often needed to be corrected."

"And have the lessons stayed with you?" Elton pressed. "You know how to please me?"

"I try, Master. I try."

"But you aren't perfect, are you?"

"No."

"In other words, I'm still sometimes compelled to correct your behavior?"

"Sometimes—sometimes you whip me simply because you enjoy doing so."

"Ah well, yes, that."

Elton shrugged and grinned at Reeve, who hadn't said a word the whole time Amber was talking. Not only that, Saree couldn't tell whether anything Amber had said had made an impact on Reeve. How could he just stand there when she was both physically and emotionally sick? Horrible as what Amber had described, what concerned Saree the most was whether her friend had been permanently damaged psychologically. Was there counseling for her and the others—if they ever got out of this mansion of horrors?

"So," Elton said, "what this takes us back to is the question of what constitutes adequate *behavior modification* for the behavior we've just witnessed on the part of both slaves." Taking hold of Amber's left nipple, he hauled her next to him. "Going by your experience, what would you expect me to do to you?"

21

A moment ago Amber had looked like a mannequin. Now naked fear dominated her expression. Just the same, she was obviously struggling to respond the way Elton wanted her to. "My—my behavior was impulsive. By leaving the position you'd placed me in and embracing my—my fellow slave, I failed you. I will ask for forgiveness by bringing you the whip I want you to use on me. But you will not accept that small token of my shame. You will bind me as you see fit before administering punishment, and when you are done correcting me, you will order me into the surf where the saltwater will sting the marks you placed on me."

Shaking his head, Elton gave Amber's nipples a hard squeeze before releasing them. "Did you notice something?" he asked Reeve. "This one still refuses to deal in specifics. She can't bring herself to spell out the details of her punishment. Once I've broken down that last barrier, I'll know she has truly given up ownership of her separate will. Of course"—he laughed, his eyes making Saree think of a predator about to make a kill— "then she'll bore me. I won't want anything to do with her."

And then what? He'd turn Amber over to someone else, sell her—kill her? With hands like that, it wouldn't be hard.

Reeve was no longer holding her wrists, not that she felt any freer. What did the scraps of clothing she wore matter when she felt as if she was sinking into quicksand?

"I've wondered about that," Reeve was saying. "A slave can hardly be fired or let go. What happens if things don't work out?"

"Depends," said someone Saree didn't bother looking at. "We have several options. Bottom line, variety is what keeps all of us—the doms, that is—interested in this lifestyle. Swapping sometimes takes place, and there are underground auctions, but you know what they say about fresh meat."

"Yes," Reeve drew out. "I do." He ran his gaze down her body and then up again. Stopping at her breasts, he unceremoniously pulled down on her top and tucked it under her mounds, exposing her. She knew better than to cover up. "That's what drew me in, taking a bondage virgin and turning her into something capable of meeting my needs."

"Exactly," Elton agreed. "Now, back to what started this conversation. Some of my *colleagues* will disagree, but I believe that you and I must teach our slaves that they've disappointed us, now. I promise it won't take long, too long anyway." He chuckled. "Then we can get on to the evening's agenda. What if, in the spirit of things, I go first? Slave, assume."

For a moment Saree believed Amber was going to run. Instead, although she looked as if she'd rather be dead than here, her friend widened her stance as far as she could and linked her fingers behind her head. She looked so vulnerable, so helpless.

"There are a number of responses for submit," Elton explained, "depending on the situation. This exposure of her body shows she is presenting herself for whatever I choose to do with it. However"—Elton turned his piercing gaze onto Saree—"I propose an alternative to the usual punishment, one that will demonstrate how far your slave has progressed in her training."

"What alternative?" Reeve sounded only mildly curious.

"As we've already discussed, there was equal error in judgment and restraint on the part of our slaves. I therefore propose that they each dispense the other's behavior modification."

This room was designed for refined relaxation, for the appreciation of life's finer things, not cruelty. And yet going by the deep mutters of agreement, the men were looking forward to seeing women in pain. As for the other women, no one had so much as gasped. Was she the only one who saw this as insanity?

"What did you have in mind in the way of behavior modification?" The question came from Paul.

"Nothing too difficult to achieve." Elton winked at Saree. "Granted, thanks to her former career, this creature is far from a novice in such things, but I don't want her to feel she's failed. She must gain some measure of satisfaction from a task well executed so she can appreciate it when it's her turn to be on the receiving end."

She and Amber were going to be forced to punish each other! Yes, insanity! As for Reeve, how could he possibly just stand there? She couldn't raise a hand against her friend! She wouldn't!

A chilling thought stole her breath. If nothing was left of the old Amber, she'd agree to anything her master commanded her to do.

And if she refused, her punishment would only be worse.

Several of the men were debating what corrective tasks could be adequately achieved in a short time given the physical setting, not that she could hold onto the specifics of their disgusting suggestions. So this was what being trapped was truly like? No matter that she'd felt countless bonds on her body, none of that had prepared her for this moment.

"Interesting," Reeve was saying. "I would have guessed that permanent restraint would have been incorporated into the room's design. Not having those certainly calls for a more innovative approach. I take it there's a supply of cuffs and ropes nearby. Otherwise, the slaves would see this space as a place of respite."

"Right you are." Elton sounded delighted with Reeve's perceptiveness. "We'd never allow that. And giving the slaves the misguided impression that they might one day make it out that door unrestrained"—he pointed toward the massive sliding glass door leading to the deck overlooking the ocean—"constantly plays on their minds."

"In other words, being within sight of freedom while tightly restrained serves as its own kind of punishment," Reeve said.

Sick. She was going to be sick! And when that was over, she'd attack Reeve with every bit of strength at her command!

"Once again," Elton said, "you've grasped the essence of our association. I'll tell you what. Why don't I give you a length of rope to use as you see fit to adequately prepare your slave to receive her punishment. I'll take an equal length and weave it over and around this creature's body in such a way that she can't forget that her turn is coming. In other words, she'll have freedom of movement and yet she won't."

Amber's arms were still uplifted and her fingers intertwined, and yet she seemed to be sinking into herself. What would happen to her if she fainted or sobbed that she couldn't do this?

What had happened to the funny and optimistic woman she'd once been? What had that bastard done to her?

"Now!" Elton snapped. He slapped Amber's cheek so hard her head jerked to one side. "You know what you're supposed to do. Two ropes. And the black paddle. That'll do for starters."

"Master," Amber whimpered. "Please—"

"Now!" Grabbing her shoulders, he shoved her so hard that she stumbled and fell. Instead of getting to her feet, Amber seemed to hug the carpet as if trying to gather strength from it. Everything from her defeated air to the exhaustion in her shoulders swept Saree back in time to when her parents had lacked the strength to get out of their hospital beds. But Amber hadn't been taken down by disease—a monster, a bastard was responsible!

"I shouldn't have to say a word," Elton said, his tone conversational. "You know what I'm capable of because earlier I allowed you to see a demonstration, don't you?" He flexed his fingers. "Where my greatest strength lies. The decision's yours. Do you want to be the recipient of that strength?"

"Please, please."

"Begging for mercy? Damn it, you know better. Now get the fuck up!" Elton kicked Amber's side.

Whimpering, Amber pulled her hands and knees under her in preparation for standing, but before she could do more than that, Elton kicked her again.

Something clicked inside Saree, a primal shift she had no words for or control over. She no longer saw Amber, the other women, or the men; not even Reeve existed. There was only the bastard cocking his leg for yet another blow. Screaming, she hurtled herself at the man who outweighed her by many pounds. Because he was off balance, they collapsed together. She started to push away from him only to find her hand tangled in her leash. Instead of shaking it off, she grabbed it in both hands, scrambled behind Elton, and looped it around his neck.

"No!"

Reeve? Not daring to look around for him, she started pulling. She'd never so much as fantasized about hurting someone, and yet tonight she knew with every fiber in her that she was capable of choking this bastard to death. More than capable, she wanted him dead! As for the consequences—

Gurgling, Elton reached back for her. She managed to evade his clawing fingers, but then he started thrashing, practically

GOING DOWN / 257

whipping her about. Scared but determined, she fought for balance.

"No!"

A steel arm wrapped around her middle. Another went around her throat. "Drop it," Reeve ordered, his mouth inches from her ear, "before I break your wrist."

He would; she knew it. Besides, the insanity that had catapulted her into action was being replaced by rational thought. Even if she managed to render Elton unconscious, his fellow slavers would do whatever was needed to stop her. Dead, she'd be of no help to Amber and the others. Dead, she'd never see her sister again, never touch Reeve again.

Propelled more by Elton's tortured breathing than Reeve's hold on her, she ordered the muscles in her arms to relax. Releasing the leash, she caught a glimpse of Amber's shocked expression. Then Reeve hauled her away from Elton.

Sounds began sorting themselves out. Elton was still trying to get air into his lungs and Amber was trying not to cry. Several of the other women were muttering, but the men's shocked and angry voices made it impossible for her to hear anything they were saying.

The men, they were still in control!

I'm sorry, so sorry! she silently told Reeve. *I didn't mean—I shouldn't have—*

For no more than a half second she longed to wrap her arms around Reeve and beg him to protect her, but if she did, she might have signed both their death warrants. If Reeve defended her, The Slavers would see him for what he was and attack him en masse. If he shook her off, he would have in essence thrown her to The Slavers to deal with. There was only one thing left to do, a single desperate measure.

Reeve let go of her throat. Not waiting for him to shift his hold to another part of her body, Saree dropped to her knees and wrapped her arms around his legs. Praying her expression was that of a misbehaving animal begging for forgiveness, she stared up at him. "Forgive me, Master, please. Punish me—I need to be—please, punish me. Teach—I have so much to learn."

That said, she released him and lowered her forehead to the ground in a gesture of absolute surrender. She even put her hands behind her, hoping he'd take her cue to begin restraining her.

What had happened? How could she have forgotten what tonight was about? Yes, that bastard had hurt Amber but—

Amber? Or her parents?

Silence, either that or she could no longer hear for her heart's chaotic pounding. At the same time she was aware of the beat of every passing second. Her impulsive action followed by her dramatic plea had dropped so much on Reeve's shoulders, but she couldn't take back trying to choke Elton. Once she'd done that, she hadn't been able to think of anything that wouldn't risk pulling Reeve down with her.

"I'll kill her!" Elton bellowed. "She deserves—"

"No!"

Risking a great deal, she lifted her head. Elton was only a few feet away, one hand massaging his throat, the other fisted. Reeve planted himself between Elton and her.

"Whatever she deserves," Reeve continued, "I will administer, only me."

"She tried to—"

"I know what she attempted." Not taking his eyes off Elton, he grabbed her hair and yanked her to her feet. Instead of letting up on the pressure, he forced her head back so she had no choice but to rest her shoulders on his chest to keep her feet. Much as she wanted to touch him, she kept her arms at her sides.

"She's a wild one and hasn't learned her place in her new world," Reeve said. "I've gotten a great deal of pleasure out of taming her, but its clear that I've allowed my enjoyment to get in the way of truly accomplishing my task."

In nearly a single motion, he released her hair and snagged her leash, pulling her head down so she was looking at the floor. "Elton, I apologize. I would have done anything to avoid this happening, but it did. Now both I and my slave must deal with the consequences." He slapped her buttocks so sharply that her knees nearly went out from under her.

"As for my amends, I propose signing a blank check and letting you decide on the damage amount. As for hers—" Another harsh slap made her quiver. "Obviously I was wrong to allow her out of her training room. I want to take her back to where she belongs. By the time I'm done with her, she'll understand her place."

Despite her tumbling emotions, she sent Reeve a silent thank-you for trying to get them out of there alive. Even if he hated her for what she'd done, at least he wasn't turning his back on her.

"You?" Elton challenged. "Despite your obvious failure, you believe you're capable of making the necessary behavior modification? Not going to happen."

Dread clutched her heart; she wondered if she was sensing the same emotion in Reeve, but all he said was, "I beg your pardon?"

"You acknowledged that I'm owed compensation for the injuries I suffered at this bitch's hand, but I don't want or need your money. I insist you turn her over to me."

"Impossible."

"No, not impossible." Although she couldn't see him, Elton's tone chilled her. "I shouldn't need to point out that you're more than outnumbered. I'd hate to have our association degenerate to the point of violence. At the same time, the opportunity to work with a rebellious slave isn't one I intend to relinquish."

Once again time broke down to one rapid-fire heartbeat after the other. If Reeve refused to turn her over to Elton, he might be killed. But if he turned his back on her, she was as good as dead, only death might be preferable to what Elton had in mind. *I'm sorry. So sorry.*

"Not an easy decision, is it?" Elton asked, sounding amused now. "Your hesitancy tells me that you have feelings for her, a most unfortunate situation and one my colleagues and I would strongly counsel you against. In fact, this has me wondering if there might be more than a slave/master relationship here. If you've been—"

A new sound, distant and yet coming closer, stopped Elton in midsentence. When Reeve slackened his hold on her leash, she straightened and cocked her head.

"Helicopter," one of the men said. "What's it doing out at night?"

Elton shrugged, his eyes clawing at her until she wondered if she'd started bleeding. He didn't want her alive, but neither did he want her dead. And beneath those emotions lived yet something else, a coldness she'd never seen before. If he'd once been a caring human being, that part of him had died.

The *whip-whip* of helicopter blades continued to grow until she half expected the aircraft to crash through the roof. One of the men unlocked the door leading to the rear deck and stepped outside. "What the hell?" he hollered.

"The fucker's landing!" someone yelled. "And there's another behind it."

Instead of looking at the two men, Saree kept her attention on Elton. For someone without an ounce of humanity in his soul, his face now gave away a great deal, rage foremost. "What the hell is this?" he demanded of Reeve. "If you're responsible—"

"You'll what?" Reeve shot back. "It's over, you bastard. You're over!"

"The hell—" With that, Elton whirled and raced over to Amber. Saree had no doubt that he intended to use her as his shield and hostage.

Releasing Saree, Reeve charged after Elton. But before Reeve could reach him, the kneeling Amber knotted her hands in front of her. Just as Elton reached her, she brought her hands down and then up, slamming them into his groin. Screaming, Elton slumped to his knees. He was still trying to cradle his wounded cock when her fisted hands struck him full in the throat. His scream became a desperate gasp for breath.

Something was happening outside, men yelling, wind whipping, powerful engines roaring, but Saree couldn't take her attention off Amber long enough to try to make sense of it. The Slavers were all on their feet, some standing and staring, others running toward the front of the house. The naked women clung to each other, all except for Amber, who now stood over Elton, cursing, crying, laughing at the same time.

Willing strength into her legs, Saree walked over to Amber and held out her hands. "It's all right," she whispered. "You're all right." At that she turned back so she could look at Reeve.

He nodded, but she couldn't tell what he was thinking.

22

"It's over," Saree said into the cell phone that one of the men who'd been in the helicopters had given her. Sucking in air, she ordered herself to slow down. "The cavalry showed up. Those bastards have all been arrested, and now Clan members are going through the mansion so—"

"Wait a minute," her sister interrupted. "What mansion? Who are you calling the cavalry and do you have any idea what time it is?"

The time, Hayley pointed out, was nearly one in the morning. After apologizing but only halfway meaning it, Saree forced herself to concentrate so she could bring her sister up to speed on everything that had happened, not just tonight but since her life had taken a sharp left turn. By the time she'd run out of steam and Hayley out of questions, her throat was sore and her eyes ached.

She was sitting in a patio chair on the expansive deck, staring at the part of the ocean that the lights, moon, and stars revealed. Although her spine ached and her buttocks had gone numb, Saree couldn't bring herself to stand and walk back into that house of horrors. Even after she'd promised Hayley that she'd call her back as soon as she knew where she'd be spending what was left of the night, she continued to sit and stare at the waves. Technically The Slavers hadn't been arrested since those who'd rescued her and the other women weren't sworn law enforcement officers, but the man who'd given her the phone had assured her that they had more than enough evidence to turn over to law enforcement. He'd mentioned that although the former slaves would have to testify, much of the weight of the case against The Slavers would come from Reeve—and her.

Where was Reeve? She hadn't seen him since the raid started. Going by what she'd heard and observed from her place of relative peace, every Slaver had indeed been rounded up and restrained. Now Clan members were pressing them for personal information, something they of course were reluctant to give. It made sense that Reeve would be part of that interrogation, although maybe he was talking to the women.

She should be looking for Amber or assuring the former slaves that they were truly free, and if neither of those things, she should have insisted she be allowed to observe the interviews of the Slavers.

Instead she sat. And thought. And tried to gather the courage to tell Reeve good-bye.

So hard, so damnably hard. But the fantasy was over, and as incredible as her time with him had been, reality now ruled. What it all boiled down to was that she wasn't—

"I didn't know where you were," a too-familiar voice behind her said. "I've been looking—"

"Have you?" she asked without turning around. She'd heard his tone so many times that she shouldn't still respond to it, should she? But she had, and the reason for the thread of heat from between her breasts to her core had only a little to do with relief because the nightmare was over. "I've been here the whole time."

"Why?" Unless she was mistaken, he was still standing in the doorway. "Maybe you were afraid—"

"Not anymore," she said, although she remained shaken. "I didn't want to be in the way."

"That's the only reason?"

She still wore the collar and chain he'd placed on her, and although she'd covered her breasts, the scant costume remained as a reminder of the role she'd been cast into. "What do you want me to say?" Although she knew better than to look at him, the effort of not doing so taxed her.

"I don't know. That's the hell of it. I don't know what either of us should be saying."

That wasn't right. Reeve was a man of action and self-confidence, courageous and determined. "What's going to happen now? Can The Clan make citizen arrests?"

"Yes, but there's no need. The police are on their way."

The police who'd want to talk to her. "What am I suppose to tell them? I don't see how I can get away with lying about how you drew me into this."

"I don't want you to do that, but you'd consider lying?"

Damn it, hadn't she just warned herself not to look at him? It hadn't done any good because now she was staring back at him, not just staring but taking in that so-familiar body and remembering that he'd once been a helpless, confused, and hurting boy. Human. Just like her.

"I don't know," she told the strong and shadowy figure standing near the closed sliding glass door. "I haven't thought—could you be charged with kidnapping me?"

"The DA is going to be a lot more interested in prosecuting The Slavers than examining the role my colleagues and I had in exposing them. Our priority has always been to keep The Clan out of the news because otherwise we won't be able to continue to operate. Obviously, we've succeeded in the past."

Something told her it wasn't going to be that simple, that

deals would need to be made, compromises reached, information suppressed, but she couldn't think about that right now. He was coming closer, and that was all she could concentrate on. Each step erased more than physical distance. His nearness complicated her world. They'd been through so much together. Their bodies had become one in more ways than she could call to mind right now, and they'd shared their deepest pains. But did she really know this big, dark man?

What did it matter?

"She's here," Reeve said as he sat in the chair next to her. Instead of studying her, his attention locked on the moonlit surf. "The coed who'd been grabbed in Manhattan Beach. They were keeping her in a cage. She's pretty traumatized but—"

"Of course she is. The others—maybe I'm crazy to be saying this, but the others have had time to comprehend what happened to them while she—"

"She's trying to grasp the fact that she's been rescued. I told her the police are on their way, but I'm not sure she could hear me."

"Not hear? What—"

"I'm a man." His tone was sober, maybe self-hating. "Right now she doesn't trust anyone with a cock."

Get to your feet. Find that young woman. Hold her. Instead, she sat.

"What about you?" he asked. "Is that why you're out here? You don't want to be anywhere close to someone with a cock? Or maybe it's just me you want nothing to do with? I don't blame you. That's what I need you to understand."

"If I could have killed Elton I would have. He deserves—"

"That's not what I asked."

What was wrong with Reeve? Didn't he understand that her emotions were still in tatters, that the way she'd earned her living couldn't possibly have prepared her for what she'd just experienced? "It's the best I can give you." She was careful not to look at him, but why the hell did he have to be sitting so close that his life energy reached her? "You can't tear me out of my world and thrust me into something incomprehensible and expect me to have it all together."

"You're right; I can't. That's what I didn't allow myself to think about when we hatched our plan, the impact on you."

For a moment she half believed he was going to take her hand but maybe she'd only imagined it. Whichever it was, too-familiar heated energy snaked through her. Her nearly overwhelming need for him at this moment had to be a result of tonight's trauma; it had to! His assignment had brought them together; otherwise, he would have wanted nothing to do with her. She was soiled goods, and what she'd done for a living danced too close to what The Slavers had been about.

"I don't know when you'll be able to leave," he said, now watching her. "The police are going to want everything you can give them. You're a key component in the case. Your testimony—"

"That's right, my testimony! So it didn't occur to you that maybe I wouldn't want that responsibility thrust on me? A means to an end, that's all I was." *Damn you for expecting me to cooperate fully when I'll have all I can do to survive you walking out of my life.* "I can't refuse to cooperate; I want to. But my name and face are going to be all over the news." Rocked by the thought, she stood and paced to the railing overlooking the surf. "And to think I used to believe I was a public figure. That's nothing compared to what's going to happen."

Mistake! Why hadn't she guessed that he too would be putting his feet under him and joining her?

"I'm sorry. For so much. That's what I came out here for, to apologize."

And now that you have, you can go back inside. "It doesn't matter," she whispered. "I'll do what I have to."

"I know you will. But when it's over, what then?"

"What do you mean?"

"Will you go back to work?"

That's all you care about? "I don't know. I need time to—what about you? Do you get a vacation?"

"This career doesn't work that way. If I'm needed—Saree, I mean it, I'm sorry for what I put you through. I was so focused on achieving the goal that I didn't look ahead, didn't acknowledge that you'd lose the anonymity I've worked so hard to accomplish for myself."

Why did his voice have to blend so perfectly with the sounds rolling up from the surf? And why hadn't she backed away from him? And why couldn't she keep her cunt from clenching? Maybe most of all, why were her fingers extending toward his?

A touch, light and yet hot. Nerve endings short-circuiting and the Southern California night breeze in her hair and nostrils and his strength sliding into and around her. Anger, if that's what it had been, dying.

When he pulled her around so she was facing him, she planted her free hand against his chest but couldn't bring herself to try to push him away. Just the same, her hand remained as a barrier between them. *Say it. Tell him how much you disgust yourself.*

"Don't apologize," she managed. "What's going to happen is bigger than both of us. It *has* to be."

"Yeah, it does."

His mouth was so close. Damn it, he didn't have to be looking down at her like that, and his arm didn't have to be around her back as if he thought she might take flight. Yet despite the distraction and dangerous potential of his body, she had things to say before putting an end to tonight. To them.

"This is the side of what I do—did for a living that I've always managed to avoid facing," she whispered. "I hid behind the word *consensual* and told myself that The Dungeon was good, clean fun. But that wasn't all there was to it. The Slavers—people like them feed off what we offer them."

"Don't." Pulling her closer, he wrapped both arms around her. One covered the small of her back while the other pressed against her buttocks. "Don't blame yourself for—"

"Of course I do!" Was she speaking the truth or simply trying to weather Reeve's presence? "We have all these controls so underage kids can't view what's on our site, but do we try to block out the sick elements of society? No! We take their money and shrug and say it isn't our problem. But it is. It is."

"Saree." His breath dampened and heated her face and throat while his cock sought a home. "I mean it, don't take on that burden."

"Why shouldn't I. It's the—"

"No, it isn't. Saree, you just told me not to apologize for what I put you through. You're no more responsible for what The Slavers did than I am for my father's rampage."

That stopped her, that and his strength and sexuality. So much evil had taken place here and yet beyond the walls, the ocean endured. "Of course you aren't. You were only a child."

"Just as you're only a woman, a sexy woman who does what she loves."

But can I ever do that again? "I think—I want to talk to those shrinks you'll be taking the women in there to. I'm so—everything is so complex."

"Yeah, it is." He pressed the heel of his hand against the base of her spine, stealing her breath and challenging her sanity. "And it's not going to get better for a while."

"I know."

"But eventually it will."

"I know," she repeated. "The way it did after my parents died."

"And after my father was arrested. Honey, the other reason I came out here was to tell you how damn proud I am of you.

You're an incredibly brave woman." He took a deep breath. "And for the first time since I became a Clan member, I'm not thinking about moving on to the next assignment. I don't—don't want to be alone anymore."

"Neither do I," she whispered.

Leaning back she looked up at him. It didn't matter that she couldn't make out his features, that she still needed to ask him if he saw her as tainted goods, to tell him that she'd have to draw on his strength to get through whatever it took to put The Slavers behind bars.

There was this moment. This ocean breeze. Their bodies crying for each other.

Tomorrow could wait. And they'd face it together.

Turn the page for a preview of
WOLF TALES VI!

On sale now!

1
_____

"**Y**ou bitch! You're nothing but a cock-teasing bitch."

Eve Reynolds twisted to one side and tried to duck, but the big guy kicked the motel room door shut with his foot and slammed her against the bedroom wall. His buddy stood to one side, watching with a salacious smirk on his face.

She aimed a kick in his direction. The smaller guy jumped out of the way before she could connect. Eve twisted in the bigger man's grasp, felt her T-shirt stretch, heard it tear. The shredded top drooped to her waist, a meaty hand surrounded her exposed breast, thick fingers dug into soft flesh. It hurt, damn it, but not as much as when he shoved his thigh between her legs, lifting her feet off the ground while he groped her other breast.

She twisted, but couldn't break free. He was taller and stronger and totally enraged. Adrenaline poured into her system. Eve's vision blurred and she fought the need to shift. It would be so easy—so utterly satisfying. Just be the wolf long enough to take them out, both of them—the big guy assaulting her and his smarmy buddy, too. She could change in a heartbeat, all slavering teeth and powerful jaws tearing into her attackers. Eve pictured the blood and the rewarding burst of terror. She felt the first frisson of change course through her body. The man's thigh ground against her sensitive pubes. She tensed, preparing for the wolf. Then Anton Cheval's words of warning leapt into her mind. The leader of the Montana pack had been deadly serious and his warning was branded in her mind.

Our identity as Chanku is a closely guarded secret. Take care no one learns what you are.

These men would know, if she let them live. Eve wasn't ready to kill a man, much less two, which she'd have to do if she shifted. Leaving witnesses wasn't acceptable, damn it all, but she really hated to do the girlie thing. Then a hand snaked down the front of her shorts and rough fingers scraped at tender flesh, forcing entrance. She screamed, loud and long, her voice powered by anger, not fear. Then she bit into the man's thick bicep, the only body part within reach of her teeth. Her human jaws lacked wolven strength and sharpness, but the combination of scream and bite, of nearby doors opening and people yelling, was enough to stop the attack.

The big guy shoved her to the floor, yelled for his buddy, and the two of them raced out the door and climbed into their truck. The shiny red Chevy 4x4 fishtailed out of the parking lot, spewing gravel and dust in its wake. Light from the garish streetlamps turned the dust to gold and the gravel twinkled like precious gems. A perfect example of things not always being as they seemed.

Eve held on to the doorjamb and gasped for air as she watched them leave. Neighbors on either side of her ground-floor room spilled out into the night. She clutched her torn shirt across her breasts, waved off their concern, and apologized for the disturbance. Then she closed the door to her motel room and leaned her head against the warm wood.

Heat and moisture engulfed her. Heart pounding, breath still rasping in her lungs, she concentrated on the thick, humid air and the silence, now that the truck was gone.

And the fact she'd managed not to shift.

Eve rubbed her left arm, well aware she'd have the jerk's fingerprints imprinted in her flesh for the next few days. Her crotch hurt where he'd shoved her with his thigh and violated her with his filthy fingers. Both her breasts were bruised.

Moving on unsteady feet, Eve limped into the bathroom. She glanced only briefly in the mirror before looking away. She didn't need to see the tangled blond hair or the bruise along her left cheek to know she looked like a wild-eyed tramp. Hands shaking, head pounding with the onset of a headache, she stripped out of her clothes, stepped into the shower and turned on the water. All she got was a tepid spray, but it was enough to wash the man's stink off her bruised body.

Eve let her mind go blank as water sluiced over her head and shoulders. When she finally got out and dried off, though, her head still ached. She grabbed a washcloth, rinsed it out, held the damp cloth to her forehead . . . and thought of Montana.

Clear skies and dark, cool forests. Trails leading into magical places where wild things ran and the water tasted clear and fresh against her tongue. Thick grass beneath her paws, the sound and scent of her packmates beside her. The sense of belonging, of being one with nature and the pack.

She'd known that closeness for such a brief time, but the feeling hadn't left her. The sense of brotherhood, of family. Of belonging. Still, she'd had a good enough reason to leave after a mere taste of what her life could be, hadn't she? Discovering she was a shapeshifting Chanku with the ability to switch instantly from woman to wolf had opened her life to freedoms she'd never imagined but always craved. Freedom she would have given up had she stayed with the man who wanted so badly to claim her.

Adam Wolf. Damn, how she missed him.

She brushed the unwelcome sting of tears from her eyes, took a deep breath, and slowly regained control of her shattered emotions. It had to be the adrenaline from the attack. That's all it was. Adrenaline and nerves. Not Adam. Never Adam.

Talk about sucky timing. She'd wanted independence her entire life. When it was finally handed to her, even beyond the amazing power of the wolf, she was every bit as trapped by love as she'd ever been by circumstances. Recognizing her unhappiness, Anton Cheval, the uncontested leader of the Montana pack, had given her a beautiful, cherried out antique Ford pickup to drive, credit cards with unlimited funds, and a pocketful of cash.

The fact the truck was supposed to go to his packmate, Stefan Aragat, as a birthday gift, hadn't seemed to bother Anton a bit. He seemed certain Eve would have it back in time.

So what had she done with his largesse? Driven clear across the country to the town she'd grown up in, parked her butt in a nicer motel than she'd ever been able to afford before in her life, and waited to see what would happen next.

So far, nothing good had come her way, and she had no idea what had drawn her back. No idea what was good enough in Tampa to lure her away from the beauty of Montana and people who loved her.

What kind of fool was she?

Eve freshened the washcloth under the faucet and wrung the excess water out of it. This time she held the cloth against the bruises on her left breast where the flesh had been so cruelly twisted. She had no one to blame but herself for tonight's little episode, but damn, she hurt all over and felt like a fool. A very lonely fool.

She'd had such a short time in Montana with Adam Wolf. The name alone should have warned her, but he'd been everything she'd ever wanted in a man . . . and more. They'd found a connection unlike anything she'd experienced. When he'd brought Oliver, the quiet young man who worked for Anton Cheval, into their bed, the sex had been little short of mindblowing.

So, what did she do? She ran. Fast and far, afraid of the overwhelming emotions, frightened as much by the changes in her body as she finally embraced her wolven, Chanku heritage, as she'd been by her attraction to Adam.

Unfortunately, she hadn't been able to leave her libido behind. Tonight, she'd lost control, and along with it, what little respect she thought she'd held on to. She'd wanted sex. She'd wanted a repeat of that amazing night with Adam and Oliver. Every night since coming to Tampa, she'd found a quiet place to run as the wolf, to learn more about her new body. The downside of the exhilaration she experienced on four legs was that damned Chanku libido. Desire, hot and potent, streaming like a living entity through her veins, and needs she really couldn't satisfy on her own, no matter how fresh she kept the batteries in her electronic buddy.

Each night she returned to this room aroused beyond belief, her blood racing, sexual desire taking precedence over all other instincts, all sense of caution. How else could she explain what she'd done tonight? She'd gone trolling for a man.

The two men from the bar had seemed nice enough at first. She'd led them on, invited them back to her room. Eve thought she wanted both men and all they promised, but when it came right down to it, she'd not wanted them at all.

She'd wanted her own kind. Her body still thrummed with the dark cravings, the sexual needs unfulfilled these past three weeks since she'd left Adam. Cravings that intensified each time she shifted, each time she raced through the night on four legs, searching for others of her kind even though she knew there were none here.

Needs she'd thought she might satisfy with the two men

she'd brought home with her tonight. Except, once again, it had felt all wrong.

They'd both kissed her, a man on either side in the front seat of the big pickup truck. The larger of the two had been the most aggressive. He'd stroked the warm folds between her legs, rubbing her through the soft cotton of her shorts, and her body had responded. Her breasts tingled, her pussy clenched and creamed and she'd thought it might work. She'd hoped her body would continue to react, but his kisses weren't Adam's. His touch wasn't as loving as Oliver's. He didn't understand the needs of the wolf and his mind was closed to her deepest desires. Would it always be this way? Would she only find satisfaction among other Chanku?

Sighing, Eve stretched out on the bed and held the damp washcloth against her breasts. It didn't do a thing to ease the all-consuming ache between her legs. The constant throbbing, the clenching of muscles too long denied, the desperate need for penetration, for sexual release.

She lay there in the dark, naked and sweating. The little air conditioner hummed and rattled, but it didn't touch the thick Florida heat. She retraced the past month of her life, the three weeks since leaving Montana. So much had happened in those few days after she'd met Keisha Rialto and Alexandria Olanet, when their wonderfully protective mates, Anton and Stefan, had rescued her from an abusive relationship turned deadly.

Why was she always drawn to losers? Probably for the same stupid reason she'd walked away from the finest man she'd ever known. She was an idiot, pure and simple. Too stupid to live . . . wasn't that how the saying went? *TSTL*? It fit her perfectly.

Her life was spinning out of control, twisting pointlessly in a maelstrom of need and arousal, of desperate cravings and unfulfilled desires. And she was lonely. So damned lonely. Eve rolled her hips against the bed, imagining Oliver beneath her and Adam between her legs, The memory brought forth a rush of fluids and a hollow, empty feeling deep inside.

She clutched the bedspread with both hands, accepting her needs, her powerful desires. Accepting, yet wondering how it could happen, how she could take this woman's body and become a wolf?

How she could take a man like Adam Wolf into her bed, into her heart, and find real love? The kind of love in fairy tales. The kind of love she'd always been denied.

Take that love and then stupidly walk away from it.

Once she'd discovered her heritage as a shapeshifter, a member of an ancient race that somehow appeared on the inhospitable Himalayan steppe so many eons ago, everything had changed. It was hard to say what was the biggest thing that had happened—shifting into a wolf, or meeting Adam, a man so tender and loving he made her ache with wanting. A man who claimed his only desire was to fix things.

Eve wondered if it was too late, if now that she'd left him, would he ever be able to fix her? Would he even want to?

Not if you keep running away, you idiot.

Nothing quite so sensitive as an inner critic. Eve moved the washcloth to her right breast. Her nipple tightened almost painfully when she scraped the sensitive tip with the cotton cloth, so she repeated the motion. Again. And again.

She shifted her hips against the wrinkled bedspread and her body felt all itchy and achy. She wanted to run. Wanted to shift and become the wolf and race through the forest. She hadn't run tonight. She wanted the wild and cool forests of Montana, not the hot and humid parks and gardens around Tampa, Florida.

She wanted to hunt for rabbits and deer, not worry about stepping on a cottonmouth snake, or running full tilt into a hungry alligator.

What the hell was she doing here, anyway?

Idly rubbing at her taut nipple, Eve reached between her legs and stroked her clit with her other hand. The tiny nub stood upright, hard and slick with her cream. She bit back a frustrated moan. Her fingers weren't enough. Her needs were too great, her body too desperate, aching for the heat and weight of a man.

She thought of the new vibrator in the table beside the bed. She'd never even used this one. Big and thick and perfectly formed to give her release, according to the advertising. *Crap.* Who was she trying to kid? It would take a lot more than plastic and batteries to ease the ache building inside.

Why had she even come back? When she was eighteen, she hadn't been able to get out of town fast enough. Away from the foster care system, from abuse and emptiness and a sense she was always searching, always looking for something just out of reach. Keisha had referred to it as quiet desperation, that knowledge buried deep in the heart, always calling to those who shared the Chanku genetics. Hinting at more, at something just out of reach, some visceral knowledge yet to be discovered.

She'd found it in Montana with the pack of Chanku shapeshifters. Once she'd started taking the big, ugly brown capsules Anton gave her, once her body had received the nutrients it needed, completed its changes and she'd finally been able to shift, Eve discovered a side of her life she'd never imagined. Never dreamed existed.

She should have been happy there, finally at home. She could have been happy with Adam and Oliver, if only she'd been able to ignore the tugging sensation deep in her heart. She'd thought it was her need to be her own woman, to succeed entirely on her own. Now that she was here, living alone and feeling lonelier than she ever had in her life, Eve knew that wasn't it at all. There was something more, something still unexplained.

For whatever reason, it had called her back to Tampa. Until

she knew what fate held in store for her, Eve knew she couldn't leave.

She sat up on the edge of the bed, her mind filled with thoughts of Adam. She missed him. Damn, she hardly knew the man, yet the image of his tall, rangy body filled her heart and her mind. Made her body anxious and miserable with wanting.

Did he feel the same? Had he missed her over these three long weeks? Would he come to her? *Why should he?* Her shoulders slumped and she sighed. *He's just found his sister and his mother, and a new family in the Montana pack. Why would he come after me?*

She glanced toward the window. Through the slightly parted curtain she saw the cherry '51 Ford pickup parked outside her room. Black and shiny beneath the parking lot lights, it gleamed with lots of chrome and expensive paint. The truck had been a loan from Anton Cheval, but he wanted it back by July 20, in time for his packmate—and lover's—birthday.

Stefan's birthday was just a little over a week away, and Eve still wasn't sure why she was even here. She really didn't want to go back without finding out what had drawn her to Florida in the first place, but she'd promised Anton she'd return the truck.

Unless, of course, she couldn't. Maybe because it wasn't running?

Grinning broadly, Eve grabbed a fresh cotton gown and slipped it over her head. She went outside, lifted the hood on the truck and stared at the myriad bits and parts of whatever made the darned thing run.

She shrugged, looked around to see if anyone was watching her. Then she reached inside and pulled a few wires loose. For added measure, she tugged a couple of unidentifiable things completely free and tossed them inside the cab. Then she went back inside her motel room and placed a call to Montana.

* * *

Adam threw an extra pair of clean jeans into the sports bag and zipped it shut just as Oliver walked into the room. He glanced up. "Are you ready, Ollie? Got your bags packed?"

Oliver shrugged and sat on the edge of the bed. Small and dark, yet always meticulous in both dress and action, he took a